GREAT AMERICAN PLAIN

# GREAT
# AMERICAN
# PLAIN

Gary Sernovitz

Henry Holt and Company | New York

Henry Holt and Company, LLC
*Publishers since 1866*
115 West 18th Street
New York, New York 10011

Library of Congress Cataloging-in-Publication Data
Sernovitz, Gary.
    Great American plain : a novel / Gary Sernovitz.
        p. cm.
    ISBN 0-8050-6777-9 (hb)
        1. Triangles (Interpersonal relations)—Fiction. 2. Sales personnel—Fiction.
    3. Middle West—Fiction. 4. Brothers—Fiction. 5. Fairs—Fiction. I. Title.

P S3619.E76 G7 2001
813'.6—dc21                                                          2001016926

Henry Holt books are available for special promotions and
premiums. For details contact: Director, Special Markets.

First Edition 2001

Designed by Kelly S. Too

Printed in the United States of America
1  3  5  7  9  10  8  6  4  2

*For my parents and theirs*

GREAT AMERICAN PLAIN

PART ONE

# [ 1 ]

His tongue was twisted, and the line didn't come out straight. He had used it hundreds of times that summer and had practiced it, mirror-practiced it, every day that spring. This was Sales, this was the Act, as Orditz had said, but Orditz, he knew, was dead. "I'm not going to lie to you. An instrument's an investment," was what he meant to say. "I'm not going to lie to you. An instrument's an instrument," was what he did.

"A what?" asked Ed's customer, a man dressed in the habit of the State Fair: T-shirt, high socks, short pants, his hemispheres bulging from the short's elastic.

"An investment. An instrument. An instrument *is* an investment."

"Like-ah, what level of investment?" The man turned to his wife, defending their boys, who were silenced by the organ before them, rainbow-buttoned, churchly, prehistoric.

"A little over fourteen hundred dollars."

The man froze for two beats longer than his response required. Ed Steinke labeled the freeze and capitalized it: The Decision. He leaned guardedly forward. The man was indeed deciding, between a *whoa,* a no-nod, and a smirk, diagnosing Ed's insanity for Ed's benefit and his boys'. The man chose the third option, reconsidered, added the first two, and collected his family. It moved to Olde Country Maple Syrup, the next-over booth in the South Exhibition Hall. Normally, Barry Steinke, the organ's player, Ed's brother, Ed's employee—he had rejected "partner" in April—would have laughed at the scene. But that time he didn't. He was otherwise occupied, staring at—watching—a girl. He watched her eyes downcast, he watched her eyes uplifted, and then he felt both of their eyes, hers and his, hoping, dancing, flirting, tangle-tripping to the floor. Then he watched the girl flee deeper into the South Exhibition Hall.

The family's departure was only the latest defeat for Ed Steinke. Earlier, at two o'clock, he had tried to wring his first sale of the dry rag of an afternoon from Connie Svensson. After six minutes of Ed's imperfect but acceptable lead-in, Connie—a schoolteacher, he could tell, her blond fallen to brittle gray—had politely asked him if she could try it out. She then proceeded to play a string of Lutheran hymns for such an eternity that Ed would have happily signed on to the faith if she agreed to stop playing and he wasn't already Lutheran. When Connie ended her recital, Ed alerted her and a small assembly of secondary customers to the many attributes of the Brackett 180-X. Bashfully, Connie admitted that tickling the ivories—the ivories were plastic—did make her feel like a girl again. Five insinuating minutes later, Ed asked her if she might, then, very well, then, be interested in buying one, then. "Oh no gosh," she laughed. "I never use the one I have."

Then, at three-thirty, he dreamed a whole orchestra for Lottie Ostergard. "Have you ever had the pleasure of playing an organ?" he asked her; he would not travel the mined Connie path again. Lottie had never had the pleasure of playing an organ. "This instrument is really amazing," he shared with her, mechanically earnest; he had refreshed his eye contact on the last word (Orditz, page 106). "It's sym*phon*ic. Like a conductor. You are. You are like a conductor." Ed winced, and winced at his wince; the inversion, the pauses, the gestures—all were strangling Perfect Execution.

"What you know." Lottie's neutrality was shifting, not to belligerency, but in that direction.

The pitch needed more sincerity, and Ed tried to add it, like oregano, a tablespoon at a time. "Now, I was a little skeptical myself the first time I sat down at the Brackett 180-X because I'm hardly a musician myself."

Lottie: silence.

"But I can sit here and describe the Brackett from noon till . . . noon till night." From the back of Lottie's eyes, the answer, taut and focused, made it clear that that was not going to happen. "But what better way is there to appreciate the Brackett than to appreciate its sound? Hear it. Right, Mr. Steinke?" At the cue, Barry missed the cue; he sat on the organ bench, staring into the crowd. "Isn't that right, Mr. Steinke?" Ed repeated, smiling the particular sort of smile of a particular sort of salesman—like the particular braggadocio of an impotent sailor or the particular late paintings of a spent artist—that could not hide the hollows underneath. Barry didn't move. "Mr. Steinke, I think this, um, young lady"—Lottie Ostergard was thirty years older than Ed—"would like to hear you play." Barry winked at Ed, infuriating, an exaggerated hee-haw, and remained still. Ed excused himself from Lottie and turned to his right. "You better stop staring at that fat ass right now," he whispered inadequately, "and start paying attention or I'll—"

Although not addressed, Fat Ass, who had been babysitting Lottie's purchases in the aisle, approached his wife and the salesman in two serious strides. "What did he say?" Len Ostergard asked. Lottie, unsure herself, shrugged. "What he *say*?" Her wifely physiognomy compacted five messages: calm down, ask him, don't ask me, let's go, not with your temper again, buster.

Ed spoke. "I was just telling Mr. Steinke here that he should *not* play 'Green Grass,' you know, 'Green Green Grass of Home,' but he should really play something to get your. Get your attention. Demonstrate the Brackett 180-X's versatility."

"Hmm," said Len, and "Hmm," said Lottie, and they moved at her urging to the maple syrup booth, hunched, replaying the scene in undertones.

Barry headed off Ed's tirade: "Don't even start, dude, it's over."

"I'll tell you when it's over. I'm not paying you to lose customers." Ed paused; his face considered. "I'm paying you to follow goddamn orders."

"You got to like watch your tongue. It's not good for business."

"How about I watch my—" Ed stopped; his cheek-skin deepened from salmon to red.

Barry, calm as always, lectured: "Let me just tell you something, okay. I was just looking at that dude because, you know, I'm not like a scientist or anything, but if you think about it, that dude should like fall flat on his face every time he stands up. But he didn't, which is like kind of strange, if you think about it." Len's gut, a repository for a lifetime of sins in that butter-built state, was so perfectly round and so perfectly huge that it carried his center of gravity to nearly a foot in front of his toes.

"I'll tell you what to think about, jackass." Ed's breath drew hard, and his temples, with a p-pump, asserted their presence. "I'll tell you— How many times do I have to tell you? We only sell these fucking things when we achieve Perfect Execution." This above all, Orditz had said, this above all.

"Perfect sex-ecution?" Barry's rackety laugh acknowledged his own hilarity.

"Perfect Execution, idiot. That means—Jesus, I've told you a *thous*and times—flawless, seamless between you and me. I don't care how fat his ass is, we need to Lead through Preci—"

"But that was like a pretty fat one, if you think about it."

Ed stepped out of the booth and looked down both sides of the aisle. His mood sank one-two-three: plaintive envy, angry envy, disgust. He knew that his promises of wonderfully alive drumbeats were undistinguished particles in the clatter of the South Exhibition Hall, where the come-ons of toothy auctioneers collided with browsers and the "maybe *ifs*" of hagglers bounced off "costs what it costs" obstinacy. It was a loud universe in the South Exhibition Hall, a concrete shoebox with a brown corrugated lid. (*Two* football fields of space, the authorities bragged, in the only reasonable unit of measure.) The Steinkes' neighborhood, the central alley, was the loudest of all. Locations bordering the twenty-foot-wide alley were the only ones available for amplified presentations and required higher fees. Although Ed didn't use a microphone and knew that he couldn't sell the Brackett 180-X like an automatic apple corer, a dozen at a time with a six-minute wows-and-bows demonstration, he chose a space in the central alley because it was, he believed, the Fair's Secret Energy Zone. According to an article in *The Journal of American Sales,* the busiest twenty percent of a shopping mall or, by Ed's corollary, an exhibition area—the SEZ—captured fifty percent of the business. However, Ed also knew, conventional wisdom insisted that the Brackett's real home was the West Exhibition Hall, where the booths were larger and the merchandise more substantial: contour chairs and home gyms, professional grills and deck kits. Yet Ed still trusted in the Secret Energy Zone, and the West Hall was a building away.

None of the fairs that summer had approached success, but this one—a state fair in the brothers' home state, the big dance—had been the worst of all. The two state fairs to the west, at least, had been more commercially minded and in that way more amenable. Tractor and picker and thresher companies brought veteran salesmen and sizable inventories to attack the farmers' last debt-saddled dime. For the city dwellers, reputable local dealers displayed big-ticket items—sofabeds, appliances, even cars—aside the gadgety buffet. People at those fairs and at the generic Home Expos earlier in the summer were ready to spend, and Ed had sneaked out a few sales between the busts and the duds. At the few large county fairs attended in between, the Steinkes had had less competition and the advantage of an aura of urbanity. Among those folks, completing a sale was like giving birth, a divine joke of unnecessary length and pain, but Ed had managed at least one sale every other site.

In the central alley, Ed did an about-face and returned to the booth; only his ears hinted at a redder past. "Why do you always have to stare?" he asked, exhausted by his brother.

"Because I want to." Barry was regularly immune to the virus of shame.

Ed dug around the petrified root. "Do you do it just to piss me off or is there some other reason I don't know about?"

"I told you. I do it because I want to."

"So it *is* just to piss me off." This summer was the longest time the brothers had spent together in seven years.

"What*ever*, dude."

"Answer me," Ed ordered. Barry's puppy face no speaka English. "You do it 'cause you're an idiot, right?"

"I do it in the morning. I do it at night. I do it with the girls in the skirts so tight," Barry sang—it was more of a recitation, his voice roaming across only three, four close notes—and the discussion was over. He stood up, hand-pressed his hipster, blue-collar tan pants, and precisely confused his hair. "I'm getting some air. Should I come back here? Because we're like probably done for today, if you think about it."

"You'll come back if you want to live."

Hands buried in pockets, Barry headed in his bouncy, slouchy walk toward the exit. It wasn't just that Barry's staring broke Ed's concentration. (Concentration—Orditz, page 174—was the foundation of Perfect Execution.) It was its triangularity. Barry would stare at someone. Ed would look at Barry and the someone. The someone would then look back at Ed and assume that he, Ed, had been staring the whole time. Then the someone would judge him, and *that* judgment would join the other judgments, the hovering wasps stinging Ed for being a salesman, for wanting to be a salesman, for reading the books he read, for saying the things he said, for selling organs, for tolerating his brother, for not being more like his brother. Every day, people did nothing but judge Ed, he could tell, but none of them knew him or his plans, knew that selling organs was part of something bigger, not glamorous for sure, but necessary. At twenty-four, Ed Steinke wasn't a washed-up loser like the rest of the jackasses on the circuit who hawked paring knives and radish rosers to tightwads because they couldn't do any better. He sold the Brackett 180-X because he wanted to.

A boy, a dedicated nose picker, stood in the central alley and regarded the Brackett: colorful, electronic, thrice his size. "You like music?" Ed asked as he bowed nearer the boy, absorbing a pang in his kidney. Ed never sat down at the fairs; that would have been undignified, an affront to customer and code. The boy stopped picking his nose, which was more recognition than usual.

"You know, when I was your age, I used to play an organ just like this," Ed lied, "and I couldn't have asked for more fun." In the central alley, two yards behind the boy, a brow turned suddenly serious and searched the underbrush. Finally, breathing again, the mother located her son, came to him, and crossed her arms over his shoulders, his head pressed against her belly. Ed looked at her hands. No ring.

"I was just saying to your beautiful, um. I was just saying to your handsome son that when I was his age I got a lot of pleasure out of the organ." Mother and child were stone-faced. "It really improved my grades. And I don't want to exaggerate, but it set me on a path. Um, to better things."

"It's big," the mother finally said.

"Yes, big and powerful." There were a number of trigger words—*piano, price, music, what's-it-do*—that could lead Ed seamlessly from this clumsy foreplay into his memorized pitch. *Big* was not one of them. "Yes, hundreds of pounds of top American engineering and musicianship." The Brackett 180-X was built in South Korea. "Really a very substantial piece of equipment." The woman had fidgeted at "hundreds of pounds," and Ed adjusted. "At the same time that it is big, ma'am, it's also compact. Really small, for all it can do."

Small was a relative term, the woman thought. The Brackett was smaller than an elephant, no doubt, but her living room, if you could call it that, was *really* small. If she bought the organ, she would have to get rid of her couch. Curious, she looked over Ed's shoulder for a price tag.

"Yep, very compact, very affordable." Ed abandoned hope for her trigger and pulled one himself. "Many people have never thought about, um." Losing his place, he petted the Brackett. "This organ is very compact, very. Yes, very affordable." Many people have never thought about why they would need an organ, was how Ed was supposed to start the pitch. He had never gotten it wrong before.

The woman uncrossed her arms from around her boy and steered him firmly the maple syrup way. She angled herself, parallel to her son, turned to Ed, and offered him a concluding look, indifferently doubtful. Much too much, no hard feelings.

Ed reminded himself that he used to be a good salesman. Pilsen's: he had held that place up himself, twenty-two years old and green, only Orditz to guide him. Perfect Execution. Goddamnit, it had worked.

# [ 2 ]

The State Fair's advertised imagery was the same every year: the State Fair was red-barn, verdant, lakes and livestock and bright, circley suns. The state's fairground, to the contrary, was set in concrete and overpasses and the blotchy siding of a downshifting suburb, set in a gray echo of the northland's five-month winters and slush-puddle springs. And so even in the Fair's late summer, when verdant was still true across the state, the fairground was city. Country nostalgia was canned, pickled, and sold.

This was not entirely lost on two who had driven past the fairground the night before. Out-of-shape skinny and his companion, out-of-shape chubby, were on summer break from their doctoral theses, driving northeast to northwest. Like all such drives, the only ammunition against the tedium of car-caged days was a literary self-awareness that they were road trippers, not straight liners, and as the Great American Plain—not just the Great Plains but the whole grain-waved ocean between the Lake of the Woods and the Rio Grande, the Rocky Mountains and the Appalachian Plateau—sailed by hour after hour, only the backseat ghosts of Kerouac and Steinbeck made the flat vistas tolerable. With a couple more years remaining as earnest and young, the men laid down one rule: they should try, whenever possible, to meet real Americans. Their performance of that commandment had been by and large sloppy, and guilt radiated from the backseat. Thus when they stopped in the skyscraper-drawn capital of the flatlands and learned that they were not far from a state fair, an event crammed with the potential of meeting untold numbers of real people, they turned right and congratulated themselves on their spontaneity.

They made the decision late, and it was past midnight when Chubby let it be known that he would faint if he didn't eat soon. Skinny took the interstate exit four miles past the hope-imploding fairgrounds and drove into an empty parking lot. On the far side, a do-it-yourself warehouse rose at the hump of an aged strip mall. Four buildings stood on the near side; three of them, the ones Chubby most needed, were closed. "Man," he complained as the car idled, "this is a disaster." Skinny didn't respond. He was weary with a weariness that had road-seeped into the car, a weariness of the road that made him describe himself, against better judgment, as weary. *Tired* didn't seem strong enough. "I'm *not* getting anything there." Chubby nudged his nose toward the fourth structure on the near side of the lot. The building was open, as always. The company that owned the eight pumps and thousand-foot store did not let anything as trivial as time halt the dollarly flow.

Skinny sighed; he wanted to sleep, not eat. "It's there or nowhere." Before Chubby could muster enough energy to mumble his assent, Skinny had already inched toward the station. They parked. Chubby arranged his insufficient hair with cigar-stub fingers. Skinny exited the car and entered the store. Leila Genet, behind the counter, looked up from a magazine and offered Skinny the same smile of benign sincerity that she offered all postmidnight customers. Only rarely did Leila greet customers verbally, and she had quit altogether that week, when the customers, almost all men, many of them Fair-drunk, saw her briefly as romance's last chance. "Hello," she had said a handful of times, mistakenly, on the Fair's first day. Hello, *yourself,* sister, baby, honey, baby.

It was nearing the end of her shift. The store was empty and, but for her bored breaths, silent.

Unprepared to see a woman, Skinny lost a step. He regained his stride, awkwardly at first, and proceeded to a rear-wall cooler. *Now, there's a real American.* Skinny, whose prolonged virginity may have been responsible for his lingering romantic idealism, glanced at Leila's waist-up reflection in the cooler's glass door. Much to his disappointment, a loose center-snapped uniform boxed in the visible half of her body. Before Skinny's fantasies could heat, Chubby's reflection crossed the girl's.

Leila worked on the second shift alone; the money was better for her than on the first shift and better still for the company: it no longer assigned to units in the station group a roamer on the second shift. A roamer had been an unnecessary constriction; margins must expand, forever, outward.

Skinny moved to the sugar-and-chocolate department, where Chubby was studying his choices. "Just looking again?" Skinny started the routine.

"Doesn't hurt to look." Chubby selected a bag of cookies.

"I thought you were just looking?" Skinny intended the comment to be innocuous, but it sifted poorly through his weariness. He glanced at Leila.

Chubby was admired by his colleagues, reservedly, for his wit and cherubic good humor. "Bite me, will you. I'm hungry."

"Clearly." Skinny peeked at Leila again.

Leila noticed the peek. Skinny, she thought, was kind of cute. If not cute then different, intelligent. He wore glasses, and he wasn't like the other guys who came into the station, all twins, it seemed, to Rusty Schmidt: grand packages of ground beef, once athletes, muscles melting.

Chubby was exhausted by the night and by the same routine from his pencil-legged companion. "Why do you keep looking at that girl?" he asked in a loud whisper.

"Jesus, keep it down," Skinny whispered in return. "She's not deaf."

"What's your problem?" Chubby asked.

"Are you insane? She's not deaf."

You're right, Leila thought. I'm not deaf. She cleaved the fleshy center of her lower lip, preempting a smile. This was fun, in a scary way.

"Are you going to invite her back to a motel, lover boy?" Chubby's whispers headed uptown.

"What?"

"You know, for a little hide 'n' seek."

I'm not deaf, Leila thought again. She released her lip; this was no longer fun, not even in a scary way.

"I swear, fat boy, if you don't shut up—" Skinny imagined or wanted or prayed that Leila had not heard his companion.

"I can see a bright future for you two. You can share all your exceptional insights into what's-his-name's 'flawed economic model.' I bet she would find it all quite fascinating. I know I do."

Although Skinny's subsequent muttering was largely incomprehensible, Chubby caught enough of the telegraph staccato to know that Skinny was close, a fig leaf away, to naked fury. But a body in motion . . . "Or, I know, maybe you can talk about her job. How she finds it challenging to keep track of the prices for, what's it, regular and super unleaded."

I'm not deaf.

"Or how she keeps the counters clean."

I'm not deaf.

"Or how hard it is to refill the fucking coffee." Rolled, Chubby rolled, but Leila could not hear him or the chipping ice or her once-bored breath over her silent chant. I'm not deaf. I'm not deaf. I'm not deaf. I'm not deaf. Skinny deposited a bottle of water into Chubby's belly and did not wait to see him balance it with the cookie sack, commendably adroit. "Pay for this, you— I'll be in the fu— I'll be in the car." Shamed sufficiently, Skinny, double-fisted, decided to finish his tirade in private. As he darted out of the station, he didn't look at Leila. She didn't look at him.

After passing over a chocolate milk for a fruit juice, Chubby brought the items to the counter and stood body-to-body—not face-to-face, not eye-to-eye—with Leila. The next morning, Leila rewrote the script from this sentence end. At minimum, she should have shared her chant with Chubby. *I'm not deaf.* Even better, if he had been gracious enough to participate, she should have taken the high road and accepted his apology with a knowing nod. But on that night, which could not be rewritten by morning regrets, no satisfaction was offered, no recognition returned. Leila tucked a strand of her amber hair, chemical-free and doll-straight, behind her ear. "Five twenty-seven." She tucked it again and gave him his change. And then he left.

When the station door swung shut, Leila closed her eyes, opened her mouth in mechanical unison. Her lips sculpted the three syllables again, this time aloud. She took a resigned, acidic breath. She tasted that slight and the others before it, tasted her cowardice and her grandfather and forty-one college credits now wasted. She exhaled; the acid left, the resignation remained. She tucked her hair behind her ear. It fell back across her face.

A man entered the store. His wide nose merged into a substantial mustache, tobacco-stained, wrapping to his mouth's corners. No one in the magazines that passed Leila's nights wore mustaches like that anymore. The man came in every day, and Leila reached above her for a pack of his cigarettes, menthols, strange for a white guy, she used to think, although she had stopped thinking about it altogether.

The man bobbed his head once—his daily gesture—and revved his phlegm. She entered the cigarette price in the cash register and waited.

"Gas too."

Leila looked out the station window and, head now down, noted the price on the inside pump reader. The man was still; silence. I should say something to this guy, she thought. But the register told him what he wanted to know, and he handed her a bill. She made change and laid it on the counter.

"How's it going?" she asked.

"Same-ol', same-ol'."

Leila tried to smile, but her lips pulled wide, a flatline, unnatural.

The next morning Leila arose unrested and cranky; glimpses of midsleep awakenings were still palatable and dry. The sitting dream, the bush, had moved beyond repetition: it had become, it seemed, a cornerstone of the night. An oversized T-shirt clung to her nudity, and she stared blankly at the ceiling from her double bed. The past-noon sun, ignoring the barrier of shades and thick canary drapes, crept into the room, and through the yellow dim, Leila watched the ceiling, watched the scratches in her oak dresser, watched the faded inches of her daisy-drawn wallpaper. She followed the rotations of her cheap plastic fan as it wheezed and goaded the stale humidity into her lungs.

Leila could have slept anywhere in the house—her grandfather's room for instance, the master suite with the thirty-year-old mattress and the three nightstand photographs affecting life. Her mother's room was also available; it was larger than Leila's, but Leila hadn't been in there for three years, and the last time had been a mistake, not wrong, but not conscious. When her grandfather had died fourteen months ago, he had left Leila the house and the benefits, a windbreaker, not a parka, of a late-idea insurance policy. She had enough to get by if she continued working, if she wanted nothing expensive, if accidents did not happen, for a while anyway. She probably should have sold the house immediately and moved someplace smaller; the old-timers in the area had started complaining years ago that the neighborhood *used* to be respectable; the real-estate market had become more indifferent by the year.

In her afternoon mornings, normally, Leila listened, her eyes closed, to the sounds of the house and to the dust marking time in corners, in closets. In the summer, at least, there was the fan; its demanding clicks couldn't erase the house's sounds, still and empty, but it measured them, plotted them, fixed them to a grid. Normally, Leila would spend her first minutes with her eyes lazing through the yellowish half-light. And she would ask herself, normally, in pulses not words, if her heart could still flitter, if her knees could still twitch. She had not felt a flitter nor a twitch in years. It had not been a choice; it was a rhythm, a deep groove: it hadn't happened today, it hadn't happened today, it might happen today, it hadn't happened today. Normally, and this was the newest addition to normally, Leila would wonder whether the years, each daily tide, could wash away the ability to act and receive and feel. If no new experiences, sandbags filled with ardor or loss, were quick-delivered, would the whole beach erode? So Leila would wonder, normally. Then she would get up. Then she would go to work. Then she would come home.

But today, today wasn't normally, and Leila opened her eyes and remembered last night. She first directed heroic endings to last night's drama: splendid Leila silences Chubby with hard glare; benevolent Leila basks in the glow of her benevolence. Then she directed more vengeful last acts. These required more effort, a personality displacement, and thus in the middle of one rant, she faltered. You know, I'm not like deaf, she should have told Chubby. I'm not dumb. I'm not like blind or an idiot or retarded. So you can't treat me like I'm just some worthless checkout girl, like that's all I'm here for, *like that's what I am.* It caught her, and she repeated it. *That's what I am.* Checking it methodically from all sides, she inspected it for discoloration. That's what I am. That's what I am. That's what I am. That's what I am. She closed her eyes for a better look, registered each word slowly, then tried to put the phrase back on the shelf. It was not the first time at the station, of course, that Leila had been insulted, condescended to, seen through, stepped on, ignored. Every day there, she met people with seeds of anger, seeds of danger, seeds of intimacy and disappointment.

Rectilinear and fixed, a railroad tie, Leila slipped her nails beneath the waistband of her underwear, snapped it back, dragged her hand up her stomach. What does that like even mean? she thought. That's what I— I mean, who cares what I am? *No one that's who.* Technically speaking, Leila was wrong. Her aunt Mary, great-aunt, cared; her aunt Peg, to whom no one had spoken in fifteen years, probably still cared too; and others, no doubt, congenital sympathizers for the lonely, also cared intensely for her.

The alarm clock read one forty-five. Stu-pid, she cursed. She had wanted to get up early that day. She had wanted to go to the Fair.

She looked at the clock, ceiling, clock again. *Two o'clock.* I have to get up, she thought. I don't have to do anything, she corrected herself. I don't have to do anything because . . . She knew one because—because she didn't have to go to work until next Monday—but she didn't want to say that. I don't have to do anything because . . . She knew others—because no one was waiting for her at the Fair, because no one was shining his shoes to impress her—but she didn't want to say those either. I don't have to do anything because . . .

That is what I am. Leila kicked off a sheet weaved around her legs—old institutional, rough cotton—and slid her finger again beneath her waistband. Her left hand wandered aimlessly, then mindfully through her body, but no pleasure was there, only duty, just checking. Finally, she pulled herself to a sitting position, *two-thirty*, walked across the room magnified by the oak emptiness between lone bed, lone dresser, lone desk, and let gravity persuade her barely cooperating feet downstairs. She stood in her T-shirt outside; the porch roof blocked the afternoon sun, but Leila, whose eyes had been purchased months ago by the fluorescent lights of the second shift, squinted. She folded over, her knees unbent, to pick up a newspaper. Hers was a body recognizable, coltish, a late bloomer's not yet convinced of its finished state. Well into her eighteenth spring, Leila, now nearly twenty-three, had let her unyieldingly straight hair grow to her waist against the advice of common sense and, more relevant, the ascending, aerosoled model of her similarly complexioned peers. Despite constant feeding and watering, no breasts had grown on her great plains until she was nineteen. To top it all off, literally, the rest of her face had lagged behind an overbite—now a graceful projection, a cornice applauded for its architectural whimsy—until the years of anonymity, slander, and empty Friday nights had had adequate time to do their business.

Leila turned into the house, threw the unread paper on top of its brethren of the last two weeks, and wiped the muggy newsprint on her shirt. She had asked the station's manager for the week off. As she did every year, she planned to go to the Fair on Tuesday, today, her first day off, and maybe again on Saturday. Leila had missed the Fair only once. Last June, her aunt Mary, the sister of her grandfather Peter, had packed Leila's clothes, sealed the house, dragged her to the car, and drove her up north to stay "with the only person you have left." Leila had come to terms with her grandfather's death, but she did not know how to handle her teapot-shaped abductress. Mary Volk had enjoyed a brief interlude of surrogate motherhood for Peter's own daughters before "that mean-spirited brother of mine pushed me out of the door." After Peter's death, an event that severely handicapped his ability to raise any objections to her actions, Mary took command of Leila's "situation." This was Mary's destined moment of triumph, return, reward after enduring years in the wilderness and passing a godly test of resolve. So Leila spent four months in her great-aunt's house, an airless mausoleum congested with photographs, needlepointed pillows, ghosts, a poorly rendered heirloom picture of Martin Luther, and a letter, the framed centerpiece, offering condolences to a young woman widowed by a Japanese Zero and the Philippine Sea. In October, Leila finally made her escape— Mary was at church—and called that night from home to thank her aunt and to let her know that the station like *absolutely* needed her back. Mary never understood how that poor girl was going to get by all alone.

Leila threw herself, back first, on the living-room couch. I should really go, she thought. A few minutes passed. She couldn't get comfortable, get right, and she tried a pillow, one side, the other side, folded, padded down. A television was turned on by remote control and turned off by the same method. The phone rang. Leila hid her head under the pillow, but the inconsiderate peal cried five times more. Leila didn't want to talk to anyone, any-more, ever; she didn't want to be *near* anyone. The phone stopped. Leila couldn't imagine any idea stupider than going to the Fair. It was resolved; she wasn't going to go. Two minutes later, the phone rang again. She commanded it to stop, and the ringing, now obedient, withdrew. It started again two minutes, exactly, later. She picked up the receiver. Hesitating for a second, she answered far more curtly than she had planned to, "Yes?"

"Oh, Leila, I think I not catch you." It was Yankel Blakov, the manager of the station. His accent was exclusively his: one part indeterminable eastern European from indeterminable place of birth; one part barreling Middle West from his years boarding with his sister and her American husband; one part Yankel origi-nal, pedigree unknown. "Hey, hey, Leila. It's *Yankel* Blakov, you know, from the station." He always said that, just so you didn't confuse him with the other Yankel Blakovs you knew. Everyone agreed that Yankel was a moron. By some unexplained inversion of the American dream, this had not prevented him from rising to his current position.

"Why did you call three times?"

"Oh yeah, I want to make sure I catch you before you leave already, you know." Yankel had ascended to his post through attrition; as his office-parked superior glumly defended himself after one notorious company outing incident, What choice did I have—he'd been a clerk for fourteen years.

"Yankel, I'm *about* to leave," Leila moaned.

"Oh yeah? I call you to see if you can work tonight, you know."

"Yankel, I have off till Monday. You *knew* about it last month."

"Yeah, yeah. But Irving can't work tonight, you know."

"Well, I'm sorry, but I'm leaving for my vacation in like exactly two minutes."

"Oh yeah?" Disappointment turned to thinking, and the combination, overloading, turned to incomprehensibility. "Uh, oh yeah. No problem then, you know. Um, I just uh, you know there, just someone else get. Okay bye." With that, Yankel decided the matter for Leila. He had soiled the house, the solitude, which had not as of yet been wholly unbearable. She could be more alone, she figured, at the Fair.

# [ 3 ]

Leila had entered the South Exhibition Hall through the west door at the same time that Barry exited through the east. She, like most, was a methodical fairgoer, and she started on one side of the hall in the narrower aisles; she studied the merchandise of the less dynamic booths, car waxes and hand creams, and tried not to notice all the stupid happiness of the Fair, the hands a-holding, the thank-you kisses for buying-me-this, the little-girl paws inside Daddy's protective mitts.

As Barry left the hall, he untucked his cotton oxford, buttoned the top button, and bunched up his sleeves to a practiced two inches higher than his wrists. His board-riding sneakers, his shirt, his hipster pants (with a ringed hammer-holder for a hammer he didn't own and nail pouches for nails he didn't use) were standard youth, Cal-Mex, and identifiable rebel. The outfit's genius was its day personality; Barry could tuck in the shirt and hide the sneakers under the organ. This was a compromise, a protested one, with Ed, who worshiped at the First Church of the Holy Necktie and believed that there was no sin worse—bankruptcy maybe, but that's it—than a salesman presuming to sell a fourteen-hundred-dollar item without wearing adequate business apparel: navy blue, all-wool, two-piece, single-breasted. But Barry couldn't do that and maintain his self-respect for he was cool Barry, good-looking Barry, Greek-beauty Barry with the porcelain skin of the Olympian gods and the beveled facial shifts of the olive descendants. With a sharp nose that, technically speaking, was too big and a crop of overgrown peanut-shell hair, which seemed to have been cut long before the invention of both scissors and barbers, Barry was, truthfully, a collection of the odd, unusual, and androgynous that should have totaled a person more homely than not. Should have, but didn't.

Half hour to burn, Barry thought, forty-five minutes at most or Ed'll like definitely go nuts. As Barry entered the Fair's main byway, he needed something, he felt; air maybe, water, food, *some*thing for something else, when he had been sitting on the organ bench, had been whirring in his legs, an abstract itchiness neither inside nor outside his skin. The summer was almost over, and he was relieved and uneasy, because the summer was almost over—yes, good—and then? He didn't know, *and then*. In his marrow, on the hairtips of his legs urging him out of that hall, that booth, that brother, he didn't know, *and then*. But dwelling didn't lead anywhere, Barry figured, and he opted for a snack. There were only two places in front of him for food. A popcorn wagon, which was closer, contained a figure, elderly and dog-faced; a trailer, a dealer in ballpark foods, was farther away, but the dim figures in it bore gayer breasts, more pampered hair, tighter skin. As Barry approached the trailer, the sixteen-year-old figure on counter duty that day, Jenny Lozach, was discussing with her best friend and colleague, Tina Jansky, the tragic fallout from Tina's cousin Nicky's triple-timing. The owners of the trailer had uniformed the girls, over their horrified groans, in logoed purple polo shirts. Jenny carried a safety pin in her purse for such occasions and cinched the shirt in back, revealing an almond of flesh above her waistline. Tina, equally thin—Was there a choice?—but deeply disturbed about her nose, a long Polish downslope, chose an extra-large edition and belted it. It made her look, as one beer-happy customer informed her, like a grape Popsicle.

"Large Coke and . . ." Barry ordered, sedated; his ventriloquist lips did not stoop to movement. He examined the window-poster pictures of ice-cream novelties, and pressed, assured and hard-sounding, the one he wanted. In a just world, that press made clear, Barry Steinke would not be bothered with trifling tedium like ordering a large Coke and an ice-cream novelty. Jenny thought this made Barry cool.

One decibel from inaudible, Jenny confirmed, "Large Coke and the double-chocolate one, right?"

Barry nodded and grinned the boomerang grin of the terminally bored. He had eaten only three hours earlier, but his metabolism, naturally fast, had been rearranged by intoxicants—man-made, grown, imported, distilled, uplifting, and down-dreaming—which had accompanied him constantly over the last six years. Barry had made a firm, polygamous commitment to them when he was fourteen; he had been affected so far by only sideways repercussions.

Jenny snapped, nervous and unnoticed, her bottom's Lycra wrapper, moved behind the soda machine, and repopped her head across the counter window. "You want like regular large or like family-saver large?" A majority of Jenny's great-grandparents were Hungarian; her high cheekbones and skin, sun-brushed that summer into a Mediterranean bronze, marked her as true exotica among the state's medium-rare majority.

"Whatever you want." Barry could see by Tina's wiper-blade glances that Jenny was giving her a sign. Jenny returned with the ice cream and a tub of soda, and Barry paid. He was too intent, too strategic to let the outrageous markup remind him of the perpetual lightness of his pockets. The transaction was over.

"My name's Barry." He offered his hand.

It caught Jenny by surprise. "Hi, I'm, um, I'm Jenny." She enfolded hers in his.

"Well, it's very good to meet you, Jenny." Barry enunciated her name open-wide. Their hands were positioned for an upright American shake, but they didn't move their locked paws; they held them together for five clamorous tom-toms of Jenny's heart. And then Barry squeezed Jenny's hand just-that-much tighter. "You like have a pretty strong handshake there, Jenny. It must be like from cooking hot dogs all day long," he said, separating the hot from the dogs, hardening the *t,* hissing the *gs.*

Tina's face scattered so quickly, eyebrows miles from chin, that the neurons got lost on their way to her lower lip; the lip dangled there, wondering if it would ever rejoin her face again. Finally, regaining her senses, Tina humphed. Although Jenny had giggled—not disappointedly, Barry had noticed—

she welcomed the humphing occasion and flipped her head in Tina's direction; Jenny's ambitious bangs, courtesy of a liberal spraying two hours before, remained at attention. "And this is Tina."

"Tina, right?" Barry had heard her name perfectly, but Tina's humph, an obstacle humph, had drawn the lines.

"Whatever."

"Oh"—wittle boy Bawwy didn't understand—"I didn't offend anyone, did I, Jenny?" Jenny rubbed down the countertop and mumbled, "Whatever," democratically stressed, meaning, It doesn't matter. Tina had exaggerated her *what* and twanged her *ever:* you're like a jerk.

"So, Jenny, like what's there to do around here? I'm just traveling through." It was a silly, setup question.

"Nothing." Of course, there was nothing to do around here. Every day of Jenny's life, there was nothing to do around here. That would have been true anywhere, but it was especially true around here.

"Yeah, you know, I'm like a musician."

"Oh, really." Jenny rested her elbows on the counter; her and Barry's lips were now two feet apart.

"Yeah, I'm like doing kind of a rock slash rockabilly groove."

"Like that's really cool. I, like, like that kind of thing." She had no idea what that kind of thing was.

"But I dunno. I'm like getting kind of tired of it. If you think about it, it's getting old. So I'm experimenting with dance beats and stuff."

"Oh, yeah, dance beats? Like that's *really* cool." It did sound cool. That was true.

"Maybe you'll get to hear me sometime."

"Like are you playing at the main stage?" The main stage, which moonlighted as the racetrack grandstand, had a capacity of fifteen thousand. You could headline there if you were a big-name country singer or a perpetual-motion rock group that had done nothing creative in the last twenty years.

"Yeah, right around there."

"Wow. That must be great." A lifetime of Jenny's bedroom-poster fantasies condensed in one vision. Barry, the gardener, took pride in what he had planted. Jenny was going to hop over the counter, tear off her purple shirt, jump into the arms of this scarecrow, travel all over the world, live in fancy hotels, and never, ever, ever go to school again.

"Yeah, it's all right, I guess, but it can be like lonely on the road."

"Oh sure."

"I'm so lonely," Barry sang the three words to four notes, none melodically ordered, a joke masking sincerity masking a smirk. Jenny, however, accepted this as the indisputable proof that he was the famous musician he claimed to be. She giggled again. Thus encouraged, Barry finished his masterpiece: "Lonely, lonely, lonely, lone."

Jenny knew that dumb, girlish giggles should not hail such a performance. She thought visibly and asked, "Aren't you hot?" Leaning over, she had noticed Barry's long sleeves and long pants, a relative mummy wrap compared to the shorts galore of the Fair.

"Yes," Barry answered, not to that question, and Jenny, surrendering, giggled herself into a beet. Barry wore long sleeves everywhere, he did not tell her. Lurking just underneath his bunched cuff was his tattoo.

*What's that, jackass?* So Ed, two years earlier, had introduced himself to the moss-green smudge, size of a silver dollar, between elbow and wrist.

"Don't you know?" Barry was curious; Ed was the first in the family to see it.

"No."

"It's Elvis."

"And that?" Ed, between scoffs, pointed to six indecipherable characters.

"E.A.P. R.I.P." Barry smiled, satisfied with the memoriam.

Ed asked the obvious. "Were you drunk?"

"Yeah, but if you think about it, it doesn't like matter." Ed requested further information. "'Cause I got drunk *to get* the tattoo."

"What are you talking about, jackass?"

"There's like a *big* difference."

"Which is?"

"You'll never understand." And the conversation, by mutual consent, was over. Barry didn't care that the subtleties of the big difference would escape Ed forever. As he explained to the designated driver (also drunk) on the way back from the parlor, he had not enrolled with EAP RIP in the ranks of the tattooed to impress "friends or girls or my family or nobody." He had enrolled because he was in The Hotels. Barry, the heart of the group, kept the blood circulating through the *corpus bandus teenagerus* by writing the songs, booking the gigs, and buying the beer. His writing, actually, was only arranging—The Hotels' live repertoire, stretched full, consisted of eleven covers—and his booking never went beyond registering for high-school band battles and ensuring that the band could still play on Fridays (for free) at The Rooster. Nevertheless, musical history will remember two achievements of The Hotels: it bolstered the reputations of the original four members at Carl Schurz High School; and it allowed the bandmates with one staff change—bassist Andy Vojchek's parents absolutely insisted that he go to college that fall—to avoid doing anything else until they were nineteen.

On those glorious Friday nights at The Rooster, Robert Gutmanis, its proprietor, a rosy-cheeked bear of a man known as

Guddy, somehow hid the rest-of-the-week drunks, smoldering violence, and implicit sorrow, and opened the bar to the local high-school kids until ten. Per an understanding with the law— "if we don't have any trouble, you don't have any trouble"—no alcohol was served on Rooster Youth Music Nights. Guddy claimed to make just as much selling cans of soda for a dollar apiece, although cups of ice sold briskly too, also for a dollar, and the capped bulges in the boys' pockets could not be solely attributed to hormonal excitement. Onstage, on those Fridays, three boys appeared at first; they were all dressed with minor variance in T-shirts, loose black jeans, and baseball caps beaten onto their noses or fiercely turned frontside back. The set began pleasantly enough: six two-chord riffs were interspersed with three fifteen-second drum solos by the not-untalented Andy Schneider. Following a considerable drum roll, Barry, less pale then, with the tight-wrapped boniness of a six-year-old at the dawn of musculature, jumped onto the stage and commandeered the show. Barry believed it incumbent upon an interpretive artist to shed (loudly!) any imprisoning fealty to an original artist's rendering of a work. Thus "number forty-seven said to number three" became "number forty-seven said to friggin' number three," and "while I get my kicks" became "while I get my stinkin' rotten-rotten-rotten-rotten kicks." After the opening song, Barry, bolstered by a combination of consumables, embarked on a cluttered journey of jumps, screams, sung-spoke phrases, and pounded chords. Midway through The Hotels' life span, Barry began to insert rap interludes into selected songs, taking a jailhouse rock, for instance, as a starting point to launch into several verses regarding prisons and the murderous vengeful exploits that put the narrator there. The raps and Barry's better-sung interludes blended well into the playing of the rest of The Hotels, who subscribed to the gospel of all punky high-school autodidacts: if you play a song twice as fast and thrice as distorted, the audience will never catch on to your missing half the notes and arriving at the same part at four different times. At the concerts, The Hotels' female fans in thigh-carving skirts or painted-on jeans alternated their adoration between prospective suitors thrashing helter-skelter in front of the stage and Barry Steinke on it. A collective sigh was heard, an immemorial swoon, during Barry's two signature symphony-in-a-box romantic solos. In The Late Rooster Era, Barry, who was more than competent when not self-distracted, would introduce his last solo by raising his left arm—*whoa*—overhead, uncited because unaware black power. Barry would read the inscription, pausing for a solemn second between each solemn letter.

Lately, however, Barry tried not to dwell on the tattoo just as he tried not to dwell on other aspects of his current situation— his brother, the organ, the expos, the fairs. A tattoo would not have bothered him, but that tattoo reeked of the unpleasant stench of a good idea gone bad. (Barry had spent a month listing ways to change EAP RIP to something else. But his other ideas—TEARDRIP, FEAR RIPENT, WEAP RIPPER, BEARYRIPPLE, PEAR RIPOFF, HEAR RIPTIDE, and LEAP, RIP & ROLL—were either stupid or required spelling compromises best not permanently made on one's skin.) I can't like imagine what I was thinking, Barry would look back in amazement, but he knew exactly what he had been thinking. School for him had always been a daydream playground—"Mr. Steinke, Mr. Steinke, are you with us, Mr. Steinke"—of stadium concerts and concocted eager groupies. The Hotels had existed to conquer global consciousness. The tattoo, like the band, was an homage (Barry had never heard the word spoken and pronounced it with a hard *h*) to the first generation of rock from the next. But the tattoo, like the daydreams, had been dulled by sunburn and scratching, blurred by hard soap and sweat.

Barry and Jenny's conversation had halted on Barry's admission that, yes, he was hot. Jenny's eyes widened. In these situations,

Barry never thought about what words would follow—that's what he liked, craved, needed about these situations. He was a natural. "I was like thinking of going to the midway for a while, but that's no fun alone."

"I like *so* want to go, too." Jenny's shoulders slouched, adolescent before the cruel facts of the cruel world. "But I got to like stay here until the Fair closes."

"Working girl's got to do what a working girl's got to do." Barry sipped from the soda—the moment, a tablet on which Jenny could inscribe her submission.

Tina, ignored, brewing, jealous, looked up from the rotating hot dogs and rained on the courtship. "You are like so immature."

Jenny rolled her eyes, begging Barry to disregard her dumb friend.

"What did you say?" Something had changed in him.

"You heard me."

"Why would you say something like that?" Barry's curiosity was genuine. Why had the entire universe decided, this summer, that its *only* purpose was to prevent Barry Steinke from having a good time? It didn't make much sense, if you think about it.

Caught in the middle, Jenny chose Barry's side. She could forgive Tina afterward. They were, after all, best friends. "Teeenaaaa."

The whine did not pacify. "Forget it. This guy's just an immature liar. He's not gonna play at no main stage tonight."

"Hey, Gina, why don't you mind your own business."

"It's Tina, you immature asshole."

"Whatever."

Jenny spun around and glared at Tina. Tina lifted her palms chest high. *Okay, I'll back off.* But as Jenny turned away, Tina mouthed it again for Barry's private viewing. "Im. Ma. Ture."

Well, that did it. "Hey, Jenny, you're like okay, but something around here sucks." His fists snatched his purchases and he walked away, walked away expressionless, walked away far enough from the trailer that he didn't witness the fight that followed, didn't hear the hateful slings, things so hateful that only a best friend could say. Like a well-trained soldier, Barry marched back toward the South Exhibition Hall. But he was upset, in-the-nucleus upset; he usually didn't mind the strikeouts, the accepted hazard of the home-run hitter. But today felt peculiar. Not just with Jenny, but with that four-wall stifle of the South Exhibition Hall, crushing and condensing, with his legs, bristling. Gina-Tina-Big-Purplina had interrupted him, the whole world kept on interrupting him, from the only thing that made this friggin' life worthwhile.

*Immature. Where does that piece of trash get off calling me—*

If Tina had called him ugly or stupid, an idiot or an ass, Barry would not have given up so easily. *Imma—* If Tina had said *anything* else, he and Jenny, he was sure, would have been interlocked by nightfall. But *immature* was the word that killed The Hotels.

# [ 4 ]

Barry was back in the booth, and Ed thanked him for being so lazy and unhelpful. Barry, never afraid of a retort (moron, suit monkey, failure), was silent. He was silent when another prospect came and went, unsold. And he was silently finishing the last of his ice cream as the bulging man listened to Ed. "An instrument's an instrument."

"A what?"

By that time, Leila had already stolen a glimpse of Barry. She had been standing at the outer edge of Olde Country Maple Syrup—her grandfather, she was almost certain, had bought a still-unopened jar here ten years ago—with no other goal than to avoid the glare of the owners: city people, distrustful, vigilant, obsessed with thieves. She looked to the neighboring booth and noticed Barry, returned her eyes to the tins and mini-cabins and mini-jugs of syrup below, glanced over her shoulder at the syrupers' policing glare, and looked at Barry again. Barry was nice looking, she thought, but the human mop wasn't—this was correct—*that* nice looking. He was awfully, recallingly skinny too. Leila had no intention of approaching him or talking to him or trying to attract his eye, she told herself the obvious. Other women in this situation, she knew—television women—were randy, whispered asides, got laughs. The closest woman to Leila was Ed's customer's wife; she wore a peach T-shirt with a multiform decal: MUSCLE CAR '66.

Leila imagined her own futile interruption of the woman: "Um, ma'am?"

"Muscle Car Sixty-six," would come a husky smoker's response.

"I think that guy's all right." Leila would flex her pinky at Barry.

"Muscle Car Sixty-six."

"But it's like been a while. Do you have any suggestions?" she would ask.

"Muscle Car, girl. Muscle Car Six*ty-six.*"

Leila tried to stifle the laugh in her throat, but a few peeps escaped into the hall's sonic stew. Two accompanying raindrops of red landed on her cheeks and flooded them with color; the blush applied itself artfully, banishing her usual nightworker blanch. Ed, struggling to Lead through Precision his deep-dimpled customer, didn't notice, but Barry saw Leila, stared, and approved. Leila sheepishly tucked three strands of her straight hair behind her ear. Barry smirked. Leila fixed her eyes on her shoes. Barry's thoughts, not all innocent, bubbled. Jenny Lozach was forgotten; Yankel Blakov who? Leila wasn't exactly a tomboy, Barry noticed, although tomboys would not have objected to her dress. As always, she wore jeans and an earth-colored top, strict by the rules: unneon, unfrilled, unbuttony, unchecked and unstriped, and unworded—especially unworded. That day, she had put on white jeans and a burgundy knolly cotton pullover that accentuated her lines and stopped at her subtle hips.

Around the cuff, Barry scratched his forearm slow, dragging; it took eighty seconds for the watch to travel a minute. He looked at Leila, who tucked her hair earbound again. Three seconds later, she tucked again. Leila's head's shape and her hair's texture colluded in a magnetic attraction between strands and right eye; the more she tucked, the limper her hair became. The limper it became, the more it fell into her face. The more it fell into her face, the more she tucked. Then, self-conscious about hair in her face, self-conscious about playing with her hair, she tucked the straight strands because she did it whenever she felt self-conscious. Three years back, tired of the whole to-do, Leila had cut her hair boyishly short, but like those veterans who reach out to scratch the leg they lost a half century ago, Leila, feeling self-conscious, would reach out to tuck the hair in front of her eyes and find none there. After maintaining the bob for six weeks, she let her hair grow long again.

A symmetry of self-consciousness was established, a mutual stimulation perhaps of the aroused. Barry's thoughts turned to action. He winked, and the wink missed. For a precocious achiever in the sexual department, a wink that did not reach its target was a tough knock, a combination of public feat and private failure, branding the doer with guilt without offering him the remedy of shame. Barry was in a bind: the wink had missed, he was sure, but if she *had* seen the first one, a second wink would probably end the story early. *But what do I got to lose?* He winked again.

Success. An amused, if not altogether acquiescing, smile lifted Leila's face. Her blush deepened; the slight overbite closed. After smiling, she did the proper thing. Her mouth lightly suppressed another coy curl, suppressing enough to not look easy and lightly enough to still be smiling, and she tucked her hair behind her ear. She glanced briefly at Ed, still working, and aimed her eyes down. Calm down, she thought. She had not stopped moving, it felt, since Yankel's call. She had rushed to get dressed, rushed to leave the house, rushed to her car, rushed to the Fair, rushed to the hall, and when she was finally ready to stop rushing, *this* had happened. *You don't know what you're doing. Just calm down.* She tried to pinch another glimpse of Barry, but her eyes sank again before they rose. *Why did he wink?* She plucked the strings, a wink and a wink and a wink. *Probably 'cause he's messing with you.* She guessed his age, and she decided to walk away, and she wondered if she had brushed her teeth, and she decided to stay, and she insisted that it was Barry's turn to offer a sign, and she decided to leave. Paragraphs became sentences, sentences became syllables; pages were lost; chapters were missing. She looked down at the jug of syrup and read its ingredient list: syrup.

Leila was right; it was Barry's turn. After her coy smile, Barry should have returned a reserved smile of his own, an acknowledging nod, and a broader smile. That, Leila appreciated, was how it worked in the movies. She looked at Barry.

Following Leila's smile, Barry had been prepared to return a soft smile, another wink, and a broader smile. Yet the nervous hands tucking and tucking the hair, the eyes so forced— fluttery—on the syrup jars, the blushing—they all declared embarrassment. Hers? Hers for him? A spot on his forehead? A stain on his shirt, a zipper half open? Barry's hands, he rubbed and felt, were sticky, double-chocolate sticky, and his mouth was—? He cleaned, tongue-cleaned, his upper lip and puckered both lips to disperse the excess saliva. But before he even had the chance to *begin,* the girl's face screamed in horror.

*The pig was just like all of 'em.* The pig had licked, slow, swampy, and lewd, his upper lip. The pig had then blown her a kiss.

Horror wasn't quite accurate; it was horror-confusion-shock-awe-disgust, each reaction not successive but a new reaction, blended and baked, inseparable and unique. *What the—* Barry had no idea what—*who*—had prompted her reaction. He turned to Ed; whenever something goes wrong, it's never a bad idea to blame a family member first. Ed was staring across the central alley, his eyes were flat, he was on the mat again, and this time, it appeared, he was just sitting out the count. *Where's that family he was just talking to?* They had seemed interested. This whole thing is too, too, too— Barry dipped into his coin purse of vocabulary for a nugget to encapsulate the absurdity. He failed.

By then, Leila was fleeing. The only word for it was *flee.*

Ed saw it too. He asked Barry, "What's that girl running for?"

"What's it to you?"

PART TWO

# [ 1 ]

Planets cannot stop their spinning. Gravity's no longer winning. Three wise men lost their way. To Bethlehem on Christmas Day.

To one side and the other, in front and in back, the booths were filled with commerce and bustle. At the center, however, the booth was empty but for two—two people, two moods, defeated and angry.

"Are we done with this disaster yet?" Barry ended a half minute of silence.

Ed's middle finger provided the response.

Barry's smile was flattened and satisfied: his brother was being childish. "Face it," he broke the souring news, "we're not going to sell anything today." Ed grunted, and Barry continued, "So I propose we call it quits."

"I propose you shut up, jackass."

These outbursts should no longer have surprised Barry, but like a sailor too used to a squall as a concept, he was often taught anew their tangible force. "Is that a 'Yes,' moron?"

Ed's middle finger responded again. In case his sign language was unclear, he added, after a blink, "No, this is a 'Yes.'" His left hand back-plowed through his hair, lifting and releasing on the upstroke, matting responsibly on the down. His face was bunched and nauseated, temporarily speechless. He watched Barry. "Why are you scratching yourself like a friggin' dog?"

"Go to hell." Barry stopped scratching.

"Oh yeah," Ed gained strength, "I forgot."

"Like what's your problem?"

His head ostrich-bobbing toward Barry's arm, Ed purred, "Well, it's not as *per*manent as yours." Ed's advantages, as he calculated them—his age, his ac*comp*lishments—resuscitated his cheeks to a composed, edgeless slack.

"Being a loser isn't like permanent?" Barry sounded less manful than he had hoped to.

"Why don't you just throw away your whole arm, jackass?" When Gene Steinke first saw his younger son's tattoo, he mumbled, with the forty-percent-off perceptiveness of a paranoiac, Who made you get that? All those shaggy-haired friends of yours?

"Did someone tell you you were funny?" Barry replied evenly. He should have punched Ed, he thought—he like *so* wanted to punch Ed in that snotty *per*manent mouth. But Barry reminded himself that he was the calm brother; he would not relinquish that title, no matter how hard Ed pushed. "'Cause if they did, they lied."

"Did someone tell you you weren't an idiot," Ed mirrored, then hesitated. The game was becoming too heavy, saddlebags; he just wanted Barry to leave. He exhaled noisily, finally surrendering to his obligation to add, "Because you *are* an idiot."

"Know what, Ed?" Barry asked after a cooling pause, the baby brother again, amnesiac.

The tone's change checked Ed. Barry wasn't serious exactly, but he was back-floating, disengaged. "No . . ."

"To be like totally honest, I don't like care about that band or like any of that high-school crap anymore." Barry had not listened to The Hotels' guiding saint for over a year now and had not talked to half the band's members for longer than that. "I just wish . . ."

"Yeah?"

Barry just wished that he didn't have the tattoo to remind him how much he didn't care about any of that crap anymore. "Nothing."

"What?"

"Nothing."

"*What?*"

"I said, nothing."

The tin gears behind Ed's face prefaced his reply: his eyes flashed first with an animating spark; his left nostril and a sneer below it twisted, as a piece, around the first words. "Then don't bother me with your crap. Got it, jackass?"

"I've got better things to do than like waste time talking to you anyway, dude."

"Then go do 'em, asshole." *Whatever them is.*

Barry shook his head, disappointed and facile: imagine your own flesh and blood acting like that. "Okay, *moron,* then I'm leaving. If I'm not back in like an hour . . ." Barry lost his sentence to drafty, wider thoughts, and his mouth, fly-catching, waited for sentence-end to return.

Proving anew that there is nothing in this world as beautiful as the love between two brothers, Ed tenderly wished Barry Godspeed on his journey: "Do I look like I fucking care when you come back?"

With another shake of the head, Barry left.

Waste of space, Ed thought and resolved not to pay Barry for the day, but he had made and broken that resolution so often that he had stopped noting it in his ledger. He and Barry had never been close. Their differences in temperament and appearance— Barry had two and a half inches on Ed, Ed fifteen pounds on Barry—had often made both brothers wonder what they would have thought of each other with strangers' bare histories. Yet it was a mundane difference, the age difference, that ultimately caulked the barrier. By now, it had been seven years since Ed had left for college a week before Barry started high school, seven years when Ed's daily activities were unknown to his younger brother, seven years when Ed's personality, which thirteen-year-old Barry had found merely square and serious, had deepened and shaded in often indecipherable tones. It had been seven years, a few summers excepting, when Barry learned of Ed's life in spills and leaks and six years when Ed only learned of Barry's in brief flashes of scandal; seven years when no one would have predicted that their paths would cross again that April when Ed invited Barry to become his partner. Ed had done it, he would have told you candidly, to save his brother. After high school, Barry was a musician, "full-time," and appeared at the Steinke home on Rue Chambois Road only to eat in or take out. No information was publicly available as to his whereabouts in the interim, and Gene and Linda Steinke painted the blank space with lurid, fantastical depictions of their son's sins, narcotic and sexual, many of which were not that far off. Linda tried to encourage her son to reconsider his refusal to even think about college with epigrammatic object lessons. *You know, Bare, I never went to college, and I've regretted that all my life.* Barry's replies were water-tight. *That's you and I'm me.* Gene's strategy initially rested on the hope that a medley of guttural grumps made whenever Linda gave Barry money would cause his son to change his mind. Ten months later, he adopted a new approach. Gene was the distribution manager for Lincoln Paper, a private four-hundred-employee paper-goods manufacturer. An enviable position by the standards of Rue Chambois Road, the job was sturdy, dissectible, geophysically fixed. The distribution manager spent a third of his day in committee meetings and a third overseeing the three clerks—down from seven fifteen years ago—who nursed the computer systems and tracked down errant loads. Gene passed the final tongue-bitten third of his day defusing the ire of customers and salesmen when southbound shipments went northbound and westbound shipments went nowhere. After hearing secondhand from Linda that Barry had been semiofficially branded one of the neighborhood ne'er-do-wells, Gene announced, "Enough's enough," pulled some levers at Lincoln Paper (a family company that regarded a nip of nepotism now and then as good for the soul), and told Barry that there was a job waiting for him in the company's warehouse. Much to everyone's surprise, Barry accepted it; he was broke.

Like a sentencing judge, Gene never specified whether the warehouse job was intended to punish past sins or inspire reform, and he was also completely unaware of the environment to which he had sent his son: the warehouse was a day school for laziness and petty vice. The pallet crew, Barry's unit, collected pallets, wasted time, kept the pallets organized, repaired pallets, took long unaccounted-for breaks, and delivered pallets as needed to the packing area. Its members were all young, born surly, and without fear. The new kid soon outdid all the cell-block toughs with the construction of NB, the Nap Box, a one-pallet-by-one-pallet-by-one-pallet cube—one side missing—which was concealed in the crew's corner domain. Barry pressed NB's open side against a wall and initiated Nap Time, everyone a turn.

It was, Barry boasted via kitchen telephone one Saturday afternoon, "friggin' paradise, dude, friggin' paradise." Barry hung up the receiver. His parents had gone to a garden show, and he assumed that he was—

"That's great." Ed startled him. Although Ed no longer lived at home, he had yet to find a laundromat as cheap as the free one there.

"What's it to you?"

"Nothing." That normally would have ended the discussion, but Barry's description of paradise, delivered with a maestro's bravado and a devil's impenitence, prickled Ed, who had heard everything. With each second of the high-noon standoff, Ed's disgust ballooned. "No it's *not* nothing," he recanted. "How can you act like that where Dad works?"

Barry, bravado and impenitence aside, was neither devil nor maestro; he *had* worried about the pallet crew's potential for scandal, tarnishing Gene. Yet Ed had violated his rights by prosecuting him with eavesdrop-obtained evidence. "Who cares?"

*"Who cares?"* Ed spoke more loudly to his own ears, which were confirming their reception. "Dad cares. Mom cares. I—" Full stop. "That's who goddamn cares."

"Then tell 'em all about it, Officer." Barry carefully selected a late-season, grapefruity orange and walked out of the kitchen.

"I will, asshole," Ed yelled after and never did. He had no particular interest in protecting his brother. He didn't tell his parents because he knew Scene Two. His father, widow's peak standing on end, face a hypertensive red denser than anything Ed would ever be able to achieve, would spew something unbearably silly: "I knew those drug-addict friends of yours would lead you to this." His mother would chew her lips to dam the tears, retreat to her kitchen, and start to mop the floor or chop enough carrots and cabbage to drown a whole family in a swimming pool of slaw.

Ed could have related the story of his saving Barry from an incipient life of downward mobility so gravely, so soberly that you would have needed to touch him afterward to verify that he was real. There were, however, other facts. In exchange for the "opportunity to make unlimited $$$$," the Brackett Corporation sought salespeople with good local knowledge *and* musical experience. Ed had the first qualification and, with Barry's musical experience, the brothers' comparative advantage presented them, in Ed's calculus, with an uncanny ability to seize the $$$$. At the time, Ed was suffocating at his job at Pilsen's Distributors, his first job out of college. The money at Pilsen's, a restaurant-supply company, was fine, fine enough anyway, but the customer base was rigid, the days wearisome, the work routine. Although Ed had risen to sales manager and third in charge (out of four), he ached for more experience creating sales from the dust, not more practice pricing spatulas or upselling barstools. Every week since his junior year of college, Ed had been mailed two, sometimes three, packets glossily hailing commemorative-stamp manufacturing or recovered-metal sales as America's next growth industry, packets topped with thanks-for-your-interest letters addressed to Potential Franchisee or Friend of Good Ideas. Of all these, of all he saved (and he saved a lot), Brackett spoke to him the loudest. Only after he decided on it did he decide to save Barry. Barry agreed to the job offer almost immediately, although Ed would never learn the reason. When they made a joint announcement to their parents, Linda couldn't imagine anything more beautiful or natural than her sons' decision. Within three days, every woman loosely acquainted with Linda Steinke knew that her boys were in business together. *Together* proved her boys were close; *business* proved them bright.

Ed didn't know why he wanted to read it again, indeed knew that he didn't want to read it again, but he reached for his brief-case nonetheless, bending down quickly, the pang greeting him, reminding him of his soldierly all-day stand. He stood up, another pang, and turned to face the central alley. His fingers gripped the case at the first knuckle-line, unsure. From the other side of the alley, the tableau of Ed in his booth was heartwarming, slightly shabby perhaps, but the business of this country is business. In center canvas, Ed was swathed in navy blue, hard case in hand, his maroon, sober-octagon tie hanging straight and proper; behind him, two Brackett posters were thumbtacked to the booth's back wall. In the left poster smiled a happy family, white and nice, blond, sweatered, and dated: BRACKETT. FILLING YOUR HOME WITH MUSIC. The right one sent the 180-X—it may have been the decade-old 120-X—floating through star-twinkled space. BRACKETT. THE FUTURE OF MUSIC.

Ed sat down on the organ bench. Sitting was undignified, he knew, but after Connie, after Lottie and Len, after Barry, after the muscle-car family, after that morning, (after Orditz), he didn't give a damn. He picked up the case and laid it on top of the 180-X, delicately, so not to scratch either instrument. His briefcase was the American standard, a cordovan fortress with eight eye-poking corners and two high-security latches—he had trusted this steed since his first day of college. He opened the case and stooped, still sitting, to examine himself in a wallet-sized mirror attached to the case's vertical half. He labored a smile, polished his teeth with his tongue, and labored another. He didn't care, frankly, how he looked now—Barry was gone, most of the customers were gone, another limping, kicked dog of a day was gone—but it was habit; he attempted to keep himself well groomed on duty; he would never, as an article in *American Salesman* cautioned, "Lose a Sale to Lice or Other Hygiene Pitfalls."

The mirror reflected only from forehead to mouth, the section of Ed's face that he didn't mind. Despite the aging effects of the case, Ed's skin remained smooth, a northern smooth, a pale sea with summer's ruddy-island cheeks, days-old whiskers straining to be seen. His teeth were white enough; his nose, unlike his brother's, did not attract reviews; his hair and eyes were, according to the crayon box, Unremarkable Brown. His profile, though, bothered him. Ed did not have a double chin exactly, but he had weakness. It had almost always been that way, but the last three month's fried-and-packaged road life had added mass to his lumpy frame. Whenever possible, he avoided turning his profile to his customers, lest they think a flaw in his inner character rendered the unperpendicular intersection between chin and neck. *Strong chin, strong man.*

He fixed his eyes on the lights of the hall overhead and ground his thoughts—thoughts about money and sales, commissions and Barry, success and success, success and success, always about success and success—into powder. He exhaled and tried to scatter the powder into space, but it hung like the summerend's humid curtain across his face. Secret Energy Zone, he thought. What a crock of shit. He looked at the neighboring booths: four selling knives; two selling juice machines; one can crusher; one set-and-forget breadmaker; one magic sandwich toaster; two cleaning sensational shammies, also magic, although evidently from different families of the supernatural; and the Olde Country Maple Syrup couple—squinty, ravenous bastards. Ed craned his neck to inventory the competition farther down the hall.

From across the alley, over attentive ears, an amplified, hammy, lullaby voice floated to Ed. "I say," it said, "I may be a simple old man from Mississippi, but I know a good deal when I know a good deal."

I know a jackass when I know a . . . , Ed muttered to himself.

"And the All-in-One Knife is just that: an a-*maze*-ing deal." Vernon Warbler had glistened his snow-leopard hair, shined his bolo, tightened his suspenders, starched his blue denim shirt and pants, and made two-thousand percent sure that nobody could de-*ny* that he was a simple old man from Mississippi who would not, *could* not steer you wrong. Ed made a formal pitch, whether prompted by a customer or forced onto one, three or four times an hour. Vernon Warbler was a knife-selling dynamo who played a continuous loop every day, eight hours straight, never stopping to eat, drink, nap, breathe, piss, shit, spit, or sit. "And it is such, I say, an award-winning modern wonder that my good friends at Olaco got a patent on the product *and* the price." Ed was not a patent lawyer, but he was skeptical whether the All-in-One Knife, which consisted of a bread knife on top, a general-purpose knife on bottom, and a bottle opener attached to the handle, apparently with rubber cement, had contributed enough to human progress to warrant a patent. He was also doubtful of "award-winning," although he had never attended a cutlery-awards ceremony. "Just look. Just look at this po' little tomato," Vernon urged as he placed a fist-sized te-*may*-toe, green-tinged, on a cutting board and guillotined it cleanly with the All-in-One. A number of the gathered nodded in appreciation of the knife's proven sharpness and value. Vernon looked at one man, the audience's skeptic (there was always one). "Mister, you don't look impressed with my little knife. Don't you like tomatoes?" The crowd laughed, but the skeptic did not change expressions. "I say, now seriously, tell me, friend, what don't you like about the All-in-One Knife?"

Vernon had absolutely, *absolutely* no idea what he was doing, Ed thought. *Never* ask an open-ended question like that at the beginning of a pitch. Perfect Execution demanded control, demanded direction—Orditz had revealed *all* of that. The salesman must take the customer's General Inclinations and funnel them, choreograph them, *precisely* and perfectly into an unequivocal decision to buy, buy, buy. An open-ended question like Vernon's would always, Ed was sure, lead to defeat. Sure, Vernon sold a lot of those stupid knifes, but that didn't—

"Well," the skeptic replied, "it looks kind of chintzy." Gotcha, Ed thought. Finally.

"Chintzy?" Vernon laughed, the humor swelling. "Chintzy?" With a juggler's alacrity, Vernon brought two more tomatoes onto the cutting board. "This is chintzy." Another knife, comically larger than the All-in-One, appeared from the air, and despite Vernon's full-throttle chop, it bounced off the tomato and slid limply down its side. "This is the All-in-One Knife." Vernon brought it down with sweet gentle force, and the tomato parted before him. The skeptic was still not impressed. Vernon continued, "I say, I got a strong feeling that you just don't like tomatoes." The crowd laughed again; they felt warm, giddy, this was the Fair, the patent-medicine man that granddad used to talk about, not a box of cough drops in a grocery-store aisle. "You know, my mama always said, a tomato a day keeps the doctor away."

Ed sighed. *Here we go again.* This jackass—this buffoon—was exactly like the rest of these traveling embarrassments. They're just out to make a buck, crack a few lame ones, keep themselves financially afloat. They have no idea, no *comprehension,* Vernon especially, about what it means to be a Salesman. It is not just a job. Orditz: humor has its places in this world. The Sales Act is not one of them.

"Yep," Vernon repeated, baiting, "she always said, *one tomato* a day keeps the doctor away."

Someone in the audience took the hook: "That's an apple."

"No wonder she died at thirty-one."

*Classic Sales: Theory and Technique,* Alfred Orditz's great, columnar, and only published work, did not spark the permanent revolution for which its author had hoped. Nevertheless, it was still required reading in rather-behind-the-times college business courses taught by rather-less-than-stimulating college business professors. It was in one of those taught by one of them that Ed Steinke was brilliance-blinded by the opening words of Part One

(Technique), the words that, as Ed's professor lectured, cracked the shell and revealed the nut of salesmanship. *This above all: Perfect Execution.* The previous generation of sales theoreticians— generations came every ten years or so—had bickered and beaten to death a poor man's debate over whether it was better for a salesman to be loved or feared, be a friend or a father, try to make the customer want a product or be afraid to be without it. That generation had agreed on the necessity of moving beyond the simplistic precepts of the generation before them, the champions of "complete knowledge," who had argued that a salesman needed only to *know* his customer to achieve success. In 1954 Orditz arrived and declared that he had no time for the "false dialecticians" who prattled about the customer-salesman relationship. What no one knew before Orditz, Orditz explained, was that the Sales Act itself could be flawless, beautiful, whole. You could master it "like the balletic arts" with Perfect Execution; you could realize Perfect Execution by mastering *Classic Sales.* In the first part of the book, Orditz disaggregated the Sales Act in three chapters and wallpapered the next eight with behavioral precepts required for perfection. ("Leading through Precision" in Chapter 6, "Understanding the General Inclination" in the second half of Chapter 9.) But the technique of Part One was only the sky-is-blue truth for Ed. Before and after Orditz, he had read plenty of paperback how-tos, six-steps, and ten-rules, half of which contradicted the other half, none of which asked you to think too long or too hard. What made Orditz different, what beatified him was Part Two (Theory), the part that no professor assigned. Mankind, Orditz proclaimed, is divided into two types: buyers and sellers. Sellers, of course, are the leaders with power over the masses of buyers, but sellers, Orditz made clear, are not just those who sell goods or services to others; in a modern complex economy, everyone acts, at times, as both buyer and seller. True sellers are those who create the sale from the dust. "Only the True Salesman," the theory climaxed on page 286, "is more important to the Transaction than the Good sold. In this regard, only the True Salesman has freed himself from the constraints of Normal Exchange. In a very real way then, only the True Salesman can say that he is a man apart from the quotidian Buyers' Culture." Every time Ed read page 286—he had lost count of the readings—he would roll the syllables slowly off his tongue, pause devotedly inside the critical capitalized words, let the lusciously exotic *quotidian* sit and sweeten on his teeth. Ed had always been apart from the Buyers' Culture. At eleven, he poured four days of sweat and spirit into a seventy-three-line poem, an epic really, on nature and meaning—"Last Winter"—only to be told that he was probably a left-brain kind of boy; at fourteen, he was advised that he might not feel quite comfortable in a class for the gifted; at seventeen, he did not have a date for the senior dance; and so at nineteen, when he read Orditz's theory, he recognized an embryo in the mirror; when he read Orditz's technique, he saw the instructions on the page.

Ed watched the huddle competing to open their wallets for Vernon Warbler and thought about the woeful, corrupt lives of those customers. Trying to override his thoughts, he assigned an income profile to several buyers. It was a good game, a strategic skill builder, another habit, at least a distraction. He had started doing it after reading in *American Salesman,* the glossier, more frivolous competition to *The Journal of American Sales,* an article entitled "Six Exercises to Sharpen Your Skillz." Fifty-two, he guessed as a woman, the skeptic's wife, handed money to Vernon for an All-in-One. An upright happy-dad showed a new All-in-One Knife to his wife in khaki culottes and their inflatably adorable children. *One-oh-five.* In the exercise, one never got the answers, which admittedly eliminated some of the interest from the game, but Ed reckoned that it couldn't hurt. A mismatched black couple, a twig and a stump, stood behind the skeptic's wife, waiting for their chance to commune with the All-in-One Knife. Ed, an heir to the northland's received wisdom—

"Whatcha selling?"

Ed turned; he couldn't imagine why anyone would have any reason to talk to him now, a brown blot on his profession, his ideal. (The memorized response: "What am I selling? I am selling a *doorway* to an enriching new musical experience." Doorway: he had liked that.) "What did you say?"

"What are you selling?" the man restated his question, slow-er.

Ed didn't appreciate whomever had sent this character with all his goddamn questions. He indicated the organ with a baby jerk of his head to the southwest. "This."

The man stood, intrigued; Ed's approach was about as soft a sell as the man had ever encountered at the State Fair. Especially in this aisle with all the amplified yammerers. "Looks pretty fancy?"

Ed shook his head, a low-tide bob, although not enough to jar him into engagement. "Yeah, it's top of the line," his monotone endorsed. The man considered the quickest exit to this situation; he wasn't interested in talking to this creep anymore. Ed, suddenly animated, spoke loudly, hawkish: "You see that guy over there?" The man looked around directionless until Ed's nod pointed him to Vernon. "He's a fucking clown." *Fuck*ing clown? the man thought. "He doesn't do anything right. You know what I'm saying?"

"I, I, uh, I don't know. I'm not sure."

"There is a— You see, there is a reality. A truth, you know, to the True Salesman. You can't act like that." As always, Ed pronounced capitalized Orditzian concepts with gloved, elocutionary care. He nodded at Vernon again. "It's just not right. There is more to the Transaction than the Good Sold. Than this Normal Exchange." Ed gazed into the man's eyes earnestly, waiting for accord.

"I suppose." The man looked away.

"But that fucking hick is—"

"I think I see my, um, mother over there." The man motioned in a direction of a female figure, notably younger than he.

"What?" Ed asked, but the specter had already slid next to another female figure and disappeared. Ed muttered something about him and something else, also not nice, about Vernon and things even worse about Vernon's customers. Then he reached into his briefcase. His hand shuffled past calculator, magazines, a nail file, lonesome invoices for Brackett Corp., notes-to-self. It grazed his ledger book. Ed had not tallied his accounts in a week, but there was no rush; he already knew more or less-less-less the discouraging news. Then he picked up by the corner the latest issue of *The Journal of American Sales*. It fell open at an ad—not a slick, understated advertisement for whiskey or luxury cars. The *Journal* contained none of those. It opened to a shadowy, black-and-white ad for sample cases, rolling, and as repeatedly assured, elegant; the magazine was a forum for great business books distilled on a page, revolutionary new notecard filing systems, computers DIRECT TO YOU at wholesale prices. With most magazines, Ed was your average reader, skittering ahead, jumping back, leaving articles orphaned and unread, but he read the *Journal* religiously, procedurally. Studying each article in order, he would eat all his vegetables before beginning the next course. This was in contrast to all of the magazine's other readers, who maintained the salesman's natural skepticism of every type of intellectual nonsense, including things with names like *The Journal of American Sales*. They read only the classifieds, which filled nearly half of the magazine. Although Ed never ate dessert first, he had no less enthusiasm than his peers for the magazine's back half, and he considered himself able, with notable precocity, to calculate the probable commissions, grosses, and nets of various opportunities from one or two tantalizing sentences. He had responded to hundreds of ads and affiliated himself with three of them—small missions, not much results—before he had found Brackett eight months ago. "Brackett Corporation, a major global diversified manufacturer, seeks energetic team-oriented team who can think outside the box for Midwestern circuit. Untapped market. Outstanding opportunity to make unlimited $$$$. Perfect for self-motivators with good local knowledge. Musical experience a must."

Last night, to keep his foreshadowing finances at bay, Ed had read most of that month's *Journal of American Sales*. That morning he had read the rest. And that afternoon, as he held the issue, it hummed, still stung, still stuck in his throat, undigested.

Gene and Linda Steinke had brought the *Journal* yesterday afternoon. The parents had seen the professionals in action only once before, at a home show in early June. At the State Fair, they had initially spied from a corner unseen, Linda oh-look-honey beaming in parental pride, Gene crankily asking why they just didn't go up and say hello. However, when they saw Ed pitch to a couple and saw the young woman nod contemplatively to Ed's words, Gene thought, What you know. He himself had never been much at sales. And when Barry played a short number—a standard, jazzed up, mechanically canned—Linda smiled knowingly at Gene, demanding an I-told-you-so apology: all those problems can't erase his talent. Gene grunted and rolled his eyes.

Eventually, the parents approached, and Gene moved to Ed and Linda to Barry. She hugged Barry, snugly, and he hugged her back, a self-release. Then she turned to Ed and hugged him; before her arms were fully around him, he pulled away. "Okay, okay, good to see you too." Gene had shaken Ed's hand as his other hand—it ended up being his wrist—gave his boy's shoulder an awkward collegial pat. "Hello, son." When Linda came to hug

Ed, Gene walked to Barry and, without the handshake, patted the shoulder of the younger one. "How's it going, Barry?" Barry shrugged, an implied I-dunno. Bumping, contorting, Gene maneuvered back to Ed and reposed in his favorite chair of a conversation: "So how's business?"

"You know, all right."

"Well, the economy's pretty good," Gene declared expertly. "Pretty good for luxury items like that."

Ed's voice regressed to a pubescent plaint. "I told you, it's not a luxury item."

"Okay, okay." Gene remembered that he had made this gaffe once before, and Ed had become all hot and bothered that time too. Gene didn't remember that he had made that gaffe four times before.

"And your brother?"

"I don't know." Ed planned to snip that conversational rivulet there; he didn't need a father confessor, didn't want to decide matters in Gene's hushed we-are-the-men-of-this-family tone, but he was getting pretty tired of Barry. "It's just weird. He just doesn't seem to care, you know."

"Well your mother says . . ." And Gene let the point drift into a void. Of the same height and relative proportions, Gene and Ed stood, American gothic, facing Barry and Linda and the central alley. Finally, Gene said, "Look at him with that hair. He looks like goddamn Kurt Gajewski." Ed laughed, even if Barry's crown of knots was only halfway to Kurt Gajewski's, the Steinkes' occasionally drug-free neighbor and the only character in their pacific neighborhood purposely devoid of character. Thirty-four, Kurt lived with his mother in a blue vinyl-sided ranch house fifteen feet from the Steinkes' duplicate in aluminum and cream. He paid his expenses—mainly cigarettes and their more charismatic cousins—by cutting lawns in the summer and, if really desperate, shoveling snow in the winter. With his shirt off, his gappy butt-balancing grin unashamed of his pockmarked flabby chest, and his lingering aroma of bacon, Kurt would drive around all summer in his paint-flaking mower. An old black transistor duct-taped to its steering column would blast rockabilly and blues.

"He sure does, Senator," Ed returned the joke, and his father laughed, a trace embarrassed for the implied comparison between his spawn and a loser like Gajewski. Kurt called everyone Senator. His mother: "Hey, Senator, these pork chops rule." His customers: "I'm sorry, Senator, I ain't responsible for that damage to your hedge." Telemarketers: "It's Guy-*eh*-skee, Senator, not Ga-*jew*-skee." Occasionally, Barry: "There's only one kind of rock and roll, Senator. It's real rock and real*er* roll." Rue Chambois Road, as a street, was not ready for the everyday use of congressional titles; Gene Steinke's reaction was the most intense of all. Every other summer Saturday, while most men of the upper Midwest watched fishless waters from a rowboat or televised sports from an armchair, Gene watched Kurt Gajewski mow the lawn. From behind the curtain of his den's bay window, he would bark commentary. "Damnit, Linda, he missed a spot. . . . Damnit Linda, I will eat my hand before I pay that baboon another nickel. . . . Damnit, Linda, I could cut grass better with a pocketknife." And to fill time betwixt and between, he would trickle the grumble: "Goddamn communist." Kurt's mower's engine would eventually return to rest, and Gene would run his hand excitedly through his widow's peak, an increasingly lonely trapezoid on a naked plate. Face reddened, loose jowls shaking, Gene would watch Kurt, self-made and deregulated, saunter onto the porch. The doorbell would ring. Gene would stall on purpose for thirty seconds, often a minute. Finally, after the third ring, he would answer the door and, without a word, hand the ransom to Kurt. Then he would wait for it to come like a punch. "Catch you later, Senator." Door slams. "Goddamn

communist." And Gene would roar that, no matter how sorry
Linda felt for Kurt's poor, poor mother, he was never ever going
to give another cent to that communist again when he had "two,
count 'em two, healthy boys at home." Gene's grumbles were not
an indictment of Kurt Gajewski's political affiliation. Not only
had Kurt never voted, he had never, as far as anyone could tell,
read a newspaper. Gene's farewells, instead, were vaguely related
to his declared state of being a true believer. In the sixties, Gene
had read Ford Thomas Seaway's *The True Believers,* a bottle-
rocket bestseller of a manifesto, and proudly acknowledged himself as one. He was a true believer at ten when the local laid his
list, a true believer during all the wars, large and small, right and
lost, a true believer when credit for the iron curtain's fall was
being apportioned and he stood in line for a crumb. And every
day those two words, *goddamn* and *communist,* were his constant
companions. The near-universal application of the epithet perhaps cast some doubt on its ideological underbody. A man with
an earring was a goddamn communist; a man who overcharged
him at the hardware store was a goddamn communist; stubbing
his toe on a baseboard required a *goddamn communist* just in case
they had something to do with it. Once, when Barry was in high
school, Gene reflected, sort of, on the muddle of habit, history,
and convenience that produced his communists. The public
introspection was as notable for its occurrence as its content.
"You know, Barry," father, pensive, said to son, "I know it's not
too fashionable to be a true believer anymore." Barry had not the
tiniest clue where this was coming from, but he nodded politely.
He needed to borrow twenty dollars and didn't want to jeopard-
ize his mission. "But *we* beat 'em in the end." Barry wondered if
Gene was prompting him—"Good job, Pops"—for a congratu-
latory handshake. "Who cares, though? Right?" Gene went on,
"All those movies and TV shows you two watch make those"—
he dismissed the direct object with a go-away flick of his

hand—"into big heroes. You kids think they're 'cool,' right?"
Cringing, Barry meant to reply, "I don't know," but he muffled
two syllables, neither recognizable English. "But it's just not
right. Those kind of guys never did anything for this country—
running around, smoking grass, humping each other, dodging
the—"

Gene Steinke had been too young for World War II, too late
for Korea, too early for Vietnam, or he was 4-F, had flat feet, bad
eyes, or a bum knee. The boys never got a straight answer from
their mother and never cared enough to risk asking their father.
Gene stopped his speech. Barry asked what. Gene dismissed the
class early.


Gene and Ed were stuck again in silence. Gene was certain that
a father should feel free, should be encouraged, in fact, to give a
son advice whenever he wanted to, no matter how old the kid
was. But he had to be careful around Ed: the kid had gotten real
touchy lately, and he had always been unusually stubborn, serious. (Good, though. Important traits for success. Better than
Barry's attitude anyway.) Gene analyzed the booth; he was not an
expert at this traveling-sales stuff, but you couldn't just dismiss
his thirty years of experience in the business world. "Well anyway," he said, "I think it is really good what you are doing for
Barry with this whole, um, thing this summer."

Ed mumbled, not a "You're welcome," not an insult, not a
protest, not anything.

"What?" Gene required a translation.

"Don't worry about it."

Gene was still unsure of Ed's meaning, and he turned again, for
clues apparently, to the organ and then to the two corner-crinkled
posters. "So, son," he asked, forcibly upbeat, "how are things
going in the organ game?"

It's not a game, Ed flinched. "Well, you know how these things work at these kind of fairs," he said. "It's a different type of customer."

Gene, dubious but fatherly, conveyed both: "Well, you're the authority."

"Yeah, there are probably a half dozen, dozen maybe, people who have said that they are going to come back either, you know, like today, or when they come back to the Fair. It's a two-part process, really." Orditz had declared sales a single perfect act.

"Earl, who you know—took him three years to turn a profit." Earl Luntz was the only rich man Ed knew and Gene's closest high-school friend, even if he and Gene didn't get a chance to see each other that often—that annually—anymore, what with Earl's busy schedule. Gene liked to say that Earl had accomplished a whole lot (for Earl), a whole lot meaning that he had bought a German sedan, married the silicone-vivacious Tammy Luntz, and staved off a series of copyright suits against his four-unit take-out chain, which borrowed heavily from others' motifs, menus, packaging, names. Gene mentioned Earl that morning because he, like other people—not just some other people, but all other people—assumed that Ed was in it for the money, another American boy seeking destiny in dollars and identity in cash. Assumptions, as they do, following other assumptions, he like everyone believed that Ed chose Brackett to get rich à la quick.

"I know, Dad, I know. You told me a f— You told me a thousand times."

"Okay, okay." Gene's feelings could not be easily bruised by a boy. "Don't get upset with me because everything is not—"

"Everything is going fine, I *told you* that," Ed corrected before his father had time to utter the libel.

Gene had no interest in getting into a shouting match with his jittery son. (He would win it if there was one, rest assured of that.) "Well, we brought you your mail."

"Thanks," Ed garbled.

Gene asked Linda to give Ed his mail, and Linda did, and then the parents switched places, briefly, to assure themselves in efficient words that the other child, the other incomprehensible child, was doing just fine. And then mother kissed and father shook and both left.

Ed had read the article in the booth that morning before the South Exhibition Hall opened. He had finally finished another article by Burt D. Carbone, a pebbly management consultant, boring even by *Journal of American Sales* standards. The article was an attempted refutation of a previous issue's negative and "preposterous" conclusions on systemized cross-selling. Ed turned the page.

"Alfred H. Orditz."

He stared at the words; he had never seen Orditz's name in the *Journal;* he had never seen it anywhere, come to think of it, except on the title page of *Classic Sales.* Heart beating apace, he tried to calm himself.

"Alfred H. Orditz . . . West Hollywood . . . 88 years old . . . disgrace . . . seminal work . . ."

Blinking, Ed cleared his eyes and blew a steadying wind to keep the ship a-sailing. He looked at the top of the page. *Closeouts.* Sure, he thought, the *Journal* included obituaries sometimes—great salesmen, author-gurus, guru-authors. He started to read again.

> Alfred H. Orditz, writer, died June 14 in West Hollywood, California. Management of the men's single-occupancy residency hotel where Orditz lived discovered the writer's body after neighbors complained of a smell emanating from his room. Police officials indicate that Orditz died from an apparent heart attack. He was 88 years old.
>
> Later marred by disgrace, Alfred Orditz is best remembered

for his seminal 1954 work, *Classic Sales: Theory and Technique.* He also apparently wrote two unpublished books, *The Iodine Conspiracy* and *The Treason of the True Salesman.* Orditz was born in—

Ed did a double take; that was only ninety miles away.

Little is known of his early days, although he is said to have been a prodigy. He received his doctorate in mathematics at 24 and served as a special assistant in the Office of Price Administration. Despite establishing himself thereafter as a respected voice among young academics, Orditz announced in the late 1940s that he would concentrate exclusively on applied business theory, although he continued to teach undergraduate mathematics. Students of the period remembered him as "slightly eccentric." In a *Fortune* article (October 1954) published after *Classic Sales* achieved international recognition, the magazine wrote, "People who knew Orditz were startled when they read [*Classic Sales*]. Who would have thought that this academic, known for his weighty prose and aloofness, if he was known for anything at all, could have written a book so clear?" Summarizing the conventional wisdom, *Fortune* concluded, "It is safe to say that Orditz has written the most important book on sales in a decade. If the second part is over the head of most readers, the first part is already essential reading for serious business thinkers. It is only a matter of time before it finds its way into the satchel of every salesman."

Intending to solicit Orditz's response to the printing of the 250,000th copy of *Classic Sales, Fortune* returned to interview him sixteen months later. The reporter noted that Orditz's physical appearance had deteriorated. The professor seemed "disillusioned and antagonistic." The reporter quoted Orditz: "Everyone who has bought my book has cheapened it beyond repair. It is not a guide to Mammon."

At about this time, according to university sources, Orditz's behavior became increasingly erratic. He interrupted his lectures

with tirades on "philistinism" and called his students simpletons, boors, and "greedy Judases." In 1957 he brought an
"unidentified piece of sports equipment" into his class and
threatened to beat anyone who disagreed with him. The university's faculty conduct committee dismissed him from his
post. It was only the fourth such dismissal in the history of that
institution.

According to the *Los Angeles Times,* local police reported that
Orditz, when his corpse was found, had not bathed in months.
He also had a "long biblical beard." Police found two large cardboard boxes among Orditz's few effects. One contained an esti-
mated 100 unbound copies of a photocopied manuscript, *The
Iodine Conspiracy.* The other contained a similar number of a different work, *The Treason of the True Salesman.* No summary of
their contents could be found. There is no record of any next
of kin.

# [ 2 ]

Leila had returned; her breathing had returned to its muted state;
her resolve had returned to a bent. She *would* leave the Fair, she
was clear, but she needed to stop here first.

The mural, twenty feet high, chronicled Thorfinn Karlsefni,
the might-be-historical Viking who had brought cattle to the new
world five hundred years before Columbus. The original artists,
funded by the WPA, had painted the heroic Thorfinn with
morose charcoal eyes and a narrow nose, both of which made
him look suspiciously like a young Roosevelt. Two of the background Vikings bore a helmet-obscured resemblance to Eugene
Debs and a Wobbly of local, forgotten notoriety.

As Leila beheld the mural on the building's exterior, three fair-goers exited the shed, silenced and reflective. Yes, she was clear again, she *had* to leave—there was no question—but only after going inside. For Leila's grandfather, this building, the dairy cattle building, had been the nave of the Fair. Every year, he would guide Leila through it, first thing in the morning, stuck-record repeating his admiration for its inhabitants. He would lose interest in the Fair afterward, let little Leila ride a few of the midway rides, cheerlessly eat some of the Fair's got-to foods, and insist, often before two o'clock, that they leave to beat the traffic. When Leila was older, Peter allowed her to stay later at the Fair alone. Those days, all she wanted to do was watch the people, the vacation-day romantics, the men sun-pinked, the women buttery.

After Barry's violation, Leila had charged and bumped through the central alley, a pinball trying to find familiar air or muggy air or any air outside the smother of the South Exhibition Hall. When she reached the top of the alley, a clumpy man in shorts and a sleeveless shirt, his gut playing peek-a-boo between them, rubbed the intimate of a woman's back. Pigs, Leila thought and hurried even more quickly to the door, where another man opened it for his wife; Leila stepped in front of her. Five yards outside the hall she inhaled, but the breath did not cleanse. It was a milkshake of steamed humanity and a sky's unborn shower, and Leila ate eyes and heads, misplaced and unlucky, of mosquitoes and gnats. *I should have stayed home today.* I should stay home every day. Stupid Yankel—"catch you before you already leave." Leila didn't ask for this; she didn't ask for anything. With apple-on-the-head spontaneity, she remembered—*remember* was the word—why she lay on the couch before she went to work, why she scurried home after her shift, why she should never answer the phone. People were mean and dirty, selfish and bad. She believed it.

Faces blurred and passed, bearded, pockmarked, and pampered faces, farm, factory, college faces, horny, lecherous, insatiable faces, ogling, winking, staring faces.

Maybe he *had* just looked at her, she pretended for a moment. Not like the rest of these pigs, but playfully, understandably. Harmlessly? *Why didn't I—* It wouldn't have hurt, he's not like a monster, I don't even know— For a flicker, she considered returning to the South Exhibition Hall. He had made a mistake, she had made a mistake—dumb, dumb, weren't we dumb, but now let's start again.

Hi, my name is Leila. Sorry, I had to run outside to turn off my headlights.

Hello, Leila, I'm Roger. I was hoping you would come back.

She looked deeper into the mural, looked into Thorfinn's Roosevelt eyes, at his thin, fading lips. She gazed at the most foregrounded cow. *Remember: they built this state.* A bouquet of flags wind-waved in the mural's corner. After a lavish unveiling in the thirties, the mural had sunk back unsung into the landscape; forty years later, the Scandinavian-American Society had commissioned its restoration, reviving its colors but not much interest. It's just too much, Leila sighed, acceptance and fear were encased in a seed in her brain; it was budding, but not yet in dark bloom. The first tones of twilight had rendered the Fair, or at least the cattle building, cottony and quiet in the long shadows. Leila stood alone and listened to the penumbra: notes and laughs and exchanges, all distant, all fragmented, all not intended for her. Chubby's slanders and Barry's lips—her cowardice—didn't hurt because of what they were; she could handle it, she assured herself; she had handled worse. They hurt because they were not mixed in a kaleidoscope of wins and losses, loves and disappointments; they were seagoing blasts—horn blasts—that left an ocean in-crowding after the echoes waned.

Leila considered a shout, its tremors toppling all, its effort rupturing her lungs. But no one would listen, taunted the mural, its acrylic flat cows frozen in wonder—Welcome to America—its Nordic explorers undaunted by the new world before them. No one would listen. *It hadn't happened today.* It hadn't happened today. It might happen today. It was never going to happen. But a shout maybe, or a return to him in the South Exhibition Hall, could kick the dynamo in motion, permanent motion, permanent change, any change. Stop it, she commanded. Just look at the stupid cows. And then leave.

In high school, Leila hadn't been lonely—not by poet-in-the-attic standards anyway. She had settled in with a group of friends, four or six at a time depending on the season. All were grains of the unfortunate silicate caught in the junior-high filter of puberty; some, like Leila, were late bloomers; some were just ugly; some were sheltered, scared, or indifferent. All but Leila knew no limits to histrionics when one of them betrayed the group with a party or a boy or a friend that they all did not share. Leila was more Indian than chief in the group, but she felt sneakily superior to the rest; the moon had promised her a future of slender glamour if she was patient and kind. She was also relieved not to be a daughter of one of *their* mothers. Her stomach looped when the girls traded trivial complaints about their mommies and looped again, so quickly it knotted, when she faced the mommies themselves. "How is . . . your . . . grandfather . . . Lei*la*?" they would ask in baby-the-old voices, an inch below the top of their lungs. It was assumed that the grandfather's senility and deafness—he was neither senile nor deaf—were contagious to the child. *He's okay.* "Really . . . wonderful. . . . Give . . . him . . . our . . . best." When Leila and the girls drifted apart after high school—a few went to college as far away as possible, a few married early the first boy who cooed about love—she did not fight the current. Leila reckoned that she also could have, theoretically, gone to college as far away as possible; she didn't because it never came up. It was not something she talked about with her grandfather, not something considered in that house, not something expected of her to do or, equally, not to do. But she went to community college—her grandfather had said only, "Fine by me"—and, there, she had made two or three friends, met Rusty, let the friendships drift, broke with Rusty, let memories fade. Organs rust. Rusty organs. Leila didn't much mind Rusty, the memory of Rusty, anymore. A few times over the past few years, she had considered calling him, not because she still had feelings for him (impossible) and not because she wasn't wholly convinced in her gut, in her sex, in her brain that a life with him would be a life unwanted and sad. But Rusty had been something. If she had called him, he might have insulted her—Who wouldn't after four years?—he might have laughed at her, he might have invited her over, he might have forgotten her name. But his reaction would have been movement; it would have been outside.

Rusty had asked questions: stupid, unfeigned, inexplicably charming questions; he had asked them about everything, and he had asked them about her. His first semester at the community college was Leila's first semester. As everyone majoring in general studies embarked on the same core curriculum, it was small coincidence that he and Leila shared two courses in the concrete-coffin classrooms. It was hard to miss him. The shorn fuzz at the top of the tower was actually beige, his scalp tinting through; his red-haired father, Bobby "Rusty" Schmidt, had named baby after man as part of a divine plan of repeat. Rusty Senior had been an offensive tackle for eleven recalled-everyday months in the pros, and in high school Rusty Junior was pious enough not to fight predestination and fleshy enough (topping off at six-four, two-sixty) to interest several college recruiters. Alas, he asked for too much crouching from his always grouching knees, and in the middle of his senior high-school season, the left one—the whole crowd oohed as it happened—told him that it had had quite enough. Since kindergarten, Rusty had divided most of his mental capacity between running the ship's logistics and memorizing the $x$'s and $o$'s of traps, draws, and halfback sweeps, and much of Rusty's eternal loop question to Leila simply filled in the gnawing gaps in his education. "What did he say what does that mean what is the answer what is that book what is it about when is it due when is it due when is it due?" But much of the question, at least at first, came from a different place, insouciant, a toddler marveling at his magic to make grown-ups share the truth of the world.

"So, Leila," Rusty asked one early-autumn day as they left class. They were walking past a lonely dirt-and-grass triangle, a parable of a campus green. His face framed by his square-headed bulk was free of agenda; his fleshy, pink-clay visage overruled any posturing by under-muscles, even if they had wanted to. "Do you live alone?"

Leila had not entered this discussion in years. "No."

"With roommates?"

"No."

"I give up. Who?" He threw his hands to his shoulders, the best he could do with a flexibility crowded by muscles and bulk.

Leila did not suppress an encouraging blush. "My grandfather."

Rusty considered the answer and quick-posited a theory. "Is that because your parents live outside of town, and you wanted to go to school here?"

"No."

"Oh, is it because you don't get along with them?" Rusty could understand that. It's a funny thing, fathers and sons. And daughters too, yes, probably, also.

Leila tucked her air behind her ear. "No."

"Then why don't you live with them?"

"You know." Leila explained by looking away, toward the parking lot—metaphoric oblivion.

"Nooooo," Rusty dragged on.

"They're gone."

"Ahhhh." The recognition. "So you're like an orphan?"

"I guess."

"That's cool in a way, you know. Being an orphan." It—orphan—had come up before, of course, even if the speaker (always whispering) had not been as enamored as Rusty by the word. But the word didn't agree with Leila; she had a good idea who orphans were, and her life didn't match the type. First—she knew, she had seen the movies—orphans were never orphans at all because their parents were never dead; orphans were just temporarily misplaced children. After years of torment, they always found Mum and Dad, and after a grand scene, they always reconciled in tears and scripted beauty, The Revelation of their fanciful past. At the very least, orphans—Leila knew, she had read the books—owned a memento of their extraordinary parentage: a browning wedding photograph described in fourteen hundred boring words; a heart-shaped locket sealing an ancient tear. Finally, all the orphans in all the books and epics, movies, and comic-strip squares were the heroes without exception of the story. Sure, Leila Genet was without parents, but she would never call herself an orphan. Mum and Dad were dead for one thing, and she wouldn't be attending a Technicolor reunion with them anytime soon; she had no mementos for a second thing, other than an album of well-preserved photographs, none of which could possibly be described in fourteen hundred words, no matter how boring; most salient, Leila knew the frame and the floorboards of her life, and although she was by default its protagonist, nothing had happened—and nothing would ever happen, she was certain—to make her its hero. There was tragedy in the life of Leila Genet, but there were no grisly scenes to be repressed, no swal-

lowed bottles of desolation to be unearthed, no quests to begin.
There were only facts. Leila's father did not come back from
Vietnam. He did not actually die in Vietnam—the war was pretty
much over by then—but in a car accident near Bakersfield after
his second, voluntary tour. Leila, who had never met him, preferred to think that he had never come back. When Leila was
three, her mother like her grandmother before her was cancer-
killed, and her grandfather found himself the guardian of a
notably dependent girl. Peter Luden inquired loud enough to be
heard but not loud enough to be shirking if there was anyone
more "right" to take care of Leila. The Genet family, frontyard
car-part and cinder-block rural, did not respond to his inquiries.
Peter's younger daughter Peg had embraced a cultural revolution
too enthusiastically to qualify for adoptive motherhood. Only his
sister Mary offered to help, but Peter knew her too well to accept
that offer. So Peter raised Leila the best he could even if he wasn't
that right himself. For like his neighborhood, Peter's words,
energy, everything really diminished by the year. Two months
before he died, he told Leila that he had tried to bring her up
"without judgment and without ambition." Other withouts were
in evidence—without communication, without encouragement,
without emotion—but those were the only ones done on purpose.
Leila asked Peter what he meant; she would have normally considered this prying, but the comment's obscurity overwhelmed
her. "I always thought you'd do a little better without it," he
answered. To clarify he added, "You know, ambition."

Peter Luden was the first generation off the farm. At the last
century's turn, his father had lost Ludendorff Farms after three
generations of quiet prosperity. Max Luden, still young, moved to
the city and, with the help of a cousin, secured a union spot at one
of the breweries. (Everyone conspired to forget that the
Ludendorffs became the Ludens around then, not long after the
Battle of Tannenberg.) Max's people had always been country

conservatives, tight and suspicious, but Max was different; as the neighbors used to say, he was smart in the head but not smart where it counted, and he tried, quite systematically, to order his experience. When he finally uncovered an answer—*the* answer, there was no equivocation—he settled on it for the rest of his life. *Obtain capital, meine Kindern. Obtain capital.* If you had asked Max, he would have declared his stand with union man and maybe the socialists too, neither of which were exactly a minority in that city. And when he left the labor rallies, he knew which side of the fence he was on, but he was absolutely sure that life was more rewarding on the other one. Relatively speaking, this liberated the son: most of Peter's friends expected no more, asked for no more than a slot at a factory or machine shop or, if they were blessed, the old man's bakery or tavern. However, Peter's liberation was only symbolic: Max gave his son more advice than assistance, and Peter's education ended with high school. And though Peter worked, outlived a depression, draft, uniform, and war, worked, married, worked, had Pammy, worked, had Peg, he acquired capital only in scraps, never obtained it whole. In the fifties, a cousin, the son of the cousin who had helped his father, glowed about the opportunities in Texas servicing the oil companies. ("For chrissakes, Pete, I told you a thousand times. Of course, I'm talking *real* money. Yes, *capital,* whatever you want to call it.") Oil-depletion allowances were all the rage in New York and Boston at the time, and Peter probably could have done all right. One January morning, he backed out of the driveway and waved good-bye to his two daughters smiling bravely for Daddy and to Elizabeth, tall and willowy and as invigorating as the spring. Elizabeth never told Peter she was sick; no one was sure if she knew it herself. When they called from the hospital four months later, he couldn't get back north in time.

Peter had done all right with Leila, though, he had thought. He never let her suffer for want, never made her pay for nothing, and never once told her about how he got up every morning and thought about it every morning and kept it to himself every morning because that's what you did. And what were people expecting anyway? He was a widower, fifty-six years older than her; his health was never exactly perfect. And he was the son of his father and a son of the North, the Protestant North, the last in a line (as things turned out) that preceded Ludendorff Farms and Hamburg-launched clippers and a Westphalian peace when that was all that mattered. Sometimes, though, he suspected his own excuses. He could have done better if— Well, for damned sure, the *if* hadn't been his choice.

Rusty's questions, probing and left-handed and irrelevant, continued for a week or so. Leila knew what was going on, knew the direction of her and Rusty's snatches of courting, but she didn't push it. Her inexperience muzzled and shamed. Finally, the question came: "You wanna go to a movie or something sometime?"

"I dunno." Leila rolled her eyes, inward. She did know.

"What does that mean?"

"Sure, I guess." Rusty could hardly hear the response.

The first date was the model for the first act. Rusty, Leila discovered, didn't just like to ask questions; he liked to answer them. Leila soon found the genre that generated the most excitement, and she gladly fed her cues. Rusty moved down a historical line from his knee's early glory to his knee's late misfortune to his knee's rehabilitation to his knee's expected recovery to his knee's future storied career—"soon as it gets fixed"—and eventual implied enshrinement, with or without the rest of him, in the American Knee and Kneecap Hall of Fame. Rusty, for his part, also still asked his overflowing toilet of questions, and Leila was still struck, fascinated by his nerve, oddity, direct current. Only Rusty could ask, "Why didn't you eat any popcorn? Don't you like popcorn?" without accusation, without a motivation, pique, or even interest in the answer. They went to a movie on that first date, and afterward Rusty asked her opinion of it. "I dunno," she peeped. "It seemed kind of, you know, stupid."

"I like see where you're coming from." Rusty pretended to have listened to her and waited, mind blank, for two seconds to indicate that they were having a conversation. "But I thought it was like really kick-ass. Don't you think?"

On the second date, Leila discovered Rusty's second most notable feature: his friends. In the group's bar-home, Leila smiled when introduced into the forest of former linemen, and for the rest of the evening, she only gave her name, rank, and serial number. There, Leila, a beer-nibbling mouse, observed that Rusty's perpetual question, even among that group, awarded him a reputation of being, intellectually speaking, subpar. The five or six male members of the group would talk about football, the three long-term girlfriends would wrestle the conversation to television or the movies, and they would all settle on gossip. Rusty contributed more than an average amount to the conversation, as measured by word count, but he was always the last with an opinion.

The third date was exactly like the second date, and on it, Leila began to notice the gestures. Through glances and flashes, not imperceptible, the established girls would instruct their boyfriends to check out Rusty and his new girl, how funny and awkward they were, their hands inside the bus. Ain't this pair cute, the gestures snickered, dumb Rusty and Silent Sally. *Cute.* Leila could see the cute, could feel that condescending cute nut-cracking her heart, but she didn't do anything about it. She longed for favor, was entombed by discomfort, and Silent Sally, cute, she remained. The fourth date was indistinguishable from the third date, and on the fifth date, Leila, convinced that she knew Rusty well enough, bored by a virginity extended by chance and not choice, lubricated by some bourbon of questionable pedigree, slept with him. Rusty, she discovered, was a philosopher in the bedroom: sex with him was nasty, brutish, and short. The last was welcomed; the three minutes it lasted that time and most times thereafter was about all that she, out-matched by a hundred and forty-five pounds, could tolerate.

For a month afterward, it was not storybook, but it was a story. She felt, she was certain, those love-lobby-advertised jitters when she saw Rusty in class and he smiled for her. *Our secret.* She came to understand the meaning of presence—a presence—so solid, so inertial, so *there* beside her. And even if Rusty's friends were repulsive, the girls petty, the boys rude—they had obviously decided that she was a waste of time, a temporary sprain—the group was still loud and alive and kinetic. Sure, they were cold to her, Leila thought, but she was new. It would probably change. *I just need to talk more and I will.* Eventually.

"So, Leila, I was wondering," Rusty introduced a thought one October night. Leila grinned; "I was wondering" signaled a ques-tion, classic, open-eyed. "Um." He looked around. He had not for-gotten the question. "Never mind." His countenance approached contemplation, an unseen face, and Leila tried to interpret the nov-elty. She knew that Rusty wasn't hiding anything—he couldn't by constitution—so he was probably just struggling with some deep emotional issues. But she was wrong. After the introduction, Rusty realized—it stunned him like a defensive end—that he had nothing more to ask her. And that was final, an earthquake split. And for the most part, he stopped talking to her. And he figured that his friends had been right all along.

Leila stayed with Rusty for three months after that. It took some of that time for certain realizations to take hold: the death of the inquisitor and Rusty's new personality, the sad truth that his friends were not a-warming, and the thought, inclusive and fundamental, that she did not like him. He was all right, she sup-posed, and he was still a presence, but the tingling menagerie of butterflies and worms had ceased to stomach-appear, and his body seemed to be ballooning larger, a mucus gelling into every corner of the room, depositing its tonnage on her chest. Most nights, Leila would find herself at Rusty's apartment, where he and his friends would yell for any reason at any team on TV. Rusty would acknowledge her entrance with a flip of the head— occasionally, "Hey"—and his friends, necks braced immovably by the box, would do nothing. Leila would sit at the kitchen table and mechanically finish her homework, picture herself (between chapters) kicking in the TV with superheroine power and poise, and wait until the two-minute warning, fourth quarter, third out, ninth inning. Then Rusty would go out with the boys, and Leila guessed she would too.

Leila and Rusty would return to the apartment, and Leila would replay to herself every miscarried conversation with one of his friends. How's it going, one of them might have asked. *Um-okay.* Her mouth would have invariably jammed with nerves. *Well, all right, right?* Rusty, at the apartment, would turn on the television, and sometimes he and Leila would exchange sentences, amputees, for a quarter of an hour. Eventually Leila would venture, yawning and ashamed, "Rusty, I'm kind of sleepy." Half the time, he would accept this as sufficient foreplay. Occasionally on those nights before *it,* however, Rusty would ask her a question, an invigorating mirage of his expired interest. Leila would perk up, answer the question with flourish, speed, elaboration until her lungs became vacuums and demanded back the life she had exhaled. It was the best she could do, she knew, better than herself. *It hurt.* But when Leila would finish her answers, no momentum had begun.

Leila supposed that life could have gone on like this forever; this might have been sad, real, mature romance in the sad, real world. She pretended that she didn't know. Sure, she was familiar with hot-hot romance on big and small screens; she read the magazines about celebrity couplings, vendettas, reunions. But she had no father who called her his princess, no mother who prayed to the white-wedding gods, no sister who could explain love sparks or spasms or positions not patented by missionary men. Leila had friends, okay, but the high-school gang claimed only one validated experience—piney grove, family reunion, second cousin, manual engagement—among them. The college friends were never that close. She did have a grandfather, but he, after stumbling on the lady pediatrician when Leila was eight, was grateful that all of those painfully feminine subjects never needed to be alluded to at home.

Yes, Leila had supposed, life between her and Rusty might have limped along forever, into marriage and breeding and death. Yes, their moments together were suffocating and eager and tense, but they were not unbearable. She didn't hate Rusty—really, she didn't—and didn't mind that the questions had died, didn't mind that she had become his embarrassment, that much was clear. Even when one of his friends would crack within earshot, unopposed, "Where's the shadow, Schmidt?," even then, when she *did* hate Rusty, she would inspect her hate permissively. She never hated her grandfather. She never hated her friends. She was discovering; everything wasn't, shouldn't be a celebration while discovering. And Leila could not dismiss his body, which she liked—not in that way, which never was good—but in its heartbeat, its vagaries, its movement. It was lovable, if not loved.

Around Christmas, Rusty had spent the afternoon at a bar where he had devoted himself to two obscure bowl games. In his apartment, Leila counted off his tardiness; it was four months after the first date.

Rusty eventually walked in three hours late, high on football and beer. I was wondering, he began. Lately wondering had hit bottom; Rusty wondered only before, "Is pizza okay for dinner?"

Leila had prepared a speech, strong sentiments on respect and thoughtfulness, seasoned with the same words that were in dozens of other speeches that she had also never given. "I'm listening."

"I was wondering," he slurred again. "Why are you so frigid?"

"What?"

"Why are you so fri*gid*? At the bar with Jason and what's-her-name. . . . They were kissing and shit. She was all over him."

Leila stopped breathing; her heart pulsed her lip. "Is this like some kind of joke?"

"When I'm doing you, you just like lie there like a goddamn log."

"Are you drunk?"

"I may be drunk," he admitted, "but I'm not frigid."

"I-I don't deserve this from you." Then, from nowhere, it came: "You pig." That baby, porcine dribble of disgust was the most strident stance she had taken in front of him, and even baby was an arsonist, consuming and excessive. She left the apartment.

A year earlier, Rusty had accused another girlfriend of frigidity, and the other girlfriend had cried; he had then rescinded the accusation, and they had capped off the evening with a snap of frigid sex. Rusty knew that it was an absolute mathematical constant that young women cried when their boyfriends called them frigid. But Leila didn't cry then, and she didn't cry when her mother's room wind-rustled from beyond, and she didn't cry when her grandfather died. Leila didn't even cry the little cries at times-of-month and bad-day ends. There was a dam in front of her ducts, possibly—a public-works project, massive and concrete that kept the salty reservoir off her face; the reservoir had succumbed to drought long ago, possibly; the reservoir had never been there to begin with.

In the driveway of Rusty's apartment house, Leila did not ask herself why she wasn't crying. She thought about why she had left—*he was just being Rusty, really, I was wrong*—and she returned to the apartment, a reflex, knowing the scene could be forgotten. Rusty opened the door, half in triumph, half in stumble, and Leila's body tried its best to be cocky at her molehill hips. In the doorway, Rusty's inebriated legs wobbled, like jello, in suspension. "What the hell do you want?" he splashed and roared. And so Leila left again, and Rusty slammed the door. His friends had been right. When she returned home, Leila, matter-of-fact and composed, told her grandfather that she would be in her room if anyone called. The next day, she light-stepped down-stairs late and asked her grandfather if he had been using the phone or anything. Peter, who had maintained a marked indiffer-ence to the whole affair, who had asked only once where she had been when she hadn't been returning all those nights, who was on the last lap of a life's race, his life's race one lap too long, grunted his assurance laterally that no one had called. And even-tually, Rusty ended, and other things ended, and she reflected, abstractly and calmly and curiously, about it all ending. Death, a sweet release, but death, an uninterrupted, unacceptable parade of eternity: day after day after day after day, the ruts and short moraines set in stone. Impossible: that was life.

Leila walked into the cattle building. Before Peter had stopped coming to the Fair, he would lead her through the shed's row and identify each part of the cow. Peter had spent no more than a month or two on a farm in his life, and all that had been boyhood visiting. This didn't prevent him—probably allowed him, a farmer would huff—from holding warm-bakery notions of the lost world of Ludendorff Farms. In his spry days, the alive days, Peter had boasted of his farmer blood and had memorized enough agricul-tural trivia to prove it. Every Fair until Leila was twelve, he would make her repeat the name of the bovine elements: barrel, brisket, crops, dewlap. If her tiny voice stumbled on the funnier ones—chine (giggle) rump (giggle) flank (giggle) stifle (giggle) teats (big giggle)—she was commanded: "Start over again." As they moved along the dairycow rows, he would expound upon the varieties: the haughty Guernseys versus the humble little Jerseys; the Ayrshires, in general, he could do without, but *not* the regal Holsteins. Matching Brownie snapshots, dog-eared dwarfs in their nicked frames, hung in Peter's living room and Mary's foyer. In them, Max Luden, seventeen on crusty boots, milked a Holstein from a three-legged stool, his shirt attempting to escape around his suspenders, his naked pop-veined forearms swelling at his rolled sleeves. In Mary's version, you could see only a sunburned neck and the back of a cap. In Peter's, Max gazed over the shoulder at the camera, serious and still. There was no humanity in those photographed eyes, Leila had early perceived, no twinkle of life, no animate refrain replayed in his children and theirs. "Holstein-Friesian are their full name," Peter would lecture on the dairy aristocracy. "Dutch, you know. Best cow there is, hands down." He would end his monologue with the same pious observation: "Remember: they built this state."

Inside the shed, the end-of-day shadows painted an early gray dusk, and hose streams and cow streams and stray slumbered hay fine-stroked the ground. A preverbal breeze escorted the aroma—essence of cattle, bottled and enjoyed—through the buildings' open sides. Leila moved deeper into the shed; her thoughts of pigs and Rusty and lip-licking tongues faded away. The fading away was not a disappearance: poof, the sorcerer waves his wand. Hers was not even a standard fading: old thoughts ebb, new thoughts replace. Hers was an active fading: she could feel her thoughts evaporate; the lake was conscious of its morning mist. She looked at the rows of barebacked cows, chewing, resting, none fretting, complaining. She could almost hear her grandfather again, but she didn't repeat the names.

Most of the fairgoers had left, but the cattle had nowhere to go. They swung their tails in boredom, offering the straggler or two a clear view of their black-and-white asses. It's just me and cows, Leila hummed, warm. As she passed one Holstein, she rubbed its haunches and let its shortened hairs nuzzle the crevices of her hand. She passed another, patted its rump, tasted the tail's tickle in her sealed palm. These animals were an elite group. They and their owners—4-H presidents, FFA treasurers—had already beaten the cows of cousins and friends at the counties. By that day, the kids had already stood guard while the judges' trained glare landed on their charge. The winners would be announced tomorrow, and a summer of rising at the cockcrow and filing, combing, brushing hides, hooves, and teeth would finally be over. Many of the caretakers had skipped off to the midway; a few depressed ones, sure that they had lost, had padlocked themselves in their trailers or the Fair's dormitory cubes; a few confident ones, strutting older than they were, had gone to the tents, to the beer, to the bands. Leila passed a dozen more animals, her hand leading the way.

She stopped. Two stalls ahead of her, a girl was brushing her pet—arcing, graceful strokes—across the top line. After ten, maybe fifteen, seconds the girl bent ten degrees over—she was almost the same height as the cow—kissed the animal, and hid a secret in its ear.

*I shouldn't. . . . This isn't . . .*

Leila took a step back and hit her heel, a two-part *cuh-lunk,* on a wooden post. The girl looked up; she seemed twelve but was probably older; her rod-straight hair grazed her belt; her upper lip snuck too far from her face. A particular feeling snared itself in Leila's gullet. It wasn't a thought, probably, because the gaseous idea never found the skeletal constancy of words. But Leila *felt,* That girl is me. She was Leila if Max Luden hadn't lost the farm and Peter Luden hadn't lost his wife and her parents hadn't lost their lives. She was Leila who never woke to *that is what I am.* She was Leila who would cry when her pet failed for its trophy. She was Leila who would cry not for her own sake but for the cow's. She was Leila who would never have left the South Exhibition Hall. She was Leila who would have returned.

For five seconds, Leila and the girl stared at each other. Leila had to say something. "Oh, I'm, um, like sorry for bothering you." She tucked a strand, heavy and limp, behind her ear.

The girl's shrugged shoulders said Leila wasn't bothering her at all.

"Um, have a good night then."

The girl smiled.

# [ 3 ]

*Jesus,* Barry repeated six increasingly angry times. What a friggin' loser. Like what are we doing here? Selling *organs*? Jesus, who in the hell buys organs? If you think about it, if you think about it, if you think about it, if we had just thought about it. *Goddamnit.* Barry usually restrained from *goddamnit* and the darker curses. Those were his father's and brother's words. *He's so full of himself with this friggin' Orditz.* Who's he kidding? Didn't help me with the girl. Acting like some moron. Just staring at his feet. Jesus, she probably thought. . . . What in the hell *could* she have thought? She was good-looking. Not. . . . But she looked *good.*

As Barry left the South Exhibition Hall, his monologue treaded water for almost five minutes more with no new themes, ideas, or even words. He clustered *moron, loser, Jesus, girl, friggin', like,* and *good-looking* in new agglutinations. Ed had not learned one stupid thing, Barry decided, since the first day of the summer. He was still trying to prove something with these organs, probably trying to prove that he was, like, better than Barry. It was pathetic—Ed was pathetic—angling to shove that dorky beast down people's throats. His cracked fake smile and his oily sentences were embarrassing to himself, to Barry, to Ed, to Barry for Ed. But that girl wasn't pathetic. Barry thought of Leila and the others, of Jenny Lozach, and even Tina, all of them reduced to a single headless mannequin—breasts, extravagant curves, Woman.

Barry marched down the Fair's byway and made sure, just on the underside of consciously, that Jenny and Tina's trailer was not in his line of view. He focused then exclusively on Leila, on her flee. Leila had been so normal one moment, ready for him, needing him. *But she was like such a freak the next,* staring down at her feet, like a nun, running out of the hall, like a—like a friggin' chicken. When she did that, she didn't understand—*why*—that she was different, that she was cool, that she wasn't like Ed. She would never say, "An instrument's an investment." She would never say, "Mr. Steinke, I think this young lady would like to hear you play." Play. I'll play a friggin' bullet through his head.

And then Barry thought, I loved her.

As a general rule, when Barry said he loved a woman, any woman, he only indicated his desire to sleep with said woman at a middling level of want. The highest level of want was, appropriately enough, want. (I want that girl.) For women at the shallower ends of desirability, Barry removed himself from the sentence altogether. (She's all right. She's doable, I guess.) Barry's love-heresy was not limited to his internal, their externals rating system. At early times in a relationship—a week, a day, ten minutes—Barry would profess the three-word bomb, no fumbling, if he thought it would ease the desired into bed. Many took this for what it was: impish charm from a charming imp who would pass casually through their lives. Others, however, took it more seriously, and then—cloppity-clop—in came riding the four horsemen of the breakup: the tears and pleas, shouts and slaps.

"Why are you like so upset?" Barry would demand.

"You have to ask?" Brenda or Bonnie or Barbara would stammer, amazed.

"Do I?"

"I don't know, like do you?"

"I'm asking, aren't I?"

"All those things you said, you didn't like mean them?"

A declarative sentence would finally appear: "Like sure, I meant them."

"Then how can you like do *this* now?"

"What?"

"What? You know damn well *what*."

"No I don't."

"You said"—she would recoil from the recalled treachery—"I l-l-l-love you."

"Uh-huh."

"Don't you *understand* what *that* means?"

"Like I guess not, huh?" More tears, more pleas, more shouts and slaps, but Barry was honest at the end. He didn't—he guessed he didn't—he insisted he didn't—understand what "that" means. Sure, Barry held *opinions* on his lovers; some were more compatible, some were more fun, some were better, a lot were worse. Yet these sentiments never moved beyond the rational facts: you are better, we are compatible, thus we should pass more time being same. Barry had never signed a letter of longing or addiction, had never felt the feverish sweat of loss on his brow, had never felt his heart pass through him into another's embrace. From the age of thirteen, Barry knew women. But like the tree that grows too fast, he was hollow and knotty; the roots were too shallow, the branches too frail.

Leila as an object of "I loved her" was different. A lot of girls had been different, Barry would grant, but this time, really, Leila was different. She wouldn't jabber all the time like hot-dog Jenny. Her hair, he remembered with the pelvic ache of a chasm between lost and now, rested so calmly, fanned voluntarily across her shoulders; it would want to spill over her and Barry as they lay in bed for hours and days. And he and Leila wouldn't need to talk then; they wouldn't ask each other to be charming, successful, employed. They would be natural—silent, empty minds, peace.

Barry had walked faster through the Fair than was his style; his cool-slouchy drag had upgraded itself to a determined march. He had been heightened and bothered since the South Exhibition Hall, and the background had blurred to an animate gray. Now the colors stood sharp, the shadows peeled off, the shapes traced themselves in black-marker lines. He stopped walking, and he smiled with faint aversion and dim recollection and a suggestion of imminent release from preoccupying nags. The midway came into full view. At one end, the five o'clock sun bathed a Ferris wheel in immaculate glow. At the other end, the same sun bounced off a Viking hull as the bow crooked over stern. It was the best time for the carnival. Manmade lights and the late-day sun danced easy and slow. The cool nighttime air whispered its first breaths as the afternoon muggy hinted it would soon retire. Vaporous diesel, cotton candy, hotlamped popcorn jammed Barry's nostrils, and the smells thickened, but his smile faltered as he passed into the gauntlet of Clock Brothers Expositions—dime-toss, ball-toss, bag-toss, ring-toss—and was pelted by the cadence of the carnies: siren in intention, in practice quite resistible.

Yessir yessir. Onedollar onedollar. Everyoneawinner, awinner. Freeshot freeshot. Comeherebuddy, giveitatry giveitatry freeshot freeshot onedollar onedollar freeshot onedollar.

Barry slowed down his drag further until it declared, I, a step, have not a care in the world, a step. In front of all these witnesses, his gait announced that Barry was never going to work for Ed again. *I don't owe him anything.* Who does that jerk think he is anyway, if you think about it, to put himself in charge? Jesus, Barry laid out the evidence, he doesn't even treat me like a brother. He treats me worse than a brother, like I'm his slave. It's totally *sick* how he's taking advantage of me.

Barry stopped in the gauntlet and watched from three yards off a carny running a softball toss. The target was three metal milk cans, quaintly battered; the mark was flustered. "Come *on,* bud, it's easy," the barker encouraged his victim to give it one more chance. "You already won a tiny bear, bud, just for stepping up. Five dollars gets you a chance at a big one." The carny motioned indistinctly to a series of bears on the booth's plywood wall. From the booth's ceilings hung the giant prizes, the pride of any recipient, the proof of any man. The carny was thinner even than Barry; his exposed skin was darkened by dirt and hairs, mystery and sun; purply tendons, substantial as bones, sliced over and through his frame; his hair shone in anachronistic glory, immersed in grease or sweat or a pomade long forgotten. His age was immeasurable. But he was not unsightly, despite his teeth's dawning corruption; his face applied classical symmetry; it was machine-pressed, angular, efficient; his eyes, a hazel set off by a freshsnow white, the white set off by his barkish skin, were sarcastic, but everyone, theoretically, could be in on the joke. "Come on, bud," he challenged the victim, "you don't want to look like a fool with some little bear. Make you look *cheap.*" He smiled at the victim's companion, and she looked away, frightened by his lazy intensity. Before that summer, Barry had thought that he was tough. For evidence, he could cite his tattoo, a bad job, three offenses sealed in his juvenile record. After Barry crossed paths with the barkers of Clock Brothers Expositions, here and earlier that summer, he knew that he wasn't tough at all. He hid a smudged tattoo. They flexed eagles and mamas, demons and daggers, jailhouse tats, tributes to the South. Barry was promiscuous. They chose from herds of lovers every night, women made of leather and peroxide, makeup and fat. Barry enjoyed altered moods. They ingested coke and smack and whiskey and pills in combinations that didn't have names and probably never would. Barry sometimes gave 'em hell; they took hell and called it their own.

Barry watched the customer-victim throwing softballs, one then two in quick, angry recoil. The rigged base of the pyramid stood still. The companion encouraged the thrower, soothed him. "Come on, Davey. You'll get it in the next one." She didn't believe in rigged games. She only believed in giant bears; her eyes did not deceive—other women had them.

"Hey, buddy." The operator noticed Barry, still three yards away. His tone wasn't Ed's: sincerity dressed in cornball smiles and I-sure-do-agrees. He was a snake, slippery and tempting and mean. "Give it a try. Everyone a winner." For the games in the gauntlet, Clock Brothers had established a corrupt rental-fee system. At day's end, the game-both operators, ostensibly leasees, owed the company rent; if an operator didn't have the money, security threw him out immediately; if he earned more, he kept more.

Barry stared at him, expressionless, senseless. *She was different.*

"Hey, *bud.*" The carny tinged his menace with a confirming buddyness. "You know I get *you* a prize. I fix you up. And it fixes *you* up." He leer-nodded at his victim's companion. The boyfriend missed his fifth and final shot. Without a glance at the victim, the carny addressed him again: "Hey, bud, you'll get it this time. I guarantee it, man. I give you four throws, two bucks. How's that? Next size bear, guaranteed. I could get fired for that shit." He looked again at Barry, as the victim fished the two dollars out of his pocket. Clock Brothers did not expect its employees to follow dogmatic customer-service dictates. The carny, through his gritted teeth, yelled to Barry, "Hey asshole, you gonna play? Or you gonna be an asshole?"

Barry stared back. Everyone at the Fair was money-obsessed, a lunatic like this one. *For like two dollars.* Jesus Christ. Ed, this freak, the whole midway, the whole South Exhibition Hall had nothing to do but try, through lies and anger and hate—yes, hate—to strip the people of their last friggin' penny. No shame— Barry cringed to himself—if you think about it. No nothing.

Barry left the carny and moved briskly down the gauntlet. He thought, I am different. Different than that dirtbag, different than my brother. Jeez, *my* brother. As the summer weeks turned hotter, unendurable, Barry had found it even more difficult to believe that he and Ed were actually brothers. How could anyone so interested in organs and Orditz and scheming be his brother? Well, no more: he would never return to stealing for the Brackett 180-X Corporation. Ed was horrible, and, and.... *He was so horrible with girls.* That was the friggin' truth. There was a scientific connection, if you think about it, between Ed's greed and his awkwardness with, his cartoon bumbling with, girls.

Several years back, the Fourth of July incarnate (red hair, blue dress, freckled face, abundant chest) crossed Ed and Barry's car in a shopping-mall parking lot. "I love that girl," Barry had said with the comparable emotion of, The pavement is black.

"Really?" Ed asked distantly. Barry had interrupted his calculations, crucial ones, about the varying net margins of non-stick, no-stick, and never-stick pans.

"Really what?"

Ed committed a quarter cup more to the discussion. "Love that girl?"

"What are you talking about?" Barry asked.

"You said you loved that girl."

"So."

"What do you mean, 'So'?"

"So I said it."

"Yeah, do you?"

"Like shut up already." Barry tried to stop the duet before an expired radio-comedy team demanded its material back.

"You can't live without her, right?"

"Like what are you talking about?"

"You can't live without her." A college roommate had once confessed to Ed that he couldn't live without her. "Her" was rotten in everyone's opinion, including the roommate's. When Ed asked why, he was told, "Because I'll die."

"You're like a friggin' weirdo, dude." Barry terminated the discussion with, what he presumed to be, an understatement.

That summer Ed had sealed the case in Barry's judgment for his permanent amorous incompetence. Four or five times, Barry had asked Ed to join him in a fair's beer tent or at a neighboring bar. Barry needed a sidekick in these situations, and hoping that Ed had developed some new talents in college, at Pilsen's, from a magazine, he thought, initially, that his brother would suffice. Barry, a peacock, would invite two or three girls to join them or inveigle the converse unbidden, and he would seat Ed or stand Ed next to the homeliest or the quietest. And as Barry would begin to unwind his charm with his girl or girls, he would glance at Ed and listen for trouble. After a few minutes about the weather or the noise or the rate of occurrence of coming here often, Ed would declare unsolicited, "Yes, well, I'm really interested in sales."

"What, like clearance sales?"

"No, not *dis*counts. *True* Sales."

Barry would stop overhearing immediately; he would underhear Ed and talk more loudly himself, scratch his forearm, refuse to admit what was about to happen. For as if programmed in her genetic code, the girl's pupils would run to an apathetic distance, and Ed would go on, "You see, a lot of guys are just kinda looking to make a buck." Her foot would search for the floor's trapdoor. "But I think without, um, a big-picture framework. You know, for example, the True Salesman—"

"Excuse me, Fred"—the correction—"yeah anyway, I have to like, uh, use the ladies' room," the girl would invariably say, then leave for the bathroom, return on the other side of Barry, and seat herself, led by a giggly eyeroll. Or she would take her friends with her, away from the whole creepy scene. Not all of those girls were snobbish, superficial, or dumb. Nobody wanted to hear about an outdated prophet of sales theory. Ed knew this. But he justified his behavior with unimpeachable, circular logic. Ed Steinke, Ed Steinke maintained, was about sales. If a girl didn't like that, she wouldn't like him.

It probably had something to do with "love," Ed was vaguely aware. All those girls—Barry too, especially Barry—stoned by television, pickled by pop songs, convinced themselves that they were "in love," or needed to be "in love," and all that was important was love, because that was the thing to do. Ed suspected that they didn't really feel anything. But with their empty, miserable lives—they had no goals, no ambition, *no plan*—they needed something. But, then again, you couldn't just make it up, could you? No, you had to make it up. No, it had to happen. But it was never going to happen. . . . Christy Kanko hadn't minded the sales talk, but she had been like the rest of them, too interested in when-oh-when-will-we-sayeth-love for her and Ed's relationship ever to last. At least that's what Ed had concluded after it was over. In bed together, naked and exhausted, Christy would kiss Ed's fingers or twiddle the frugal hairs on his chest. He would squirm. She would prattle childishly—"I'm so happy, Edzy"— and he would cough. She would offer; he would excuse, herself, himself: "I'm sorry, Christy, I have to get some sleep." Yes, she had listened to his talk of flatware sales and door-to-door sales and True Sales, but she had just been in a holding pattern, Ed recognized, until she could land on that other stuff. But Ed didn't want to talk about it. *I'm really sorry,* don't be mad, it's just . . .

Barry, still walking out of the gauntlet, restated his thesis of Ed cosmology: just 'cause he can't get any, he's always taking it out on me. Well, no more, Barry repeated in declarative resolve, every beat a clenching fist. He moved from the gauntlet into the midway's open area, a cleaner collection of rides and fun houses and larger amusements. He stopped, instinctively, at the Be-a-Star, three recording chambers for too-serious amateurs and caroling drunks. A wolf pack of baggy-panted boys was howling, wrists pretending to hide mouths, at the wavering long notes and off-pitch high notes and mishandled words and broken transitions of the current star, a nine-year-old fish-eyed screecher. *Be a star,* Barry scoffed with the boys. Be a loser. After The Hotels had decided to make the leap to the next level of fame, they had made a demo tape. They had emptied passbooks and parents to pay for it and had hired the only affordable studio, a basement room of a hermetic former studio musician. If The Hotels' final cuts had not been good by conventional standards, the band had managed to play, more or less, the same part at the same time, an appreciated innovation. They had remained in their strum-and-ranting souls a cover band—or, as Barry wrote in the liner notes, practitioners of "interpretative alternative-tribute metal (not heavy)"—and Side A contained eight hard-driving favorites. Side B, however, the side kept under blood-oath secrecy, contained four never-heard-before originals, three of them by Barry. The boys had regarded Side B and its lyrics—all variations on the themes "I want you" and "I want you bad, baby"—as especially promising.

And Barry could still taste it, a rank burp from yesterday's meal. Be-a-Star—these people, whoever owned this thing, were like all the rest, like the softball-toss dirtbag, like Ed: they were criminals, busi*ness*men, trading off poor little ugly girls' dreams. The star came out of the recording chamber. Her mother woo-hooed in congratulations and shielded her from the baggy-panted pack, two of them now clapping with bullying sarcasm. Barry looked harder at the girl. If her head grew faster than the rest of her body, he proposed helpfully, and added mass around her eyes—like pushed them closer together—then maybe she could end up not all that bad looking.

She had been pretty and right, Barry thought, about Leila. He had wanted to crawl into her pants, so innocently snug, and hibernate the rest of the summer, the winter, the life. He emitted a sound, a groan scrambled with hum, in stimulated anticipation. If he had it all over again, he would have just told her how he felt. You're different, Melissa, or, This is like way out there, Ashley, but I want you to know that I think you and I are like the same. That was a worthwhile life, saying that to her.

Yesterday, Linda Steinke had completed the maneuver as planned: hug Barry, hug Ed (quicker than it should have been but there was no time to worry about it), and return to Barry in confidence. No one suspected prearrangement; the family always paired this way. Yet that time Linda had returned to Barry with a more determined urgency than usual. "How are you doing, Barry? Is everything all right?" The night before, she had tried to marinate her tone with practiced meaning: I understand you, I understand what it's like being in this family.

"Yeah, Mom, it's fine."

"Bare, I brought you something."

Barry laughed, a tickled baby's laugh. "Oh yeah?"

Linda reached into her purse for a folded paper bag, hospital corners, Boyster's Bakery. Barry didn't need to open it to see the chocolate macaroons inside. "Mom, like I have enough to eat," he protested mildly.

"Bare, I know how hard you're working, and it doesn't hurt to have a little treat." Barry loved these cookies so much; Ed liked them too, but he didn't love them.

"You're the bestest," Barry said as he and his mother smiled. That was their little joke: you're the bestest.

He's getting thinner, Linda thought, but he was always so thin, and it was hard to tell, and there were more important things to talk about. "Between you and me, Barry," she whispered in gesture, not volume, "I know you-know-who can sometimes be a little rough."

*Why can't we like just talk about cookies?* Barry groaned and opened the bag roughly. This gig sucked, but he didn't need any sympathy from his mother. "Whatever."

Linda wouldn't surrender to Barry's macho-man routine (he was obviously not eating right), and she glanced at Ed and swallowed contritely. "Remember, you have to stand up for yourself. It's just a matter of temperament. You're more artistic than he is."

"Whatever." Barry didn't mind the relative comparison, but he wouldn't hear of it in the absolute. He looked hard at his mother; neither he nor Ed had ever attached the slightest adjective to her corporeality: she was normal looking, on the thinner straighter side, and anyway, it was none of their business. A two months' separation, however, alerted Barry to dumpling changes in his mother that must have been progressing since he left high school; a clear-mission life was slackening in her lower stomach and thighs; a girdle, it seemed, was being gradually tissue-filled.

"You *are* more like that, Barry. And Ed takes after your father in so many ways." She guiltily eyed Gene, who was occupied with Ed, far enough away. They were probably talking about business, Linda thought, resigned to the truth of the cliché.

"I dunno."

"So just keep being who you are"—she smiled, a sun-mother smile, the source of all life—"perfect."

"*Jesus,* Mom, like drop it already."

"Well, I want you to know that *we* support you in everything you do." Barry had been a more pleasant boy before this summer adventure.

Barry wanted to change the subject—it had come up before— and he held the stopper that closed the drain. "You talk like you don't even like Ed." By animal instinct, Linda froze to decide whether she should laugh to dismiss the absurdity of Barry's comment or scold him on its sinfulness. Barry noticed the pause.

Linda Steinke was an exemplary mother, wife, and woman (order intentional) by the standards of Rue Chambois Road. Both Barry and Ed were healthy. Both were respectful to their parents, or as respectful as one could hope for from boys of their disposition. Neither of them had been in trouble, except for Barry, but those had been little troubles, his record was felony-free, and the past was the past. *Now* her sons were in business together.

"Business together?" the bridge players had repeated.

"Yes, they *are*."

Individually, as required, the women tax-paid their compliments.

"How *wonderful*."

"That's so nice."

"Lucky *you*."

The women were not as impressed as they pretended to be. Sure, Linda Steinke had things to be thankful for, but so did most women in Kopekne Green, an upright subdivision closed to drunks and philanderers. Candidly, Linda never felt humbled-to-tears thankful herself, but last-can-of-corn-at-the-supermarket thankful, a pretty paper cutout dress on a pretty paper cutout doll. Really, she thought, the girls go too far sometimes.

"What's your *secret,* Linda?" Penny Ropcek asked, almost as if she were interested in Linda Steinke's secret, as if Linda Steinke had a secret. She was no better than the rest of them. Especially with that Barry on her hands. Boy oh boy. The stories she'd heard.

"My life is an open book," Linda declared humbly, sincerely, mutely giggling. Despite the extruded lower lips and contemplative nods, none of the women were sure what to do with the response so they—"Whose turn is it?"—continued the game. Linda wasn't sure herself if the phrase meant anything, but it was

Gene's favorite line, his claim to the universally correct opinions on socialism, liberalism, atheism, and homosexuality. Linda liked it too, in her own particular context.

"That's fantastic about your sons, Linda," Penny Klepka, the hostess, congratulated. She led a club to dummy's ace and sighed. "Sons are great, aren't they?"

"So are daughters," Alice Zalapsky, who had three of them, corrected primly as she ruffed a diamond winner.

"I guess . . ." Penny K. sighed again. Alice and Linda and Penny R. looked to one another through the upper floors of their eyes. "It's just"—the words struggled out of Penny K.'s mouth— "I think, oh, it's strange, but I think I like Jim more than Shawn."

The bystanders, dinosaurs all bound by no careers, no degrees, inhaled—never, it appeared for a moment, to exhale again. Alice, finally able to speak, stammered, "But-but-but-but." She, for one, couldn't imagine how a sane woman could even *think* something so perverse. Of course, they all knew why. Shawn, a prom princess with the mouth of a teamster, was horrible to her mother. Jim, a mild-mannered angel, was respectful and clean. Yet if Penny had certain feelings resulting from this situation, she should have kept them to herself, or phrased it differently. Jim was at a more agreeable stage, or Jim was more like me and Shawn was more like her father.

"It's amazing that you can *say* that," Penny R. scolded.

"I know. I know."

"*Really,*" Penny R. expanded on her point. For there was *nothing* in creation, Linda, Alice, and the two Pennies knew, worse than favoring one child over another. If you sucker-punched your children or sold them into slavery, it was fine as long as you punched them equally hard or sold them for the same price.

"I know. I know."

Linda tisk-tisked—that was all from her. She assumed that Penny K. was just not herself that day and speculated afterward that she might have taken an extra swig of Irish cream in the kitchen before bringing it to the table. Linda was regularly more compassionate than the other girls, but this time her compassion for the ineffable was amplified by understanding.

Ed had been—Linda could hardly admit it—an ugly baby. He wasn't a monster, but Linda could see the double takes and swallowed compliments—"he's, er, gorgeous"—when people saw his lopsided mug for the first time. His appearance improved as he got older, but that was the only direction possible. Baby Barry, however, was huggable-plump, strawberry cream, blond with a smile that could light the heavens. When people saw him, they lost the lid to their effusion. Perhaps they were grading on an inflated scale after Ed; perhaps they were thrilled not to have to lie again. Yet even strangers would stop Linda to compliment her for begetting such a beautiful, darling, delicious, Christian marvel (and that other little boy too).

And Ed was always so *serious.* At twelve—Linda swore she could remember the day exactly—he stopped playing with balls, blocks, cars, trains, and other children, and took on, increasingly, the adult airs. Then the businesses began; a new one every month, it seemed. Gene, of course, encouraged all this, patriot-proud of his capitalist sperm. When at fourteen Ed announced that he no longer required an allowance, Gene almost cried, overjoyed, no doubt, to save the seven dollars a week. Linda did cry. But Barry, Barry was always her boy. When he was eight or ten or sixteen, he would run into the house, caked in dirt and sweat, and drag playground mud across the floor. "We don't live in a zoo," she would shout. When he was six or nine or seventeen, he would return from school and demand a snack. "I'm not a short-order cook—" *Please.* . . . And Linda would make it, not unhappily. When the real troubles began, whiskey-woozy mornings, sea-of-C's report cards, the car hood smashed (and abandoned), Barry was even *more* her boy. He needed her. He would admit it too. No one ever discovered where Barry's affectionate side came from. It didn't come from Gene, who equated emotional exhibitions (anger excluded) with fruit-loops. And it surely didn't follow from his brother's lead. "Love you," Linda would call after Ed as he left for college, apartment, work. *Okay, then.* Yet when she would make Barry those snacks, he would kiss her on the cheek. When she would slip him ten dollars before a night out—she was smart or fearful enough not to ask how he planned to spend it—he would say in that funny-bragging falsetto of his, "You're the bestest." Of course, Linda was absolutely delighted that Ed was her son and that he was such a fine young man, nothing but good news (when there was news at all). But he was the businessman, perpetually carrying on about the next big thing, just like Gene, she suspected, had done at that age. She never talked about this with Ed—he wouldn't have participated in that conversation as a matter of principle—but she gathered from his private, man-business references at the dinner table to gross margins or this Alfred Orditz that he dreamed practical, sensible, businessman dreams about gross margins and Alfred Orditz. Barry, however, was the artist. His stuff, it followed, was tortured-noble-deep, sensitive, also stirring.

*Just like Marcia.* When Gene said his life was an open book, he told the truth. His pages were clearly written, plain American English. He was a good provider, faithful husband, dutiful father, loyal citizen, frank and honest and hardworking man. Linda's life was different; secrets hid in her heart. In the voting booth, especially, that warm womb, the curtain of democracy swaddling her conscience, Linda always pulled the lever on the left. This was noteworthy only that, around election time, she feigned political apathy, or, more commonly, passive agreement with Gene. Since Gene's sole test of a candidate's merit, it seemed, was how much the fellow reminded him of John Wayne, everyone figured that

Linda voted the same. But she never did. Gene, she could explain the taproot of her reasoning (if anyone had ever asked), idolized her father, Ed Kroeger. He could recite Ed's war stories so word-for-word pure, both the near-death and the comic collections, that one might think that he had spent the war in Ed's rather large nose. If a name passed in conversation that was coincidentally similar to one of Ed's protagonists, Gene would prompt his father-in-law, "Ed, weren't you in the Pacific with" John Smith or Lat Runge or that short guy named Vurkovich? "Oh yeah, there," Ed would wind up. "Ralphie 'Da Runt' Vurkovich from San*dusky,* Ohio. Now, he wasn't *technically* a midget, but he was da smallest sailor, I was told, in da Pacific theater. I remember one day . . ." When it came time to christen their first son, Linda and Gene decided to name him after one of his grandfathers, either Ed or Gene's father, Joe. Joe, like his son, was from an off generation. A small man, too old to fight, he worked unassumingly during the Last Great Campaign in the same food-processing plant in which he had worked every week before and after the war. The choice was no choice at all. (There was no meaningful story behind Barry's name. Gene for some reason wanted to call him Larry. Linda, feeling lyrical and brave, suggested Bryce. They comprised—with a heavy tilt in Gene's favor—on Barry. It was better, Barry used to say, than Lyce.) Gene and Ed held the same opinion on everything, and they held the same opinion of Marcia—tragic for Ed, for she was his daughter. For her first eighteen years, Marcia had been modest, unremarkable, a little plain (no harm), and she had done nothing to identify herself as anything but Kroeger Child Number Four of Five. Then, with little forewarning, she became involved in the women's movement and briefly acquired a colorful enough local reputation to raise eyebrows in the homes of her father, his neighbors, and general newspaper readers. One Thanksgiving, Ed and Marcia tangled in a fight that was so brutal and odd, a fight in separate tongues—

"This patriarchy must end." "Anybody know what da heck she's talking about?"—that no reconciliation was possible, arranged, or desired. Marcia left in tears and left forever, and Ed cut her off his life like a toenail past due. Linda already had her two boys, the ugly and the cute one, when it happened. There was nothing I could do, she would tell herself years later. I was scared, she would confess. If only I were younger, Marcia's age, I would have . . . , the regrets would percolate. Well, woulda, coulda, shoulda, Linda, no use getting on about it now.

Marcia and Linda talked on the telephone every six months or so. Marcia didn't particularly want to, although not for the obvious reasons—because Linda was a housewife in an age of housewifely obsolescence, or Linda never stood up to that reactionary husband of hers. No, Marcia didn't enjoy calling because the conversations always started the same way.

"Hello, Linda."

Linda would pause to change into appropriate tones: big-sister, piteous, with magnitude. "My gosh, Marcia. Are you doing all right, dear? Really, are you?" This was twenty years after Marcia had resigned from the family, twenty years in which she had created a new life for herself in a community of the rein-vented and the free, far away from their man-arrogant fathers. Yet Linda still treated her like the seven-year-old who had lost her hamster, consoling but circuitous. Marcia still cared for Linda—at least Linda tried, unlike the rest of the family—but she couldn't handle more than two conversations a year. Linda, who thought her sister called infrequently because of the fight's still-painful bruises, froze Marcia, an idealized Marcia, in her bosom's cleaved core. Marcia was her surrogate fighter; Marcia was *out there* because Linda couldn't be. And in the private sanctuary of a voting booth, Linda shut her eyes, touched her chest where her sister lived forever in long skirts, ironed hair, and silver-and-turquoise rings, and voted the opposite of Gene.

Linda asked Barry if he needed anything.

"A life."

Linda wasn't sure if this was a joke; Barry showed a peculiar funny bone at times. "Really, do you need something, Bare?"

"The summer to end, how 'bout that? Like can you do that?"

"Speaking of that," Linda said transitionally.

"Like I don't want to talk about it."

"Well, *have* you decided what you are going to do when the summer ends?"

"I'm going to fly to the moon, Mommy dearest. Fly to the moon." Barry flaccidly tried to set the moon to a song; it was cheap charm, unsuccessful, eventually reddening.

Linda neither dismissed nor encouraged the performance. Verifying that Gene was still talking to Ed, she tiptoed onto the subject. "Barry, I've looked into some coll—"

"I'm like not having this conversation."

"Well, how about Lincoln Paper? Your father always said that he thought that, well, that they thought that you were doing a great job there." Gene had never said that; he probably had never thought that either.

"I can't do that."

"Oh, I understand. It's not your *thing*."

Barry exhaled: Linda had been watching too much television again, all those shows about young-adult angst, targeted to thirteen-year-olds, offering parenting advice to mothers confused and eager and modern. "No, Mom, it's not that."

"Well then?"

Barry looked at his brother and father, who had reached the dead end of a conversation. He drew his mother's thirsty, imploring eyes to the family's other half and asked, "Don't you like want to talk to Ed for a while?"

It was *that,* Barry knew. He couldn't return to Lincoln Paper. He wouldn't have returned if he could—the pallet crew's fun was film-thin and repetitive—but Barry couldn't return. So there.

Barry had met Cheryl Pfeffer at Lincoln Paper's Christmas party, a motel banquet-room affair notable for the severe tilt of the room toward the open bar and the *oomp*s and *pah*s of a brass-heavy combo that Jerry Claus Hozenfelder, the company's CEO, insisted was the greatest in the world. (Although Lincoln Paper's letterhead contained a silhouetted profile of its namesake, the company had nothing to do with the president, who was not in the paper-products business. A neighbor of the company's immigrant founder, Uder Claus Hozenfelder, had explained that Lincoln was the runner-up to Jesus in those parts, and Uder thought the name sounded much, much more American than Hozenfelder Papiergesellschaft.) The first woman in her family to attend college—she still gloried six years later in her B-plus (almost A-minus) average and a double major in business and psychology—Cheryl had vaulted to the position of manager, operations administration. There, Cheryl worked closely with Gene Steinke and came to appreciate his jowls-jiggling defense of the operations function, his straightforward all-bananas-taste-the-same reliability. It was thus not surprising that she was positively disposed to his son, and it didn't hurt that, at the Christmas party, he was "unbelievably cute" and she was unbelievably drunk. For the next two months, Cheryl and Barry's relationship was casual and discreet. Cheryl, a model employee in every regard, lived heart-sworn by Lincoln Paper's code of conduct and felt uncomfortable fraternizing with a fellow worker. (Barry's offers to fraternize her never failed to tickle and please.) They had an open, once-or-twice-a-week relationship then, which meant that Barry was free to pursue other girls and Cheryl was also free to do whatever she wanted, which usually involved reading four or five pages of a women's magazine, wondering what Barry was doing, putting the reading down, and telling her cat that she was sadly unable to concentrate that night. Other problems besides the code of conduct blocked a more serious relationship. Barry was two months short of twenty, and four years—plus a bucket of motivation—short of a college degree. Cheryl's mother's line had not (as a rule) married intelligently, and Cheryl feared the lineal recidivism of falling for someone whose gigolistic tendencies were so prominent. Nevertheless, the bond between Cheryl and Barry congealed. She continued to find him physically irresistible. And he professed to love her true. Cheryl and her double majors were too sophisticated to believe him at first—"it could be *pup*py love," she traded hypotheses with a friend—but she was also approaching the age when alarm, deep want, and ascribed biology helped the believing along. For his part, Barry found Cheryl's businesswoman demeanor—hair pulled back, her vocabulary a boil bubbling atop its natural skin— pleasantly different, and when she forgot about the demeanor after a quartet of beers or a two-rounder beneath the sheets, she was kooky, girlish, a circling windup toy. He liked that too.

And then there was the geometry of her frame. "What's up, dude?" Barry had greeted a pallet crewsman at the Christmas party. His comrade assumed the position next to him and began to urinate. (At this point in the evening, the pallet crew was still using the bathroom.) This specific dude's name was Christian Paul Zbrenokowski, which was a fine designation for a composer-conductor or prisoner of conscience of moderate, esoteric fame but was probably too ambitious, Christian worried, for the likes of him. He preferred "Z-Shock," origin unknown, when individuation required something other than "dude."

"Not much, dude, and you?"

"Making time. Making time."

"Who's that vintage betty you're talking to?" Z-Shock was a dictionary of catchphrases, pop references.

"What?" Barry shook off his nozzle.

"The betty. She's vintage."

"Huh?" Barry flushed the urinal.

"Vintage!" The howl ricocheted off porcelain, mirror, tile.

"Dude, you're out of *con*trol." Barry zipped and left, unmoved. However, when he returned to the banquet room and resumed his sly courting of Cheryl, Z-Shock was reborn a prophet. Cheryl *was* vintage, fifties-detective-novel vintage, sailor-locker vintage, a wet dream of a bygone generation. Her sweeping soft curves, Barry learned that night, grabbed you inside her. Her pillows bounced and giggled—he could actually hear them giggle—when freed before the act. Barry had slept with plenty of women that society deemed more attractive: girlish waifs and athletic bundles, wispy reeds and dynamite sticks. Nothing felt as good as Cheryl Pfeffer.

Cheryl had not been lucky in love, she would admit. Men were intimidated by her combination of brains and looks, was her theory; and she proved this by extracting from nervous, off-put prospective suitors their résumés, grade averages, and positions on issues of worldly importance equally thoughtful to the ones she had picked up from newsweeklies. Even in her "fun" relationships, she intimidated the men and lost them, so she related, because they were emotionally incapable of managing a second date. "You know, your problem with serious commitment probably has a lot to do with a dysfunctional relationship with your mother," Cheryl would advise a monthlong beau. Or she would tell an unplanned encounter at the morning unease, "I think women, as nesters, are fundamentally healthier, and that's why we like live longer." If the men couldn't take her, well, it was just proof: men just weren't ready for a smart attractive woman in that backward timber lot of a city.

Barry, of course, was sui generis, and she didn't expect much. However, and this was the greatest surprise, Cheryl noticed that Barry listened to her more seriously and appeared to understand her more fundamentally—she was certain of this—than some of these so-called professionals.

And so from the bed one night, she decided to eradicate a long-vexing pest. "Barry?"

Knowing "Barry?" meant no good, he oinked, "Yes."

"I think men are not loyal to women because of evolution."

Barry was operating on two hours of sleep; he and some of the pallet crew had, scientifically emboldened, combined various substances the night before. He muffled a yawn. "Yeah, that's interesting, if you think about it." That usually got him off the hook.

"Yes, I think it's *very* interesting how all these millions of years, these gender roles have been building up." She *had* read a fascinating excerpt in college about evolutionary psychology, but that was not the point.

"Yeah." Barry didn't muffle his yawn this time.

"Are you listening to me?"

"Sure. Gender roles, dinner rolls. Very interesting."

Cheryl laughed. Barry was listening to her, she could tell, but he was uncomfortable about this subject, as a man, as a per*pe*trator.

"So tell me, *Mister* Steinke, why do you think men compulsively chase women?"

"Like what's on TV?"

"Ha ha. Answer me."

"I dunno."

"*Rasp*berry," she whined.

Barry hated that nickname—she knew that—and readjusted himself in the bed to skin-shed the willies crawling out of Cheryl's whine. He then snorted a protest, which maybe could also answer whatever friggin' question she was asking now.

"Really, why do they do it?"

"Like who's they?"

"Men, Barry-Barry."

"I said, I don't know. Drop it."

But, that night, at intervals, Cheryl kept asking.

Barry closed his eyes and a dreamstate, numb and liberating, poured into him. If he could be like this forever, he could float over this ocean forever and ever, forever and ever. . . . But Cheryl's vintage body, impatient in the bed beside him, shifted in demand. He lifted himself from near sleep slowly, the numb sinking to his toes, his body protesting. He switched his mind to Think. He bounced open his eyes and turned his head quickly, a ghoul awakened from the dead. "If I tell you, will you promise never to ask me again?"

She lied.

"Do you swear?"

She lied again.

"Because it's filling." This was not a stock answer; Barry had never uttered those words in that sequence before other than to defend himself against another helping of his mother's Tuna, Nut & Noodle Casserole.

"Huh?"

"Like I do it . . . we do it . . . I don't know about we, but I do it because it's filling. When you're there, out there, trying to get some girl—sorry, *woman*—like that's all there is. And nothing else matters, if you think about it. It doesn't matter about your job, your family, making money. It doesn't matter about like, you know, your music."

"Huh?" Cheryl said again. When Cheryl had asked Barry about EAP RIP, he had told her that it was part of "like some messed-up kid's stuff." The Hotels were history; he had matured.

"You're there, and it's real," Barry continued, "and it's like all right, you know, *all right*. Because, if you think about it, it's natural. Everyone else does it. Every part of you, without even thinking about it, is pointing in the same direction. And it's filling. Everything else is secondary—doesn't even like register."

"That's really it?"

"You said you would never ask me again."

Cheryl objected, "But this is part of the *same* conversation."

Barry overruled. "I don't care. Just drop it."

She tried to ask a few more times that week but never got past "leave me alone" again. She attributed his reticence, despite his transparent sincerity, to systematic repression, a psychological malady of her own invention. This was primal human pathology and probably also socially coordinated, so she didn't blame him personally for his inability to answer frankly.

Barry and Cheryl's relationship went smoothly after that until Cheryl's younger sister Carrie threw a "kegger." Carrie, equally vintage, hadn't followed Cheryl to college or lower management. Tragically, according to Barry, she also had like a lot of whacked-out issues with her sister, some of which manifested themselves at the party when Carrie led already-wobbly Barry to her parents' bedroom. There, if one is to believe Barry, "The girl like practically raped me." Amy Igelfeld, Cheryl's best friend, noted Barry and Carrie's contemporaneous absences—Cheryl was napping off a drunk at the time—and after Cheryl called Barry the next afternoon and his responses were nervous and clipped, Amy too gleefully presented the evidence to her friend. Barry had a sixth sense for oncoming feminine aggression and prepared for imminent assaults with a thoroughness that a Pentagon whiz kid would have admired: "Mom, um, if like any girls call for me, I'm not home."

"You're not in trouble, are you?"

"No, no, *obviously* not. It's just . . ." Barry couldn't explain the situation to her. He hadn't even told his parents about Cheryl with all *her* complications: age, work, Dad, serious.

"Okay, Barry, as long as there's no trouble."

Thirty minutes later, the phone rang. "Hello." Linda was sunshine gay.

"I need to speak to Barry."

"I'm sorry, he's not home right now."

"Tell him Cheryl called."

Two hours after that and two hours after that, Linda was sunshine gay again. Two hours after that, Linda was not so sunny.

"Is Barry home yet?"

"No, he's not." Linda, who had experienced these fire drills before with her sought-after son, turned stern. "He's out, and I have *no* idea when he's coming back."

After another day of "Please, Ms. Steinke, I need him for two seconds," Cheryl made the decision. She apologized repeatedly to the Lincoln Paper code of conduct and walked from the corporate offices to the warehouse. She found Barry lounging outside the Nap Box with three other perpetually on-break delinquents from the pallet crew.

"Barry," she taffy-pulled the first syllable.

"Oh *shit,* dude," a member of the chorus sang.

"Barry, I *am* going to talk to you."

"Whoa, dude. She's angry," the rest of the chorus debuted. Over a chin-tickling blouse, Cheryl was wearing a banker-gray suit. To firm up an alibi, she had put on pink socks and tennis shoes and had told her secretary that she needed to run an errand for something. For the dudes of the pallet crew, nothing, not her chesty figure, not her cream-smoothy skin could compensate for that outfit.

"Can't you see I'm busy?" Barry protested, although she could see only that he wasn't. In the early days of the relationship, Barry, potent and invincible, had told Cheryl about the crew and the Nap Box.

"Yeah, I know exactly what you and the rest of these bums are 'busy' doing." She loaded her magic bullet. "And I'm not afraid to tell someone about it."

The chorus turned on the hero. "Yo, dude, don't *screw* us up."

Barry and Cheryl walked to the other side of the pallet area, away from the boys giggling about Stinky—"dude, that was *awesome*"—and the steaming blond. Barry accepted all. Cheryl began to cry. He said he was sorry. She asked him how could he. He blamed it on her sister. She said Carrie had done it before. He said he was so, *so* sorry. ("So-so?" "No, so, so, *so* sorry.") She proclaimed something about trust. Barry had his own magic bullet: "It doesn't like matter because I love you."

Their relationship revived that night, but the patient, Barry knew, was terminal. He couldn't allow Cheryl to hold the livelihood of the entire pallet crew over his head. Three weeks later, when Ed offered him a position at Ed Steinke, Incorporated, Barry didn't listen to a word he said. He did, however, realize that he had found the keys to his cell. Everything went fine with Cheryl in the Indian summer of their romance. *He* knew it would be over in six weeks, and they still had fun.


In the midway's breathing space, Barry stared at yet more girls, but not with his usual wolfish eye or his occasional architect's eye, which concerned itself with size and form and overall meaning, but with an exhausted eye. He wasn't going to return to Ed, that was for sure. *Be-a-Star: yeah, right.* They had sold him that bill of goods already.

But she was not like the rest of these dumb girls, Barry thought as churning shrieks and groans of the Tilt-a-Whirl waved behind him. Something inside her (not that way) was the answer, he was certain. Her running away was like weird, sure, and kind of funny, if you think about it, but because there was a mystery there, because there was something to find, there was a reason to find it. As he walked, a terrestrial cloud of the day's-end humidity swallowed him; it had been blasted, open-oven, from a ride's diesel engine. His stomach flinched, and his cheeks prepared to catch an emission. It never came. *What am I friggin' doing?* He looked around the midway's heart once more. It had been fifteen minutes since he had left the South Exhibition Hall. What am I friggin' doing *here,* he repeated with more accusation. He knew the technical answer to the question, and his thoughts, wisps of thoughts, floated through The Hotels, Ed's offer, the pallet crew. They dawdled at Cheryl Pfeffer and sped by The Rooster, chocolate macaroons, Leila. But all those events were little things, ordinary things, things that had happened *to* him. None of them were *eventful.* Barry's life wasn't a tower where each experience was built on the last. His life was a soup; ingredients were added here and there—inclinations, capitulations, garlic, basil, expectations—and its essence was little more than its strongest, latest flavor. He shook himself from self-pity, melancholy, the Cherylish analysis of every friggin' thing. *Well, there's like nothing I can do about it now.* He went to get a drink, an always reasonable plan when there was nothing you could do about it now.

# [ 4 ]

Leila would go right home, she decided—again. But first she would eat. She wanted to go home, but the Fair held her, its movement, its memory, and for a half hour, the pendulum swung: I must go home, eat. She walked by food, sizzling and tempting and inedible, and did not stop. She planted herself on the pendulous bulb and shut herself to all but the arc. Go home. Eat. Go home. Eat. Just don't think about rubbing cows, that cosmic twin, those gaseous ideas, that gobbledygook moment demanding untangling. Untangling and entangling are only a letter apart, and the pendulum doesn't have time for either. Locked swinging, Leila was hypnotized, freed of personality, opinions, freed of history, doubt, a future. Eat. Go home. Eat. Go home. Eat.

Once, small and curious, Leila had asked her grandfather why wars happen.

*Life's tough.* And to demonstrate it, he grinned and bore it.

She had exited the cattle building as if ordered by the police: slowly now, easy now, *calm*. She squinted as she passed the mural wall's stretching shadow. The sun bending in the horizon crashed into her view. She held her jaw, thinker-style, thumb notched under her cheekbone ridge, and let the sun toast through her eyes' closed lids. Her hand moved over her mouth, her fingers distributed across her face.

*I'm hungry*. Hunger was good, hunger reassured her. Hunger, unlike love and meaning and identity and recognition, was easy. *I'm hungry*. Hunger has an answer: I need something to eat.

For months now—it had been just under a year since her escape from Aunt Mary's—Leila's life had reached a still rest. In that rest, she was promised, you had certain privileges: you did not have to endure uncanny experiences, you did not have to consider life's alternate possibilities, you did not have to swell and tear. You just had to go to work eleven days out of fourteen, eat a little, drink a little, and pay the bills reasonably on time. But today had violated those privileges. And so she would leave, and today would end, and it would happen tomorrow. The experts would label Leila a time bomb, but she wasn't a bomb, she was a soldier. That was *her* dream, her regular haunt: the drop was chaos, someone lost the orders, her platoon missed the flight. "This is it," the grinning pilot pointed to the jungle below. Leila couldn't hear him over the chopper's blades. "But—" she protested. "Want some advice?" But— "Watch out for the mines, he he." Alone, on the jungle floor, she could barely see over the bush. "Well," she promised herself, "*I'm* not going to walk *into* a bullet." And she set her pack down, sat on it, never to move again. Every grunt, the machine guns cried, the reaper applauded, Leila agreed, gets it in the end. But by sitting, Leila wouldn't get *herself* hurt, get herself killed, wouldn't struggle, wander, demand, want, fail, pretend.

*I'm hungry.* After a half hour, she accepted no second thoughts, tolerated no objections.

The culinary Babel at the State Fair strained the appetite's ability to regulate, register, survey. Vendors, from the carts dispensing licorice whips to the moguls commanding two-hundred-seat burger barns, vied for the affection of the grazing hordes. Fat and sugar and salt were the godheads of the faith. Few vendors matched the pride or profits of the agricultural associations who commanded the fair's best locations, best customers, best quality, best propagandists. The potato growers dismissed any question of their importance—this wasn't exactly potato country—with a nod to the hungry masses waiting for one of their taters dressed in butter and bacon and chives. The apple association didn't let the Fair's inopportune timing, a month before the true apple harvest, stop them either; they covered their apples in caramel and pecans and pretended not to notice when the customers, ex post candy, threw the mealy fruit away. But as everyone knew, the Fair was Dairy, Dairy Über Alles. From its first minute, masses would swarm and antsy lines of piety would form, lines of switchbacks snaking the hall, lines waiting to buy ice cream or *receive* a cream puff. To the foreigner, to the traitorous, the puffs weren't much to speak of; the coat of powdered sugar poorly disguised the bread's kinship to a burger bun; the filling, a cup of whipped cream, tasted like the clouds, which meant like not much at all. The traitor's sacrilege would have sparked eloquent reproaches if the mouths of the cream's defenders were not busy puff-stuffing two in a row. For you *had* to have a cream puff, like you *had* to visit the poultry building, because even if you were an accountant or a mechanic or a housewife—especially if you were one of those—you were still part of the land that fed the cows that provided the milk that made the cream that filled the puffs that made you fat that made you dead and part of the land. We are all, we are all, we are all farmers, farmers who have lost our way.

Outside the halls, the state's immigrants had written their history in food. Most of them, it seemed, had floated to America on sausages: sausage-stuffed bellies, sausage-linked rafts, sausage canoes. Their heirs' tubes blanketed the fairgrounds, nuzzled fifty at a time on half-barrel grills. Most natives were too conscientious for an ordinary hot dog. They shunned the pink processed packages for the manlier sausages: the knockwurst, the Polish, the Italian, the kielbasa, the bratwurst—the last, the state's pork-veal mascot of all that was good. The sauerkraut-stained hands of Mitteleuropa's descendants dominated the sausage trade, but the red-faced paws feared no one. The Italians may have lent a facsimile of their encased patrimony to the generalist, but they sold the real thing themselves with the beef sandwiches, with the fried eggplants, with the fried mozzarella, the local fried favorite. The Swedes sold pancakes, the Greeks gyros, the Danes kringles, the Belgians waffles. (The Belgians were actually only one Belgian and he wasn't even Belgian; he had bought the irons from a neighbor, also not Belgian, who had retired four years ago.) The newcomers, Asians and Latinos, still a novelty to the oldest country folks, set up booths in disproportionate numbers to sell stale egg rolls and processed-cheese nachos to the gringos and guailo. And if the Anglos and the Saxons, the Irish, blacks, and Jews, didn't attempt in the main to profit from their culinary heritage—some for very good reason—they still made a summer buck from melting-pot comfort food.

Unlike puffs or cinnamon pear pie, corn was no monopolist's moll. There were a dozen or so stands operated by Legionnaires, Lions, or the odd Shriner. (Lions claimed that all Shriners were odd Shriners, and vice versa, but the clubmen were kept far apart.) The fairground's local Legion post ran the Fair's busiest corn stand, next to its tallest structure, an eight-story rippled slide of yellow plastic. For thirty seconds, children rode down the slide on potato sacks; the adrenaline produced was constant and low, and thus only the smallest children were able to notice a thrill.

Leila held up one finger: one ear, please. Her unbreakfasted stomach was in no condition for sausage or cream. "Anything to drink, girly?" asked a Legionnaire, who had called every woman "girly" for eighty-one years save mother, wife, and the Blessed Virgin. He operated the booth with twenty of his comrades and members of the ladies' auxiliary.

"Root beer, I guess."

He wrapped the husk in a paper towel and handed her the soda and corn. She dipped the cob in a paint can of butter but forwent the salt and pepper. "Ex*cuse* me, girly . . ."

Leila blushed. "Oh, I'm sorry." She gave him three dollars.

She had been hungry. Now she had food. Eat. Hungry no more. She sat at a table, her back to the streaming crowds, and began like a well-oiled typewriter to work methodically from the left. The corn was perfect, firm and summerend sweet. On her fourth pass of kernels, she noticed, happily surprised, that she was not thinking about Rusty, about the organ boy, about anything. The kernels burst with nectar, cavity-tickled with their gristle. Eating was the right answer, going home was the right answer, everything was the right answer but agitation, people pressing their rights, her rest breaking its pact.

And so, of course, someone called out her name. "Leila?"

She held the kissed cob motionless.

"Leila?" She turned around, the cob in the towel in her right hand, held like the liberty torch. "Leila Genet, right?" Just like she remembered it, his polar hair sprouted silly-willy from his head, jolts from the big brain below.

"Uh-huh." She could still run, she reckoned. Of *course,* she could. Or she could throw the corn in his face. It wouldn't really hurt him, but it would slow him down long enough for her to break away. What was it, three years? This wasn't the right time for this: she was late, *so late,* she needed to get home, she needed to like do stuff around the house, she needed to report to work, she needed to—

"Because when you didn't answer, I thought maybe I was—"

"No, no. I was, um, like caught up in my thoughts, I guess."

"It's been quite a while, Leila." His companion, a woman, lingered four yards behind. Over two gypsyish hoop earrings, her autumn-toned hair waved, encircled—en*oval*ed—her face, a model of symmetry and carved grace.

"Uh-huh."

"I didn't mean to bother you."

"Uh-huh."

"But it was a nice surprise to see you there—here." James Nancy already regretted opening his mouth, and his mouth had been open for less than a minute. It had been a reflex—not libido, never—and a boobish thing to do. How stupid can I be, he thought. I haven't seen this girl in— I should have ignored her. His Adam's apple, two sizes too large for his neck, slid down his throat.

"Well, you know . . ." Leila ended the awkward pause.

"We never did get to finish that conversation."

"Um, like, I had sort of family business."

James assumed it was a lie. After twenty-two years at the community college, he was used to it; every semester, his classes shrank by a fifth at the midterm and another fifth at the final, and he never heard from the students again. James didn't care about most of them, but once every few years one of them came along that was, at the very least, interesting.

"Nothing serious?" James hoped that this comment, somehow, would accelerate the end of his error.

"No." There had been no family business, not then anyway.

"Well, that's good, I suppose." He smiled, and his wrinkled mask revealed its columns and rows. James's life had crossed with Leila's briefly, but he had recognized that germ of *one*ness inside her. He was disappointed—this was a distant disappointment—that nothing had happened later on. James was the son of Benjamin T. Nancy, famed American historian and confidant of two generations of the state's more liberal governors and congressmen, although James early on had caught an absolute, fanatical hatred of Daddy's bourgeois brand of polite progressivism. Accepted at Benjamin T.'s alma mater out East, James refused to register for classes, attended those in which he was not welcome, and disrupted all of them with inappropriate, vicious, perceptive outbursts. They expelled him his sophomore year. Although no longer a student, James became a Student Radical but was soon disgusted by the petty politicians and the sandlot demagogues who lorded over their private insurrections. Then he moved to New York and lived on brown rice, but the filth of the city and the hypocrisy of the poets who rhymed take-a-bow with Chairman-Mao in the morning and slept with debutantes at night—that wore on him too. So he disappeared for five years until one midnight, in yet another communal mirror in yet another European capital, James saw a man who looked thirty-five but was a decade younger, he saw a man who lived in a heralded age of idealism but saw ego on all. He returned home and told his father that he would do what the fates had always spun: he would teach, although never the plastic sons of brokers and bankers; he would teach the working class.

"Jesus," he had screamed as he corrected his first students' essays. James's vision of uplifting hardscrabble American youth through poetry and prose, of *being* inspiration, survived for exactly seventeen months. In his fourth teaching semester as he stared again at his reflection, at a face that looked forty-five though it was almost fifteen years younger, he confessed, factually, a runner breaking the tape, "It's over." About that time, the friends of Sylvia, his common-law companion, had begun to plead with her to leave him. Yet she stood by him, stood by him when he drank two scotches every afternoon before four, stood by him when he sent bestsellers—"in *what* country does this crap . . ."— crashing, spine-cracking into walls, stood by him when she learned of The Two, as she called them, the Biographer Woman and the Girl. (The Two lasted only a month each; after that, James could no longer act charming, interested, or even civil.) And she stood by him when he made their lives impossible by compulsively arranging his own disillusionment. Without warning, like that day, he would wake her up and insist that they go to the State Fair or a shopping mall because, in the muddled logic of morning rage, he couldn't stand her contemptible elitist friends. As soon as they arrived at Fair or mall, James would complain about the smoke, the smell, the prices, and, of course, the people: shortsighted lumps of co-opted material aggression. But she stood by him even when they went home and he sulked and drank another glass. Sometimes she said he was a puppydog.

Leila had enrolled in James's omnibus course, English: Approaches and Styles, in her third semester. In the fourth week, he assigned a short-story composition, as he had every fourth week for twenty years. With the stories on his lap, he would recline in his den chair, his red pen too overwhelmed to correct, and lament the end of Western Civilization. "What are these high schools *doing*, Sylvia?" he would yell. "Teaching these kids how *not* to write?" If the movie-sired plots weren't dubious enough— a girl loses and finds her terrier Cheyenne and realizes, somehow simultaneously, that she loves her mother, Diane—James also had to cope with grammar that was potentially acceptable in a language other than English, spellings invented for cruel sport, handwriting unimproved since primary school. Once in a long-wasteland while, however, he would be reprieved with a story that reaffirmed his faith in the assignment, if not universal progress. Leila's was one of them. He had already noticed her in class, dewy eyes, beguiling overbite, handful-sized breasts (and he had handful-sized hands).

Leila could never account for where she got her story: a girl enters a store "one Saturday afternoon" and finds it abandoned by employees, customers, "and even sounds." The premise was intriguing enough for James—he read it after finishing "Supercat," whose title character had no super powers, as it were, other than being notably lovable—but fifteen words on Leila's second page made his hair, hairs stand further on end. *She was outside the ice cream case. Her hands made sure she was not alone.* James leaned back in his recliner and watched, close-eyed, the lithe frame of that innocent flower shivering and smiling on top of boxed gallons of caramel cashew. Fantasy concluded three minutes later, his red pen wrote—it wrote on page two, James too charged to turn to page one—"Leila, 'Grocery Store' is a tremendous story. Please come see me after class. A++." He capped his pen, paused, uncapped it, and with a showman's ta-da added another plus.

Leila couldn't understand why the top of her paper was blank. "Didn't I get a . . ." She flipped to the second page, and her face stopped, screwed off in confusion. She looked up and found Professor Nancy's stare on her. *It's all true,* he nodded. Even the third plus.

Despite The Two, James was not a dirty old man on the make, he would explain tersely, dispassionately, truthfully. Those affairs, he sighed, were just one more cliché on a beaded life of clichés. *Oh, the disillusioned professor,* he could laugh about it, the aging radical recaptures his youth enwrapped in what's-it, the "lithe frame of an innocent flower." How many movies and memoirs and novels *and lives* were based on that line? James, alas, knew the end of everything before it began; the powers that be—or

The Power That Be—had never allowed him one instant of illusion, had never allowed him one single embrace free of self-reference, self-loathing, self-mocking. But he went along with the affairs (the impulses, the whispers) anyway because, what the hell, he figured it was more honest to be a second-string cliché than to pretend that you were not.

After class, James pulled two chairs, desks built in, facing each other. He would have preferred a location less depressing than the classroom, but he shared an office, even more depressing, with ten colleagues, most of whom were going to leave the school at the first opportunity. "Please, sit down, Leila." He pointed to a chair as they both sat. "I don't think we've formally met. I'm James Nancy."

Leila looked through the desk and tucked her hair behind her ear. "I know that, Professor Nancy."

James winced. His father was Professor Nancy, famed American historian, the front-page obituary read, and confidant of two generations of the state's more liberal governors and congressmen. "Please. James." Leila turned in her left shoulder cheekward; she wasn't going to call him James. "I wanted you to stay after class because your story was truly remarkable."

Leila didn't quite understand him. "Really?"

"Yes, of course. I wanted you to know that I've read, as you can probably guess, a considerable amount of student writing, and I think your story was exceptional."

"It just kind of like came to me."

James recognized that he had a shy one here; the removal of a conversation would require masterly, dental precision. "That is how a lot of great literature is born." Leila tugged her stiff tan jeans; great literature made her greatly uncomfortable. "I see you're nervous." He smiled softly. His creased face looked more appealing around his rare smiles, he knew, a comfortable, professorial slipper. "Why shouldn't you be, right? It's just that there are a lot of people in your class incapable of writing one clear English sentence. I wanted you to know that you're not one of them." Leila tucked her hair behind her ears and remained silent. James changed paths. "Are you from around here?" She told him where she lived, a five-minute drive from campus. "At home, still, with your parents?"

"Yeah, okay."

And paths he changed again. "Let's see. Why don't we do a little exercise It's a trick I learned when I was a young tramp in California. But that was a lifetime ago." He waited for her to be bemused or bedazzled by the exotic or even the agreeable. (Tramp in California, eh? Tell me more, Handsome Older Man.) It was a lure dangled pitiably in the water, and she didn't see it to sniff it to touch it to take it. "Anyway, I want you to read your story aloud. That way, I can follow your, um, authorial emphasis and better appreciate the rhythm of your style."

Leila hadn't read anything out loud for a decade. Her grandfather had never read to her out loud as far as she could remember. Her heart, a hard systolic clap, asked her to crawl—and fetally curl—beneath the desk. "Do I have to?"

He laughed. "No, of course you don't *have* to do anything. This isn't prison, but I think that it would be a worthwhile exercise."

Leila wanted to read the story as quickly as possible, but it came out ponderous and shaky, a fee-fi-fo-fum giant in a little man's land. "One Saturday afternoon, Jenny O'Brien looked in her refrigerator. She needed some milk and she needed some, um, orange juice too." Leila's right hand started to shiver, Leila's right hand started to quiver, Leila's right hand started to tremble, and James, naughty James, took it in his. It was an old act, a bold act that he thought he would have been over by now. Through the conduit, he felt, faintly on his side, a shiver bolt down her spine.

"It's okay, Leila. There's no reason to be nervous." Advice aside, he began—his thumb began—to rub her middle knuckle, gentle and clockwise. No one had touched Leila like that, like anything, since Rusty the year before. James's skin was mid-grit sandpapery and damp. This is not like happening, Leila rush-snuck the thought between stumbled-over sentences. She inhaled, her bladder contracted, she shuddered, and her bladder itched. She read, "Her hands made sure she was not alone." James's knee started to bounce. *Why did I write that?* Leila clenched her teeth. *What kind of stupid idiot would write that?* Her reading faltered three or four more times—*What does that even mean?*—and she looked up with imploring eyes a like amount, but she finished. "She called out again, but no one in the grocery store was there. She called out again and again and again and again. And then she left."

James released her hand. "Like I said, Leila, that was a very, very remarkable piece. Is it part of a larger work?"

"What?"

Over five seconds, he paused, scratched his temple, and approached from a different runway. "Do you consider yourself a writer?"

Leila had kept a journal for six months at a high-school teacher's urging but had abandoned it when she realized that she didn't do anything worth remembering. "I don't really know what you're asking me, Professor Nancy." She tucked her hair behind her ear.

James cupped her hand tightly, a priest counseling a parishioner, pregnant and unwed. Attempting to disarm any fear, he forced the corners of his mouth upward again and laughed, gently but unnaturally low. "Leila, I want you to know that I think that you have talent. And I've seen lots of children—students—here let their talent go to waste." He let go of her hand.

Leila had written the story, a throwaway assignment, in three hours; true, when she had reread it before handing it in, she had liked some of the words, the ones she repeated, the repeating.

Now Professor Nancy had ruined it. Leila said hurriedly, "It's just a stupid little story."

"Don't say that, Leila. Please, don't say that." He was losing her to the same disease to which he lost most of his students. Anger—general, political, dusty—shone through his tattered muslin of allure. "I don't want to instruct you on how to live your life." Leila gulped. "But you have something here that you should develop. I wouldn't lie to you. This story is truly indicative." James was probably telling the truth, the Monday-through-Friday truth, when he said that he would not lie to her, but he had been backed into the corner. As Leila's terse unreplies continued to thwart his efforts to make the conversation friendly, he returned with more praise for "Grocery Store." In no time, he would call it the most important story ever told and let her know that, in his modest opinion, she was the freshest new voice in American literature since Hemingway.

Their exchange hopped like a drunken frog from topic to topic. He asked her what she liked to do. She said she didn't know. He asked her about the class. She said it was fine. He explained its name. She said that that was interesting.

"You know, Professor Nancy."

"Please, James."

"Um, okay. I have to go."

"Okay, but I want to say that I know that in your circumstances, you don't often receive encouragement in your academic pursuits." The last sentence—James tasted its filth while it polluted his throat—was the kind of condescending bourgeois horseshit that his father used to spew. "And I think that it's crucial that you think about your talent."

"I guess."

James understood what he was about to say and understood how he would justify it later. He would declare that Leila had been a fountain of purity; he would claim that he had trusted *in* her innocence; he would bandy about a trite poetic line like "savoring the last autumn day before winter"; and he would believe not a penny of it and detest himself for every word that he uttered and for every moment that they spent together before he frightened her away. He understood that he would do that too. "Why don't we meet somewhere next week?" He let none of the above change a thing. "Outside these walls, for a drink"—Leila's eyes unfolded from slits to circles—"or something to eat." Having done this only a few times more than twice in the last twenty years, James had almost forgotten to add the detergent: "I think we have made a lot of progress here, with your writing. I think that it has some real potential that should be explored."

She mumbled, "Uh-huh."

"Should we set a *time* now?" James understood not to use the word date.

"Um, whatever."

He wrote down the name of a dark Gaelic bar on the back of a reading list—dark and Gaelic were as close to dark and literary as one could muster in that part of town, and dark was actually musty and Gaelic actually Irish. He proposed a working session in three days. She twitched. In hindsight, James would come to admit that her reaction, that twitch, might not have been a cousin to an assenting shrug. As they walked out of the room, he placed his left hand legally cautious near her collarbone. "Great, Leila, then . . ."

"Uh-huh?"

"Then I'll see you then."

At the fair, James turned platitudinous in the void of Leila's silence. "Less serious troubles are always better than the other." He checked on Sylvia behind him. "If there's anything I can do to help . . . ," he added, more mannerly than volunteering.

Leila inspected her corn in her hand and looked to her shoes for release. "No, you know."

"I tell you, I think the school really does have some competent—fine—writing programs," James changed the topic, bogusly energetic, and checked on Sylvia again. After the classroom meeting with Professor Nancy, Leila had rushed home. In her grandfather's workshop sink, she had scoured her hands, scoured off the professor's pawing crumpled advance, his damp sandpaper hands, with steaming water and pumice-stone soap. She wasn't being dramatic, she insisted to herself; she didn't know why she was washing furiously, but she wanted to, thoroughly. *So leave me alone.* And then she went to bed in midafternoon and told the advancing crumple not to join her beneath the sheets. She informed the echoes—his I-wants and I-thinks, his unnatural laugh, gentle and low—that they were unwelcome as well. Leila had done this before, she noted with no-amateur pride. She *could* keep thoughts away; some people can choose not to remember. And the echoes and crumple heeded her word. When the time came for the date—the date for the time—Leila didn't leave the house. As James sat under a neon shamrock, alone and aware that alone he would be, Leila yielded her thoughts to a television below Max Luden's empty gaze. She dropped out of James's class, naturally. One paid by the credit at the college, and she could have received a refund if she officially withdrew. But she didn't bother; she just stopped going. Taking only three classes, all unbearably easy, she answered Yankel's help-wanted ad. Somewhere to go, she figured, something to do other than watch her grandfather wind down to a cold hacking still. At semester's end, Leila didn't register for the next. She didn't know why she had been going to that stupid school anyway. Yes, she had considered the obvious, teacher or nurse. The college, two-thirds of whose students were female, turned nurses and teachers off the assembly line by the cartons and case. Yet Leila didn't have any particular affection for children—so

no teacher—and didn't enjoy science or death, two preferences
that she suspected were required in a medical career. And anyway,
she was tired of seeing Rusty where Rusty wasn't; she had heard
that he had transferred to a school with a football team, where he
could at least watch. But still, every blockhead was him from afar.

James and Leila both looked around for hints and prompts
and subjects. Finally, James said, "I think the Fair is more
crowded this year than last."

Leila mumbled in recognition that he had spoken.

"Well, *then*," he said and exhaled. Leila watched him fidget
for his next words and looked then, her eyes embarrassed and
sovereign, at his face. Underneath his white-chaos hair of snarls
and complications, his forehead folds counted campaigns like a
general's chestborne ribbons. Pouches below his eyes sank
under the weight of disappointments seen; his laugh lines were
not lines at all, but muscled ramparts about the jaw, swollen
from years of exhaustion, alcohol, unsmiling afternoons. Leila
knew nothing about James Nancy, the only son of Benjamin T.
Nancy, famed American historian and. . . . She had never met
the student, the wanderer, the defender of English in his den.
God, Leila thought as she touched her own chin, I'm never
going to look like that. She didn't *hope* that she was never going
to look like that; she declared that she was never going to look
like that; she had declared it long ago. She sat on her pack in the
jungle and refused to step on a mine. She could see his face's
marks, its bags and creases, painful now, painfully acquired.
James, the lines bore witness, had circled and searched and challenged an abyss and had come back to die under these flat hori-
zons, to lie under the rows of corn and soy and wheat, under the
rows of years a-coming when the struggles, like him, were all
clichés, when the unborn generations had already seen it all
before.

"Well, I expect that you should be graduating soon," James broke another silence. He glanced over his shoulder for the last time. Shit, he thought, now I'm going to have to jump through fire to explain the truth to Sylvia. He didn't clarify what he meant by the truth.

Leila stared at her lap. "Sure, I guess."

"Well, I hope you're still finding time to write."

Leila didn't want to get into that either. "Uh-huh."

James scraped together some half-recalled phrases from their three-year-old encounter. Unfortunately, he didn't put them into sentences. "Remarkable story . . . real indicative, yes indicative . . . think about your talent."

"Um, Professor Nancy."

"Please. James."

"I have to go meet some, um, friends over there."

"Yes, yes, of course. Where?"

Leila flipped her head toward a bar area not too far off. It was crowded enough that a few of its inhabitants could plausibly play the role of her friends. "Over there."

"Well, then you better go and meet them, I suppose."

"Yeah. Like I guess I better."

"I'm sure I'll see you around."

"Uh-huh."

She stood, exerted a benign behind-the-counter smile, and held up her hands, corn in one, root beer in the other. Obviously, she couldn't shake his hand or anything like that. James said good-bye, turned around, and rolled his eyes—*Can you believe it?*—for Sylvia's benefit. Damn students: always stopping me with a request. Sylvia was expressionless.

Leila stalled as she considered what to do with the soda and corn. She threw them away rather than have Professor Nancy think that she was meanly avoiding him. To complete the ruse, she walked to a tented bar. *Go home.* Go home. I'm going. As she came closer to the bar, it roared. She reached the entrance and looked into the crowd. *Go home.* Go home. I'm going.

And then someone shouted a name.

# [ 5 ]

During the last year of high school, Ed resold—he fumed at the callous word ˈscalped—concert tickets. It was not a business; Ed was quite specific about which of his high-school enterprises, a collection of variable success, achieved the haughty status of business. It was a series of opportunities. For one sought-after show, Ed's first two customers were John Husinec, who had grown up with Ed but whose three-sport achievements precluded any friendship between them, and John's girlfriend, Shannon Wasnicki, the school's fair-haired girl on whom and on whose locks and gymnast's body most boys at Carl Schurz High School had a mad crush. Unlike most boys who had a mad crush on most girls with narrow-gauge curves similar to Shannon's, Ed did not dilute his affection for her on any lesser models of her gender. His solitary manifestations were concentrated and respectful. It was less than chivalrous then to charge Shannon his standard thirty-percent markup. Had she asked for a ticket for herself, Ed probably would have given it to her at cost. Had she by some act of heaven agreed to go with him—he, of course, never dared to ask—he would have taken her for free. But he'd be goddamned if he'd give John Husinec one dime off.

Ed's standard thirty did not please John. "Screw you, Steinke, I can read the price on the ticket." Neither Ed nor Shannon knew why John had announced this fact. This was the first time that

John had spoken to Ed in two years. "And I'm not going to pay that much. *Ever.*"

"Like don't be so cheap." Always-current Shannon reprimanded John's violation of a too too obvious fashion rule. Unbeknownst to Ed (or John), Shannon was having second thoughts about the relationship. She didn't want to see the concert—she like thought that the group was so bad—but she needed to test her theory that John wasn't really willing to do anything for her.

"It's not about being cheap." John glared at Ed as he massaged the tickets with grasshopper strokes. "I just don't like being taken advantage of by a criminal."

"He's not like a criminal," Shannon corrected him—*Is Shannon Wasnicki talking about me?*—"he's being smart." She then smiled conspiratorially at Ed. That, at least, was her intention. Ed received the smile as promising, alluding to a chance in this world for Ed Steinke and the blond angel. John bought the tickets. Neither he nor Shannon ever spoke to Ed again, though John did scowl at him in passing for weeks afterward. Yet those scowls couldn't prevent Shannon's grin from starring in Ed's tumescent dreams, and they couldn't disprove Shannon's comment, which might have been more important than the smile. Ed's teachers, who automatically gave him B's, never told him that he was smart. Linda Steinke praised him for being "clever" on thirty-nine documented occasions but never the shorter word. But Shannon Wasnicki said he was smart, even if only once; Rudy Pilsen called him a genius for outfitting an entire pizzeria, even if only once; and, even if only once, the insurance salesman with whom he apprenticed one summer used the word *prodigy* in reference, Ed was certain, to him.

The first time Ed finished reading *Classic Sales,* five and a half years ago, he didn't close the book—he placed it on his chest, open-faced, and inhaled its scent. It was the smell not of chemicals or glue but of Truth, with an uppercase T. After a second or a minute or an hour—lost time—he clamped the book's edges, turned to the first chapter, and, humbled, read the whole book again. Ed wasn't a wanderer, prone to cultist idolatry, and Orditz wasn't the messiah. But Orditz made sense. Orditz, Ed thought then, knew about *his,* Ed's, Buyers' Culture, the culture of Rue Chambois Road and two-car garages and overcooked rib roast and John Husinec's scowls, and because Orditz knew, he also knew the way out: the way of the True Salesman. Every day, Ed tasted the waking nightmare of not finding the way out. It was a wife broiling chicken every damn Thursday; it was an overdue promotion to regional VP; it was putting up storm windows in the fall, thanks, honey; it was planting annuals in the spring. It was living in a zero-gradient nirvana of forests and fields and having the world tell you that you were lucky to be there. It was the world being right.

But the way out was collapsing; that was how Ed understood Vernon Warbler's occasional glances. "I'm just selling a nineteen-dollar knife," Vernon would I-say, "and it ain't gonna change your life, but it will make it easier for y'all to cut and open and chop-chop-chop." Ed swatted at the flies of disdain in Vernon's voice for him, a—he could hear the Mississippi drawl stretch-stretching the first syllable—*lo*ser. The syrup sellers agreed with the diagnosis, so said their squeals of dollar-love, the quick snatching of bills and rushes to a strongbox. They too told him, that way, how he was the most awful spectacle of a salesman who ever lived. It wasn't just that he wasn't successful; a lot of good salesmen—great sales-men—shared fishermen tales of months-and-months droughts. No, they laughed at him, Ed could tell, because he still believed that selling organs was something more.

That afternoon Ed slumped, subdued, as he held the scrolled grave copy of *The Journal of American Sales.* But even his non-committal grip—the *Journal* dipped right-angle to his forearm—

could not silence the contents within: the biblical beard, greedy Judases, philistinism, *The Treason of the True Salesman.* Ed had known nothing about Alfred Orditz before he read the obituary that morning. Fancying the dignity of the minimalist blue hardcover, he had thrown away the dusk jacket of *Classic Sales.* And when he read the obituary, when the words remembered continued to up-push through the tarp of the work-don't-think day, the thorns piercing the nylon blanket from below, he could only ask, initially, How could all that happen? Death too? You see, Orditz wasn't a *man. It* was a concept, a concept that sales could be more than a base occupation, a concept that sales—no, Sales—could be a path, a calling, a Perfectible Art. So all of that didn't make sense, death and scandal and disgrace. The *Journal,* Ed was sure, had gotten something wrong. They didn't understand. No one but me understands. When Ed had asked his college professor why Part Two of *Classic Sales* was not assigned, the professor had garbled something about that mumbo jumbo being unsuitable. When he had asked his classmates what they had thought of Part Two, they had reminded him—"kiss-ass"—that it was not assigned. There were others; there were the girls. Jesus Christ, the girls he talked to about Orditz, even casually, were as incapable of understanding Orditz as they were of peeing standing up.

Ed watched Vernon, and Vernon was irresistible. The central alley had thinned, a few loose particles about, and Vernon was speaking to just one customer, a great-granddad in blue jacket, blue pants, blue socks, and white brandless shoes, who was being drawn into the light, Ed seethed, of Vernon's incompetent, money-magnetic whirls. The man pinched a piece of fabric on his thin zippered jacket's breast and brought forward a pin for Vernon's viewing. Vernon agreed about the debt we owe our veterans. "One myself, course." Incapable of looking at that nauseating display anymore, Ed opened *The Journal of American Sales.* He did not read the obituary this time; he regarded it, his nostrils flaring away from the sour milk of the lines, dots, crosses that were all supposedly letters. They were not—they were scratches, symbols, unreadable. *Simpletons* and *boors* coalesced on the page. Ed's face crimped ugly, repulsed; his tongue scraped between his teeth.

*Am I supposed to care about this?* A brackish glue of cotton and sweat had pasted his shirt to his back beneath the navy wool. *Does it matter?* That was the question, wasn't it? Ed stared at Vernon again, looked in his direction, any direction but down, for the answer. Vernon was chopping carrots casually, wrist loose and playful. The veteran was impressed. *Does it matter?* Ed needed to know. *Classic Sales* was still right, right? Ed had no reason *not* to believe anymore in those capitalized words, True Salesman, Perfect Execution, Leading through Precision, those concepts that just happened to be named Orditz, those concepts still glowing with the Teutonic aura of clarity and revelation. Ed had never cared about *him* before.

Does it matter? Nothing has changed.

Does it matter? No. Period.

Does it matter? Well, maybe. A problem still bristled: Ed had always assumed that Orditz was the True Salesman. It wasn't that he pictured a man wearing a diamond-encrusted name tag, *A. Orditz, True Salesman,* but he had never before doubted that a contented, self-aware True Salesman existed—as his parents existed, as *he* existed—a True Salesman who had mastered buying and selling, who had broken out and broken free, who never ate rib roast. That man had to have been Alfred Orditz. Who else could have written the book?

Does it matter? He didn't know. Authors and their work, preaching and its doing, mattering and not mattering—But *does* it matter?—started to hurt his head. He tried to concentrate on Vernon: he couldn't think about it anymore. He tried to concentrate anger on Vernon: he wouldn't think about it anymore. The veteran declared that he had an awful lot of knives already, and

Vernon shrugged and said, "Well, if you do, you do." *Victory.* Ed's anger grew, its pus bubbling, as his thoughts stabbed Vernon in the ribs of his ignorance. Ed knew that you could *never* let a customer admit his doubt, *any* doubt into the sales process. You must bring the Sales Act above conversation. It is a Perfectible Art. But between Ed's recitation of the facts, the brain-branded question— *Does it matter, Edward Steinke?*—shouted and snuck, whispered and gnawed.

Ed felt a scream collecting in his belly. It was *not fair.* Vernon was not fair. Not fair. The Fair. The scream metastasized and—

Vernon laughed exaggeratedly at an obsolete joke about Japan. Ed stood up, without forethought or intention, and marched across the central alley until he was six feet away from Vernon's counter. He stared at Vernon. Never long without words, Vernon exclaimed, curious and mocking, "I say, if it ain't my organ-ic neighbor. Finally came for your All-in-One?"

Ed stated truth as truth should be stated, plainly: "You know, you don't know what you're doing."

The veteran and Vernon looked at each other, and Vernon, with a raised eyebrow, humored the boy. He looked to the sides of his booth, over his shoulder, and across the counter to ensure that the booth was not on fire, falling down, misspelled. Finally, winking at the veteran, he said, "Well, that's a thought I've never heard. I say, you're a boy with big ideas." The veteran laughed, an old man's coughing, death-laden laugh; Ed in that suit did look kinda dubious, a know-it-all big shot if he ever saw one.

Ed's voice rose: "Don't joke with me, it's not funny."

"You're going to have to excuse me. I'm just a simple ol' man from Mississippi." Vernon winked again at the veteran. "But what in the heck are you talking about?"

"You don't know anything about sales, True Sales," Ed, trancelike, read the news.

"I say, I never thought I was so bad."

"Come off it. You're a philistine." Ed rhymed it with *Palestine*.

"A philistine?" *Blue suit with big words.* "That's awfully nice of you to say."

"I don't think you're fucking funny."

A gust blew the veteran and Vernon back, and Vernon warned for the protection of the veteran's ears, "Kid, watch your tongue."

"One, I'm no kid. Two, I'm too fucking busy watching you make a travesty of Sales. You know—it's like—" The motor that had driven Ed across the central alley stalled. "It's a . . . treason to the True Salesman."

Vernon was peeved; one more sale would have been a great end to a great day, *but* this boy was the best laugh he had had in a while. "I say, you are definitely not speaking my language."

He couldn't explain *does it matter* to Vernon, Ed realized, but he could convey it. "You're just, I don't, I—" He struggled for the word. "A hack. You think this doesn't have any meaning. Any importance."

"Kid, I tell you what. You're what my mama used to call"— beat for the punchline—"a nut." The veteran chuckled. Vernon had scooped low the *n* of the *nut* and brought the rest of the word up. "Meaning? Importance? This fella has done things with meaning and importance."

The veteran turned to Ed and nodded soberly.

Two glaring eyes, white glaring eyes, without which, Ed's face, a tomato. "I'm sick of that crap."

The veteran grunted. Vernon didn't want to lose the sale. "I say, I think you ought to return to your organ, son. We wouldn't want to miss any customers, would we?"

Both of Ed's palms, parallel and electrocharged, screeched to a halt a half foot from his ears. Vibrating and lost, they moved higher—as if to join, almost, in delineating the borders of a helmet. His palms froze at the apex, the vibrations too tight to be noticed, and then he slapped them down, without introduction, against his thighs. "Jesus, man. Can't you fucking understand?"

"I guess I just ain't so smart."


Ed had returned across the central alley, but he could hear—or thought he could hear over his own echoing, rancorous thoughts—the veteran and Vernon's dissection of his visit. The veteran, he imagined, was declaiming that the country was going to pot, kids today, no respect. Vernon would still be trying to sell him a knife. Ed was sick and goddamn tired of Vernon's smug routine, his incessant success, his not-a-care-in-the-world good humor. *He,* of all people, should care. He was good. But no, he was a plug-it-in plastic cog—a cashier. Maybe Vernon—Ed glimpsed at him again—*was* lightly fueling the veteran's denunciation of Ed and the youth of today. Ed had heard *that* before, too, had heard it from his father, from his grandfather, Ed Kroeger, navy man, Double-u, Double-u Two. For God's sake, Ed lived in it, on every street sign of his youth in nice, bleached Kopekne Green. On D day, Bob Kopekne, later the subdivision's developer, then an ambitious private with some sense for historical drama, had promised Almighty Jesus to name his first son after the battleground if he survived. But after the Last Just War, Bob and Mrs. Bob were unable to conceive, and Bob worried, half seriously, that Almighty Jesus might punish him for not living up to his side of the bargain. As a proxy, Bob decided to christen all the streets of his first success after Norman towns. "Better than naming a son anyway. More lasting and such." With atlas in hand, he originally planned to call them all Rue something-or-other (Rue Mondeville, Rue Cherbourg, Rue La Madeleine, etc.), but the state transportation authorities cried foul at the irreverent baptism of any American roadway a *rue.* Bob tacked a *road* onto all the names.

Sitting on the bench, Ed faced the organ, his back to the central alley, to Vernon and the veteran (now parting ways, commerce completed), to the twilight bastards who never bought a thing. He took a rabbit glance over his shoulder at Vernon. He took another at the syrup sellers; from the giddy enthusiasm of two stragglers there, you would've thought the sellers were giving away eternal youth in their log-cabin tins. He took a third, longer glare at Mr. Magic Shammy farther down the line, a crater-faced man with the surrendering hulk of a former linebacker, counting and double-counting a five-inch stack of green. He glared at *The Journal of American Sales* lying atop the organ, rolling, sealing. He watched it for movement, for renunciation, explanation, assistance. His scream was collecting again, the pain in his kidney was piercing again, the sweat on his back was itching again, and he wasn't going to get kicked around anymore. He banged his fist against the Brackett's lower keyboard. The calamitous chord of the simultaneous scale howled forth. The lingering eyes of the South Exhibition Hall jerked toward him. He froze.

*Jackass.*

Barry had forgotten to turn off the organ.


Three weeks ago, in their van driving through the empty midwestern night, Ed had blamed Barry for another disastrous outing; Barry had made it clear that he wasn't to blame.

Ed continued, "Why are you such a pain in my ass all the time?"

"Why are you always like so bitter?"

Ed believed, a central axiom, that bitterness was a sign of a defeated man. He couldn't be bitter because he wasn't defeated; he wasn't defeated because he had not yet entered—really entered—the game yet. Ed's answer to Barry skipped over this reasoned argument and over his usual responses to Barry's comments. He asked instead, "Why not?"

Having expected the standard response, Barry swashed through a "Huh?" and a "What?"

"Why shouldn't I be bitter? Look at me. I know I can do more than the rest of these jackasses. I know that I'm smarter and harder working than sixty, seventy, eighty, *ninety* percent of the people out there. I know that I shouldn't have to settle for two cars and two kids and two *poo*dles and a house." The house motif haunted Ed; it was his very vision of hell. "And look at me: I can't seem to get it going. They just think I'm a loser."

Barry told Ed that it still wasn't cool to be bitter.

"I didn't say that it was good to be bitter. I just said that it's natural when you can see it, but you can't do anything about it."

Barry still did not understand. "Like what's 'it'?"

Ed started to burn. "What don't you get here, moron? *It* is everything. You know, the True Salesman, getting out of the Buyers' Culture."

*Ah, Bored-its—here we go . . .* But maybe, Barry then thought, a little Orditz, a little redirection could drop a ramble-ending ice cube on Ed's three-hundred-degree pan. "What's, um, like this Buyers' Culture again?"

"I've told you a thousand times. It's *all* of this." Ed waved an angled arm; a quarter circle captured the passing night and the universe beyond. "It's all these people at these things running around and making noise and selling crap *to each other* for no reason."

"And how are we like different?"

Ed, stumbled, wasn't so sure anymore. "Well, I know how *I'm* different," he recovered. "I have a plan to break out of it."

"It or this?" The shifting pronouns confused Barry, or he acted as if they did.

"It's all the same. This. It. Everything." Ed, who like all Steinke men usually spoke with his mouth, not with his hands, waved his arm again, this time more quickly.

"But if *this*"—Barry added an aping, floppy wave of his own—"is like everything, how can you like have a plan to break out of it?"

"Are you trying to be an asshole, or are you just one?"

Barry laughed. "Why are you getting mad at me? It's just, if you think about it. . . . It like doesn't make sense."

"Neither has anything you've ever said in your whole life, jackass."

"Answer me."

"You *can't* look at it that way. Yes, 'it' is everything, but you can still break out of it, the mediocrity of the quotidian Buyers' Culture by Perfect Execution." Ed nodded thoughtfully. "Then you're above it."

"So what does this have to do with you being bitter?"

Perhaps Ed dashed the conversation's circular route because he didn't know the answer. Perhaps he did it because he didn't want to set a precedent. Ed could think about his quotidian place in the quotidian world every moment of the day; he found talking about himself for three sentences repulsive. He had picked this up from his father who had picked it up from his people who had picked it up from the winter and the water and April's thawing earth.

Barry and Ed returned to their corners as the miles, the midnight black, passed through the mood. Ed turned up the radio. After a dozen dumb minutes, Barry offered helpfully, "There's like got to be a better way."

"What?" Ed turned down the radio. The cocoon of a car on an open road had washed the day pale and distant and smooth.

"There's like got to be a better way," Barry repeated.

"Better way to do what?"

"You know."

Barry was incapable, it seemed to Ed, of uttering two declarative sentences in a row without the second one being *you know*. "What do you mean, 'You know'?"

"Like a better way to make money."

Ed's civil defense units—Attack! Attack!—sounded the alarm. "You think I don't know what I'm doing?"

"Why are you like getting angry?"

"I don't know, why are you a jackass?"

"Just answer me." That summer, Barry had developed the ability to force-march a conversation through Ed's brambles of *jackass*es and *fuck you*s.

"The only thing *you* need to know is, I've done my research."

"Whatever. Like who even plays organs anymore?"

"Plenty of people."

"Okay, like tell me this. What moron, if you think about it, is like going to come to a fair and just like decide on the spot to spend fifteen hundy, like on some organ? I mean, Jesus."

"It would surprise you."

"*Who'd* do that?"

"You've *seen* people do that."

"Yeah, friggin' weirdos."

"What'd you say?"

"Whatever, okay. Just listen to me: do you know how much the keyboard I played, like how much it was?"

"No, and I don't care," Ed said, though he should have. Barry's synthesizer had cost a third of the 180-X and had featured a digital interface for custom sound programming and a compact body that would not *totally* mortify a sixteen-year-old to be seen behind. It wasn't a guitar, of course, but it was more permissible than Brackett's nostalgia-inlaid assassin of any cool boy's good name.

"Like I'm trying to be helpful." Barry turned to Ed and thought that his brother was finally losing it. "If you like look at other, um, business opportunities, I'm sure you will find better ways to, um, make money than selling organs."

The black sky had erased the passing prairie. Ed switched the van's headlights to low beams as he overtook a hatchback on the left. He started to laugh. If he hadn't been Barry's brother—it might not have mattered—a laugh like that on a sleeping highway like that would have foreshadowed his passenger's certain grisly death.

"What's so funny, moron?"

"You."

"Yeah. Ha. Ha."

And Ed didn't say anything else.

A minute hushed and Barry resumed. "Why was that like so funny?"

"Because you think that's what this is all about."

"Well, I know it *isn't* about your love of organ music."

"So."

"So what?"

"Just because it's not about selling organs"—a truck's Doppler swoosh crossed from the oncoming lane—"doesn't mean it's about money."

"Yeah, but there's like other things that you could do, right?"

"Like be a ballerina, you homo." It wasn't clear if this had been a joke. When it turned out not to be funny, Ed decided that it hadn't been a joke although he didn't then decide what it was supposed to have been.

"Don't be a moron. You like know what I'm talking about, like other business stuff."

"You think so?" Ed acted the innocent.

"Yeah, I do."

Ed felled the impending advice with an axman's versed efficiency. "Then what am I supposed to do?"

Barry stared, impassive, at the back-speeding median.

"Tell me, what am I supposed to do?" Ed chopped.

"Like lots of things."

"Like what?"

"Come on."

"Like what?"

"Like a lot of things."

"Like what?"

"Anything. Just name it."

"No, *you* tell me, what am I supposed to do?"

Barry stared, impassive, at the back-speeding median.

*Timber.*

Ed Steinke lived in a no-name town, a hundred thousand souls, in postindustrial America. That was fine maybe for a hundred thousand souls minus one, but he needed more. It was not a want: "I want a piece of pie." It was a need: "I need a new liver." Ed's whole life, the bastards had judged him for being bitter, for being a loser, for being average, for being a salesman, for being another anonymous jackass from another anonymous strip of God's-country soil. *What am I supposed to do?* He chuckled at the sad absurdity. Barry, sulking, had turned his head toward the black.

Greatness, Ed knew, didn't invite you over for coffee when you were from Rue Chambois Road. Ed couldn't become great working for a corporate bureaucracy like Dad, that was for sure. None of those interchangeable parts, as far as Ed could tell, glowed with everlasting greatness. Even guys like his uncle Frank, a utility vice president on the rise, even the baldest ones at the hill's holy top, were three days forgotten two days after they had gone. Maybe, for argument's sake, things were different forty years ago—how, he had no idea—but good white-collar jobs, all white-collar jobs, in middle America were disappearing like the rain-forest canopy, acre by bleeding acre. Ever since the Memorial Day Massacre, when Lincoln Paper eliminated one hundred and sixty clerical, manual, and managerial positions, Gene Steinke's digestive hold—"Since when can't you eat *two* pork chops?"—had eroded by the week. Only a few years back, the CEO of the nation's second largest paper-goods company had fired half its employees, strapped it kicking to an auction block, and sold it to the largest. The Canadian pulp producers were integrating downstream, the American lemmings were right behind, and after every merger and acquisition, middle managers, especially *distribution* managers, came home in the early afternoon, shaken, stunned, and unemployed. (It might not even take a merger. Gene had seen "The Program" at a trade show, and this was not good. N-GED: Next Generation E-Distribution, the shiny-toothed salesman shared the wonders of his lethal injection, allowed any company to seamlessly integrate *all* its supplier-client systems, just like the big boys, without excessive, costly distribution personnel.) Gene knew that if you miraculously kept your job through the corporate square dance, you faced an ice wall of salary freezes, benefit freezes, promotion freezes, and other conniving freezes you had never heard of, no matter how well the company or the economy was doing. Over the last year, Gene's stomach had worn away further—"you haven't eaten *any-thing*"—with the prospects for Lincoln Paper itself. The goddamn truth: it was a midsize derivatives company in a cyclical business where only two words mattered: efficiency and scale. Yes, it was the good guy, the regional firm that maintained its customers by maintaining its values: honesty, quality, service. But the customers had their own problems; they *needed,* with regrets, to save those pennies per carton. More ominously, the customers were kinda pleased with the high-tech homogeneity that the multinationals could offer.

While Gene's fellow managers died on the vine, the independent atoms of the service economy—the lawyers and consultants, the doctors and agents—filed their claims to inherit the earth. Yet these atoms, measured not by the numbers they employed but by the riches they conjured, were no closer to greatness, Ed reckoned, than the junior vice presidents at International, Inc. The knowledge workers, as they preferred to refer to the bodies of their brains, crowed about personal franchises and unfettered freedoms, but they were too comfortable, too busy at hospital or firm to worry about anything more than their hourly fees. *What am I supposed to do?* The question, of course, had only one answer: be an entrepreneur. Since the Virginia Company—White America, Day One—the entrepreneurial way was the *only* way to greatness in the U.S. of A. for the unpolitical, unathletic, unartistic, unattractive. Acknowledging that fact, Ed learned early on, didn't help you do anything about it. Most of the great entrepreneurs had acquired historical fortunes in bygone chances to dominate iron or oil or rails. Or they had lucked into obscure fortunes, alchemists' gold fused from wiper blades or superglue or fungicide, compound D. There were, of course, the great ones who had made their billions in consumer franchises, but those ideas were already taken, those billions already made. Who needed another razor blade or canned cola, wax paper or chocolate bar? Even if people did—or if someone, through sheer force of will, convinced them that they did—the barriers to entry were too high, the competition too entrenched, the capital too distant, the commodification too near. Yes, Ed was aware of the geniuses behind the fast-food empires and retail giants, everything-marts and category killers, the restaurants and stores that germinated on three sites for twenty years before swarming the suburban flatlands—dandelions in June. Yet the shopping malls were already full, the strip centers already anchored. Your idea for a pet-food warehouse is brilliant, sir, except for the two pet-food warehouses that just moved into town.

*What am I supposed to do?* Ed read about these things. He knew about the "modest" local fortunes, the ones made by bulbous-nosed gray men who spent their sunset days on the seventeenth hole. But they, too, were historical. By that time, every city in America was generations past the pioneers, the first with the movie theaters or the supermarkets or the newspapers. And now those men (or their widows, or their children) fretted about, or welcomed smiling, the faceless conglomerates who eyed their sinecures greedily and ate them like shelled peanuts, a dozen at a time. Ed could have aimed his sites further down the scale to the happy land of moderate successes, Earl Luntz and all that. Yet those people differed from his father in the size of their houses, not the essence of their achievements. *What am I supposed to do?* Yes, Ed heard Wall Street's boasts of wealth and democracy. Yet he didn't even know how to become a paper entrepreneur. The outside envelopes of his father's monthly pension statements provided the alpha and omega of his exposure to finance, and the oligarchs of Manhattan didn't draw blood from his kind of college or divulge the stock-and-bond secrets to his part of the world. *What am I supposed to do?* Ed, who was nobody's dummy, knew about the silicon goldrush. He bitterly followed the stories of spectacled misfits—misfits younger than him, and he was a pretty young misfit—who designed a gizmo on Sunday and became a billionaire on Monday. But even if Ed had had his life to live over again, even if he had devoted his whole existence to the trinity of electro- and cyber- and compu-, to a monomaniacal quest to become the next technological wunderkind, who's to say it would have worked? Who's to say that he would not have sunk into the ocean of processors' appendages, programmers dreaming of public offerings but getting only paychecks? Ed no longer bothered to fantasize; these were hypothetical questions twice removed from the depressing reality: twenty-four stinking years old and it was already too late.

Ed thought about what he was supposed to do; he thought about it all the time; he often thought about nothing else. *But he was already too late.* He was too late to build America, too late to invent its tastes, too late to destroy the clichés of conventional business, too late to profitably entrench himself in one. If he wasn't too late, he didn't know the rules. He wasn't born into a family that taught its children about P/E multiples or semiconductors, forward swaps or network routers. Ed lived at the end of history, when all the great opportunities were the opportunities just missed; he lived on the melting edge of country and town, where the farthest point on the horizon looked like the soil between your toes. And *that* was the brilliance of Orditz. Orditz proved, unquestionably proved, that it wasn't important where Ed was born or when he was born, wasn't important that his name would never grace an art museum or campus crest. As long as Ed mastered Perfect Execution *on his own,* he could become a True Salesman *on his own.* No geographical bad luck, no generational bad timing could prevent him from lifting his toes off the ground; he could prevent it, of course, but the True Salesman, the ideal, was great and possible. Ed *had* outfitted an entire pizzeria, ovens to spoons. In June, he *had* sold three organs to three sisters at an All-Home Expo—everything he had said had met with enthusiasm and accord on that glorious day when magic dusted the air. He had felt the rush of the flawless pitch, the Perfectible Art, when his voice had become the voice of authority, divinity, command. He had given himself the power to make this person buy this product because he said so. He had touched the shadow of the True Salesman.

And if you asked Ed did that then make him great, he would tell you, if you were his brother, for instance, to shut up. That was the problem with Orditz. It was all a little goofy. Ed, like anyone, knew why those commercial heroes were great—rich, powerful, rich, famous, rich, immortal. But the True Salesman was great for, well, abstract reasons, which Ed, who didn't much care for abstract anything, could never quite clutch. Obviously, to Ed, one could not logically object to Orditz's page 278 contention that "the True Salesman is the *real* entrepreneur. He manages a perfect enterprise free of organizational manacles. The so-called captain of industry only pretends to." But was the True Salesman then great because he could sell an organ—or a car or a house or a new-and-improved K-nifty K-nife—to every customer to whom he spoke? Was he great because his feats were not business feats? Because he had powers, as Orditz said, that transcended the realm of Normal Exchange to the realm of Control Exchange? Was he great because the True Salesman had no other definition besides greatness personified, the man above the quotidian?

"I don't believe you." Barry's mind had tumbled motivation and money since Ed had silenced him ten minutes earlier.

"Huh?" Ed, who had turned up the radio again, turned it down.

"I don't believe that you don't care about money."

"And I don't believe that you're not a jackass." *Classic Sales* declared that a True Salesman could never find motivation in the selfish pursuit of material rewards. Certainly, Orditz said—or Ed assumed that he said—that material rewards would accrue to the True Salesman, but money was the proof, as rustling leaves are the proof of wind, and parting seas the proof of God; it wasn't God or wind.

"If you can look me in the eye," Barry tried to force an admission, "and say that money isn't—"

"I'm driving."

"Don't change the subject."

"No, I mean, I'm driving. I can't look you in the eye."

"Very funny."

"I thought so."

"If you can look me in the eye and like say that money has no part in it, I'll shut up."

Ed figured that Barry would anyway, turned the radio up, and let the passing farmland's black infinity answer the question.

The mumbling started in earnest when Ed's chord, or discord, sailed across the central alley. He mumbled about Vernon and Orditz, the veteran and Barry, the True Salesman and Lincoln Paper. Even Christy Kanko appeared, a cameo role. Much of the mumbling made no sense, and most of it was dreadfully coarse. It was good, mothers would say, that Ed was getting it out of his system, but the pressured pot released just enough steam to prevent a ka-boom. Everything still cooked inside him—greatness and Orditz and *does it matter*—until the meat slithered off the bone, the vegetables lost their shape, and the lot devolved into a gelatinous mess. Ed wasn't a bad guy, he thought. He wasn't lazy or dumb. He wasn't even a jackass. He was just trying. So why was everyone on his back all the time? He stared at the copy of *The Journal of American Sales* curled atop the organ. Under its cover was the emptiness, and it demanded to be read again. But Ed refused. He reached for his briefcase under the organ and opened it roughly. He entombed the magazine beneath his papers. *Does it matter* would not bother him again. That was for sure.

Ed's ledger waited in the middle of the case, its crisp block letters of EDWARD E. STEINKE, OFFICIAL LOG: BRACKETT CORPORATION, REGION NINE guarding the front cover. It had been weeks since Ed had done the books; he had been irresponsible, uncharacteristically, but he knew enough to know the gloom inside. He hadn't wanted to know more. But now— A graveyard grin came to Ed's face. *Let's see the disaster.* The coincidence was poetry: Orditz dead and Ed's enterprise, teetering and frail. Ed reckoned that he had three, four weeks left until his operation reached the critical stage and that he might as well figure out the day now. He removed—the professional restored—two manila envelopes, a calculator, and a fake fountain pen from his briefcase. He placed them next to the Official Log on the organ's flat top. In separate sections of the ledger, Ed had divided operating expenses by category: transportation, housings, meals, "incidentals and sundries." Once a week, he emptied the receipts from one envelope, recorded the amounts in the appropriate section, stored them in the other, and transferred the weekly expense totals to the ledger's income statement. Ed lifted his leg to straddle the organ seat, the Official Log and receipts now strewn in front of him. Luckily, Orditz was dead, or this might have killed him. (Chapter 7: "To destroy the performance is to preclude Perfect Execution. A salesman in the public eye must always be a salesman so defined: a man for sales, not a prankster, a gossip, a grouser, or an accountant.") However, no one in the almost empty, almost–six o'clock hall was going to buy an organ now. Even Vernon was packing up his show. Ed picked up a receipt from the Woodland View Motel and entered the amount in the lodging section. The brothers usually stayed in one of the chain motels, frugal and featureless, that crowded interstate exits. But it was State Fair time, and every affordable room in the city had been booked for months. Management of the Woodland View, fourteen rooms along a frontage road fifteen miles out of town, charged the Steinkes sixty-five dollars per night, which was higher than the winter rate by only forty-six dollars. The motel's sign promised air conditioning and hadn't been painted since the in-window units were space-age wonders. "Yeah, uh, the air conditioner doesn't work," Ed had complained on the first day of their stay. The clerk tried to appear mildly surprised but managed only to appear alive. "Must be broke in that unit." Can you fix it? "It's possible," assented Otto Felder, the clerk and management and ownership, before he returned to his television and never thought about it again. If the brothers opened their room's window that week—the window faced the backlot woodland of woodland-view fame, an area that they knew contained their preceding guests' buried victims—they wrote a personalized invitation to every moth, mosquito, and fly in America to come on in. So they kept it closed and couldn't breathe—"open it, Ed"—through the honey-paste humidity. So they opened it and were eaten for snack-or-supper—"close it, Barry, goddamnit"—by a bug army of scriptural tenacity. Fortunately, just one naked bulb hung from the ceiling. The brothers could thus only feel the mattresses so thin that a man could measure them, like rum, by fingers wide. They could thus only suspect the details of the cardboard sheets. Otto's cleaning process, which had conquered cotton's natural texture, was somehow impotent against the sheets' comprehensive, rainbow stains, each one of which could tell a story, some of considerable length.

Ed transferred the lodging expenses and shuffled a dozen meal receipts. The brothers had eaten more meals than that over the last two weeks, but Ed often and Barry always did not ask for proof. It was offensive to Barry's sense of stoic cool and embarrassing for them both to request a permanent chronicle of a three-dollar, kraut-covered purchase from a mountainous sausage prince. Ed usually jotted down the cost of the meal on whatever he could find—checkered paper dish below the corndog grease, politician's leaflet near the tax-cut promise—and stored the scraps in his breast pocket. Barry disregarded the whole thing. Ed wrote 252—six times two times three times seven—in the income statement for each week, pulled his neck, and cracked it to the side to relieve the pain murmuring from his lower back. *Does it matter* and Orditz, even Vernon, receded to the shadows and the sidestage. Work was the show, what was important, paid, real, and dense; the actors thought about nothing but their next line.

Finally, Ed entered the last expense category—*I don't even know why I'm . . .* —Barry's wages. Before Ed had asked Barry to join him, he had presumed that Barry would agree to become the junior partner of Steinke and Steinke and divide the profits in some equitable division. When Ed offered a seventy-five, twenty-five split, Barry offered Ed an invitation to kiss off. Barry didn't want a different split; he didn't want to be partners at all. Even after Ed *personally* guaranteed bushels of green and silver, Barry didn't budge. "This is *terribly* conservative"—Ed's voice tightened—"but under the split, let's say we sell just two units a day." Barry looked at his fingernails and wondered if they needed chewing. "Listen to me: two units. *One* organ every five or six hours. You would make, let's see . . ." Ed punched the calculator keys with inflated suspense; he had known the answer for a month.

"Dude, I don't like want any part of it," Barry closed the case. He had seen enough of his brother's underbelly schemes for one lifetime and knew that if he ever, in the future, decided to take all this business junk seriously, he would do it differently than Ed: he would build cities, earn millions, put a something-or-other in every home in America, and live the life of a duke. "I said I'll work for you, okay, paid by the hour." Ed shook his head and shook it again in disgust; he could hardly comprehend the "sibling bull-shit" behind Barry's decision. It was inch-sighted, mulish, illogical. It was also the best business decision Barry had ever made, the lack of competition notwithstanding. Ed paid Barry twenty percent above his pallet-crew salary, plus expenses, in cash, at the end of each week. At the time of the agreement, Ed had thought he could afford to be generous; even under the two-unit-per-day scenario—he named it the low-case scenario, not to be confused with the breakeven case of one unit per day—he would make a killing. And under the mid-case scenario! And under the high-case! The only problem was that, as the summer turned out, they had never sold two units per day except on that hallowed three-sister day in

June. The one-week record—that June week, of course—was 0.857 units per day. In five days at this state fair, the home-state stingies hadn't bought a single note. When Ed set up the Official Log, he taped Brackett's convoluted commission schedule to the inside front cover. Often that summer, he would close his eyes and swim through the printed series of breaking points, above which top-tier performers received a larger take of the gross. No matter how often he had looked, eyes open, at the numbers, however, they had never seemed other than irrelevant. Ed admitted that he couldn't even blame the whole disaster on Brackett and that lying bastard of a sales director with his no problem, no problems. *Can you show me where your research says that two-thirds of all married adults would think about buying an organ?* No problem, no problem. It was Ed's responsibility to sell organs, sell anything despite itself. Perfect Execution, sales over substance, seller over sold.

Ed's sweat glands started to dance, something spirited and Latin, the mambo maybe. As the drumming grew louder—something decidedly not Latin, more like a metronome—beads assembled at his temples. Work's omnipresence had sprung holes, and the numbers, swirling on the page, began to reveal the vortex of an answer. Ed subtracted the cumulative operating expenses from the cumulative revenues. The number was negative, of course—it had been every week since they began—but the number was fatter now, redder now, sanguine no, heart bloody. *This is not right.* Ed kept the Official Log pristine, but he was less halfpenny-meticulous with his cash. He had brought several thousand dollars with him, and he and Barry spent it as needed, card-charging everything else. Ed knew the rough amount of his plastic debts, but sometimes—once or twice a week, that's all—neglect lost a charge. He had thought that he could afford to be sloppy, occasionally. By the fall, so the original business plan had envisioned, he would have received three or four payments from Brackett in amounts miles higher than any working-capital debts. If the cash held out until that first check, liquidity would not be a problem. If he had a strong run at summer's end, profitability was salvageable. If he did not dwell on the bad and the worse, if he remembered that three new sainted sisters, buy-ready customers *could* appear again tomorrow—Why just three sisters, why not six sisters, seven brothers every damn day?—he could continue. If, if, if.

The percussion had moved to his forehead as he added the charges. At the debts he looked; at the revenues he looked; he thought about the cash remaining. *I'm busted.* Then came his first reaction, unexpected: Woodland Fucking View.

Decrepit Otto Felder, who was not unknown to call the motel that name himself, had laid down the rules. "You need to pay the whole amount right now."

"Sixty-five, right?"

"Uh-uh, the *whole* amount."

"What?"

"For the whole ten days."

"Why's that?"

"'Cause that's the way it works." Otto nourished himself through empty-motel winters with dreams of abusing travelers in the summer. His father had been a gloomy crank. That would have been hard on his mother, but she had been a gloomy crank too, so they got along okay, but Otto left home when he was fifteen. His one break—yes, one break in an entire life—had come forty years ago. He had been a clerk at the Woodland View for only three years when the original owner decided to start over out West and sold Otto the motel for a song, on installments no less.

"Well, I don't know. It doesn't seem . . ."

"Just so you do *know*, there ain't no other empty rooms for thirty miles."

"Is that true?"

Not a muscle twinged on the pallid crinkled bluff.

"Do you take credit cards?"

"Never have."

"Well, do you take—"

"Never taken no checks either." And Ed went to the van, removed the wadded cash from a money belt below the seat, returned to the nicked, ash-strewn counter, and gave the devil his due.

Ed's forefinger woodpecker-pecked the calculator as he added the debts again, all of them, from the beginning. His original number—*damnit*—was right; if he had included the neglected charges, it would have been higher still. Ed didn't need to recalculate his earned commissions; that running tally was always present and ready, like a palace guard, at his frontal lobe. *How could I've not . . .* He stood up, stripped off his suit coat, and tossed it over the organ's top. Pinkish pools of his shirt were swamped in his body's nooks. Not right, not right, the tail end of his thoughts sputtered aloud. He struggled with the lower buttons of his shirt—*goddamnit.* He untucked it, finally, and a halfhand dove into the front of his pants; his excited fingers, however, were not dexterous enough. He relocated both hands to the back of his pants; they yanked, twisted, jerked the knot until the money belt came—*motherfunding*—free.

Ed sat down again and counted the belt's dwindled, lonely, comic stash. It was the same amount as the last time he checked. *How could I've been so—* He dug his wallet out of his back pocket and counted its greenery; there was enough for food for three days.

Credits are blacks. Debits are red. Make more of the first and you'll get ahead.

*I'm busted.* My God, I'm busted. That's beautiful. Barry and— Vernon, this fu-fu-fu Fair. And now I'm busted. Ed brought both of his palms to his face as if to pray to a Muslim god, but flattened them against his flushing cheeks. He covered his forehead and eyes with his unthumb fingers. His peppery expectorating *b*'s—busted, *bust*ed, *busted,* it doesn't make any . . . —sprayed onto his hands.

Ed moved his palms away from his face and examined them disconnectedly. *Disgusting.* The wet hair tips under his arms were visible through the cotton, faraway beetles behind a faraway screen. He looked across the central alley. Are you happy? he asked Vernon Warbler, ready now to leave the hall. Are you happy, assholes? he asked the beady-eyed syrupers reveling in their take. Is everyone fucking happy? he imagined he asked them all. He slapped his hand across his eyes again; it slid, fingers trailing, toward his mouth.

He laughed. It was the same laugh as the midnight laugh at Barry's sad absurdity. He stared down the Brackett posters, tittering on the booth's back wall. "The future of music": the future of my bankrupted ass. Ed shut his eyes and ground his thumb into the bridge of his nose. *I'm busted.* His thumb ratcheting at his nose's bridge swirled his thoughts. His lower back, awash, sharpened and stung.

Does it matter?

*What are you talking about?* Ed wasn't sure why Ed wasn't sure why Ed asked Ed this.

You're busted, remember.

He's dead.

*You're* busted.

The clouds, once distinct, blended into a blanket minutes before it poured. Ed jumped up. He front-pocketed the cash and left his suit coat, Official Log, and open briefcase scattered across the booth. He had to get out of there. He had to tell Barry that it was over.

# [ 6 ]

A pitcher and plastic cup sat attentively before him. He looked into the cup, Narcissus before the pond. Oh! this contemplative bohemian, his tousled hair and long pants, otherworldly they seemed among the acres of crew cuts and cutoffs, his thin, stone face and woeful-boy eyes weighing the heaviness of his soul, his movements unhurried, deliberate. You could almost hear the poetry, musings amidst composition.

Jesus, Barry thought, his elbows leaning on the table. Look at all these guys about to get laid, and I'm sitting here like a jerk. He sipped his beer. *I should be home right now, if you think about it, not with like a bunch of middle-aged drunks.* The drunks were not middle-aged; they were, for the most part, in their early thirties. *Look at that freak.* Freak had a chicken wing in his mouth, or halfway in his mouth, and was displaying his unusual talent of cleaning the meat off the bone in one fluid sweep. His girlfriend found this neither freakish nor unusual but proof positive of the big catch he was. Barry surveyed the crowd again over the cup's plastic lip as he emptied it into his liver. *These people are so friggin' ugly.* Barry pushed the cup away; ugly had fallen from his lips and contaminated the beer. He stared at two couples at a table five yards away. *And the women look like cows.* The women, truthfully, had left their cow costumes at home, although a cow might have approved of their squeezable denim outfits. Their menfolk wore T-shirts, jeans, and baseball caps free-advertising their favorite brand of truck; both had mustaches that had been on their faces since the first whisker appeared. Two empty pitchers, which had been filled and emptied twice before, waited to be filled again. One of the men stood up shakily and told the others that he was feeling nice and that it was time for more. The Declaration of Inebriation met with two cheers and one exuberant "You betcha." As Shaky walked to the bar, Barry watched each unsure step, and when Shaky sat down again, five minutes later, he found Barry's eyes still on him.

*You all suck.*

The two couples tried to ignore Barry. They looked at one another, at the table, at the tarp, at nothing (right), at nothing (left), like four strangers straining to ignore a copulating couple on an elevator floor. Finally, Shaky's buddy suggested that they kick Barry's ass. The women asked them not to. They were at the State Fair; it was summerend; all was good; don't ruin it now. None of these arguments seemed especially compelling, but before the story could reach its violent end, Barry—now bored—stood up and sat down again in the opposite direction. He now faced the tent's back-wall stage. On it, a huffing boy, clearly too slight for the job, pushed a hundred-pound amplifier into position.

She was different, Barry remembered, her image an ideal, summarized and indistinct. She wasn't like Ed or Cheryl Pfeffer or his father, even his mother. All that Orditz crap. She was different. Those eyes of hers, which had been stuck downward, didn't scream all the time for attention. That little overbite was an imperfection, but she was comfortable with it, relished it. Barry knew this. She was like him; she didn't have time for Ed's bullshit, for his parents' (her parents') nudges and suggestions, for Cheryl's concern about my career this, my degree that. She *wouldn't* have time—that was it. If he had just been able to like talk to her, he thought. If he had just been able to explain away whatever made her flee, explain that she was like him. And that that was important.

Barry exhaled, long and twice, as he watched the stagehand unweave the cords with a jump roper's flick.

The Hotels had mailed thirty demo tapes throughout the state to venues that sounded rocky from their yellow-page listings and fifteen more to places that might be. For two weeks, they heard nothing. The other members, stewing mutinous, accused Barry of not affixing enough stamps to the packages. In the spirit of modern science, Barry mailed a tape to Andy Schneider with the same amount of postage; Andy reported two days later that the tape had arrived. For three more weeks, they heard more nothing. They could not fathom why the bars or clubs (even two podunk veterans' halls) had not at the very least sent the tape back. The boys had instructed the recipients to return the demo if, by some miracle of bad judgment, they were not interested in booking the band. Finally, a response came, the only one they would ever receive. Opening it like gold-wrapped chocolate, his tongue exploring the outside hinge of his mouth, Barry found two items: the demo and a yellow, two-inch-square piece of paper. It read, "Immature." Barry initially thought that the note was a joke played by one of his drunk friends, but the postmark—three days old and from the state's largest city—and the return address, "Tim Knudsen, Molloy's," belied that hypothesis. Barry then tried to understand what immature meant. Tim Knudsen, who had bought Molloy's, a raggedy Irish pub, and had transformed it into the city's unbiased center for new music, thought it would be obvious. Tim cared about contemporary music and that less-than-contemporary area, and he forced himself to listen to every unsolicited demo tape and CD end to end. When Tim played The Hotels' demo, "Enter The Hotels," he initially thought that it was a joke played by one of his drunk friends, but upon listening to Side B, he realized that these kids were serious. Running a bar and respecting every submission demanded more time than Tim had; he wasn't about to write a four-page critique of the opus. Yet he had showed the civility to return the tape and include the negative—*and* helpful, he thought—comment. Had Tim had the time, he would have written that the keyboard seemed cheap, the guitar needed tuning, the drummer needed downers, the bassist needed lessons. Immaturity, in fact, clouded every note the group played. Side A was gimmicky, superficial, barren. Side B was worse: it was disappointing. For a couple of bars here and there, The Hotels—Tim was as surprised as anyone—flashed integrity: the lead singer dropped the contrivances and opened to the music; the band fell into a rhythm and communicated a sincere sound. But they always pulled back, almost immediately. Had he had the time, Tim would have written that The Hotels were cowardly, hid under the covers—literally—and hid behind that well-worn mask of overdrive, teen rebellion. Tim didn't know what they were hiding from, but he sensed that—except for the bassist (what a zero)—they were hiding some real substantive talent in the process. He would have concluded that, of course, they couldn't play that crap at Molloy's, but they should work hard. Jeez, every band was once immature.

After Barry read the note, he first thought that Tim Knudsen meant The Hotels were immature to send an unsolicited tape. Following the great postage experiment, Andy Belsen, The Hotels' guitarist, argued that it was "wagged in the head" to believe that a big-city bar would book you from one demo; you needed to open for similar-sounding bands before any respectable "locale" would even consider you. (No one knew when Andy Belsen had become an expert on the topic.) Thus Barry initially imagined that Tim Knudsen's comment was strategic. Yet when no other replies came, and the band accepted that its entire critical feedback consisted of four vowels, four consonants, and (maybe) one period, Barry locked himself in his room, ignored his mother's calls for breakfast, lunch, and dinner, and meditated on Tim's meaning. Maybe immature meant that his voice wasn't deep enough, and Barry tried on his baritone, his basso, his foghorn, his frog. Maybe immature meant that the band's covers stayed too close to the originals; maybe immature was a mistake and the piece of paper had stuck accidentally to—; maybe immature was a compliment, and it meant that The Hotels were young and fresh and—; maybe immature meant nothing at all; maybe immature meant baby-cow-manure meant maybe-baby-more meant gaily-women-tour meant lately-I'm-not-sure meant . . .

Sometime around midafternoon, Barry slowed down. Maybe, a flake of maybe, immature meant that The Hotels' music—everything abut the music—was too easy.

Barry drove past the unpleasantness. This Tim Knudsen was right. The Hotels *were* immature. Immature was bad. The Hotels were bad. As musicians, they stank. As songwriters, they stank. In every way, they like stank as bad as a stank could stink. The next morning, Barry called the other members and told them to face the truth: The Hotels were like friggin' history.

And later he regretted it. That day, twice stymied, facing another week of imprisonment in the South Exhibition Hall, his stomach wall was chafed by the obvious regret: his life now stunk too. Ed forced him to play, on call, show tunes or pop songs or children's songs in the most atrocious, treacly style imaginable. Worse, Ed, who couldn't hum "Yankee Doodle," habitually enlightened Barry as to how to perform the songs "more snappy," how to make the 180-X more marketable, how to better display the range of that horribly embarrassing two-keyboard monstrosity. And when Ed spoke to a customer, Barry was demoted to an organ grinder's monkey. *Show them the string sound, Barry.* Ma'am, you're going to love this. . . . *Show them the rumba beat, Mr. Steinke.* This is really fantastic, right. . . . *Show them the piccolo, maestro. The oboe. The piccolo again.* Hear the difference? That's amazing, isn't it? If that living hell hadn't already punished Barry a thousand times over for his life's misdemeanors, Ed then practiced self-synthesizing opposition dialogue, an Orditzian concept, although any sixth-grader could have identified it as good cop, bad cop. "Barry, don't be a hog," Ed would say, shooing his brother off the organ seat to ingratiate himself to another horrendous customer. "Let Mrs. Gribovich's son—Johnny is it? Oh, I'm sorry. Jimmy, of *course,* Jimmy—give the 180-X a try." These Jimmy Griboviches would invariably suffer from some sort of low-grade mental disorder and would proceed to hammer and twist the organ keys and produce a primal wail so wrenching that even Vernon Warbler would skip a comma. And every week the brothers would lug the three-hundred-pound cross of plastic and wood to and from the van, and every night they would share a double room in a bunker motel with no girls, no amusement, scratchy towels, no way out. That was the obvious regret, the kind of regret you have if you join the army for money and the bastards send you to war, but it was only the cake's first layer. Barry also regretted that he had wanted to do it, wanted to give up the band, wanted to quit. *I am,* Barry had finished the sentence the same way ever since a noun was socially required, *a musician.* He surely wasn't a student, and he was never much of anything else either. He wasn't a farmer or a plumber or a cop, a Democrat or a plutocrat, a Gay Man or a Black Man, a Jewish Man, Spiderman. He wasn't a born-again Christian, a born-free Indian, an Asian-American, a Hawaiian-American, a Dash-Hyphen-Dash-I'm-Not-Lying American. Barry Steinke wasn't a Survivor, a Victim, a Success, a Casualty, AN INSPIRATION, an Abuser, an Abused who would be appearing on television, radio, news, sports, weather, and information every day (on the hour) at one, three, seven, and nine. *Now,* Barry Steinke wasn't any of those I-am-what-I-ams. Now, he wasn't anything. But he used to finish the sentence the same way: I am a musician.

He had taken that responsibility seriously. He read books, three of them, about The Hotels' forebears and lectured the band about Memphis, Mississippi, and the Arkansas mud. He tattooed EAP RIP on his arm out of vodka-clarified respect, not caprice. When Barry told his parents that he had "decided against" going to college because of the music—there were other reasons, but that's what he told them—his sincerity was so evident that Gene allowed him to continue eating his hard-earned food even if the decision was unacceptable. Obviously, Barry wasn't monomaniacal about The

Hotels. He stirred fun, stirred trouble, chased girls, caught girls, released girls off the line. But if that disqualified you from being a musician, America would be silent and dull.

Yet when the weeks went by and nothing came, Barry changed. Afternoon after afternoon, Barry would wait for the mail from behind the ranch house's front bay window; afternoon after afternoon, he would count seventy seconds for the mailman to drive three houses down; afternoon after afternoon, he would scurry down the driveway in bare feet and unshowered limbs. It was January then February those afternoons—eight months after high school—and the midday subzero would beg water from his eyes; the asphalt's wintry epoxy would grip his naked soles. Barry would do it anyway, afternoon after afternoon, so he could check the white-bill bundles of mail. And he would always be disappointed. When Tim Knudsen's note came and nothing more, Barry raised the flag of surrender. Sure, if The Hotels had been allowed to play anywhere other than The Rooster, had gotten just *one* paying gig, the end might have been different. But no one wanted to hear them.

A few hours after a bruised Hotels' practice—the penultimate one, it turned out—Barry and Andy Belsen went to a record store; it was as good a way as any to kill time. "Just look at this crap." Barry fingered through the bargain bin of stillborn careers.

"Yeah," Andy agreed, "at least we don't like suck like these losers."

"Like what are you talking about?"

"You know, like we're not as bad as this," offered Andy, frightened of another misstatement.

"Then like why do they have CDs, and we can't even get any-place to book us?"

"Um, because, you see . . . " For five seconds Andy slumped standing while he remembered the answer. "It's not *what* you know. It's *who* you know." Andy's father worshiped that saying as gospel.

"Who told you that crap?"

"My dad."

"He's as stupid as you."

"Dude, Barry. *Dude.*"

"Just look at this. *All* of this." As commanded, Andy's eyes circled the store. "I mean, what can like we do that all these people haven't done?"

Andy suggested, a desperate throw at the final buzzer, "I bet there's like some shit that isn't here." That megastore, like its megacousins nationwide, would not allow Andy to get away with the slander. Every album ever created by every band they had ever heard of taunted them from their megacases: ha ha, we've already been done. Musical categories that they had never imagined—Andy to Barry: "Like what the hell is Baroque?"— shouted at them to give up now.

"What, Andy? *What?*" Barry demanded. They both looked around the store again, as if harder concentration would allow them to discover the one gap in the history of music on this planet. But it didn't work; every note had been played; every combination had been tried; every instrument and style had already been magnetized onto vinyl and tape and mirrored disc. They couldn't even reject everything originally; even *that* had been done. The studio hermit who recorded The Hotels had played for them his wreck of a masterpiece, "Crash and Bang Symphony No. 2: Forlorn." The name, except for the forlorn part, was spot-on. "Like what do we do after Crash and Friggin' Bang *Two*?"

Andy laughed reflexively. As of late, whenever the practicing Hotels fell into a cacophonous mess, Barry, in an anchorman voice, would announce, "Ladies and Germs, that was the Crash and Bang Symphony Number Two." The rest of the band would applaud, chuckling.

"Stop laughing, you idiot."

"Dude, Barry."

"I'm sorry. Like it's just not funny."

"It's kind of, you know."

"Not anymore. We had something. The Hotels. . . . But with all this . . . " Barry's left hand pointed to the dreary weight of precedent lining the store. "It's impossible."

And he quit. Barry knew what the future would smell like if he hadn't quit, and quitting wouldn't hurt as much as that because quitting was *his* decision. The Hotels could have played for another three or four months at The Rooster, but then the younger kids from Carl Schurz would have complained that The Hotels were ancient and losers; they would have threatened a boycott until Guddy hired *their* classmates' band. That's how The Hotels replaced The Daniels and The Daniels replaced Skeeball and Skeeball replaced Scroogio and Scroogio replaced French Lick. And if The Hotels had tried to protest, Guddy would have responded with the same words that he responded to everything: I got to do what the customers want. I'm a business-man, I got a family. Guddy didn't actually have a family, but it sounded better than, I got a cocaine habit, for example, or I got a large and growing investment portfolio.

Barry wouldn't stammer p-p-p-please while blimpy Guddy Gutmanis exiled him. He told the world that he wasn't a musician—*Steinke, how's the band?* Moving on, dude, moving on—before it told him that he was a fool. Barry hadn't cared— well, hadn't cared that much—about admitting that he was unem-ployed or on the pallet crew. Sure, no one respected the crew boys, but they knew it. They weren't vulnerable; they weren't like Ed with his magazines and his Orditz and his perfectly asinine execution, people friggin' laughing at him all the time.

Barry poured himself another cup of beer as the stagehand, checking the sound, tap-tapped the microphone. Just like last night at this time, Barry's eyes circled the bar, out of duty, for obliging mall girls or farm girls, teenage seductresses or aging painted vamps—come out, come out, wherever you are—but landed, unsuccessful, on a sign above the stage, MAMA'S ALE HOUSE WELCOMES YOU TO THE STATE FAIR. Tonight, languor had crept into him, and he returned to his companion in the cup. That half acre under a blue tented tarp was a temporary outpost of a statewide Mama's empire of four Mama's Ale Houses and two new Mama's Microbrewery, Bar, and Grills. The six Mama's lazily attempted a Southern good ol' boy theme, although its owners never pushed it too hard. They knew that Saint Success didn't care if the old movie poster clashed with the butter churn, the Confederate flag with the mammoth German steins; the saint only cared if singles ran a tab after ten and families crammed the booths before nine. Mama's State Fair Ale House was a poor man's version of its permanent sisters. Only the cups' logo lady and the bartenders' shirts differentiated it from a dozen other places within a hundred yards; the fastfood Mama's Burgers and tepid Mama's Wings and bottomshelf Mama's (vodka, tequila, rum punch) Shooters protected the outpost against charges of immoderation or originality. However, as its owners knew, neither decorations nor food quality made one nickel of difference to Mama's profitability at the Fair. The three *l*'s—location, layout, and loud—did. Many of the fairgoers who had been to a Mama's before, suburbanites who went once a week, country couples who still wistfully recalled the blur of their one visit, eventually passed the giant slide at the Fair's heart, saw Mama's nearby location, and stopped in for a drink. Although the layout seemed box-standard, Mama's placed picnic tables only in the structure's west side, unlike its competitors; this ceded more room for the big and open, pack-'em-in-paying bar. The half acre's back section held the stage necessary for the third *l*. Mama's, the institution, wanted its customers talking loud and laughing loud and cheering loud, and it wanted the music playing loud. Loud brought attention and attention brought customers and customers brought money. After eight, a variety of midpriced rock bands rotated party songs, style unimportant, innovation discouraged. In the early evenings and afternoons, Mama's manager would book just about anyone for a half hour—a cappella groups, yodelers, high-school troubadours—as long as they could make some kind of noise.

The manager, bug-shaped, a convex belly joined to thin-stick arms, stepped onstage. "How are you all doing today?" The roared responses of the night crowds, the rounds of I-can't-hear-you and yet louder roars did not meet the question. It was five-thirty, and the mood was fractured, transitional. A table of wiseasses in the corner laughed; no one else looked up at the manager. (Barry was facing the stage, but he didn't count; he had been doing it for three minutes.) This didn't upset the manager; the same hour-numbers followed on the same clock every day. "Are you all having a good time *at Mama's*?"

"Go to hell, you loser," the comedian-king of the wiseasses cut under his breath.

"Okay, we got a great night for you this Tuesday." The manager tried to mimic the ringmaster's cry but settled, as always, for parody. "And it all starts *right now!*" Beer sloshed, teeth gnashed, chatter rolled, and the elusive sound of no hands clapping was heard. "It's my pleasure to present for the first time ever at Mama's Ale House"—he consulted his notes—"oh, I see, for the first time at the State Fair anywhere from way, way, way, way up north—I mean *way* up north—Little Lisa Zielinski and the Stone Lake Players." A few bartenders, capturing the lull, applauded in slow motion. The bouncer, a goateed whale with twenty-inch biceps and the tattoos to match, whistled between pointer and pinky.

Little Lisa, thirteen, wore an ill-fitting stuffed-shouldered lime-peel dress whose previous inhabitant, the evidence suggested, had been a rather unhappy bridesmaid. The all-male

Stone Lake Players—a guitarist, a fiddler, an accordionist, a stand-up bassist, and a drummer, varying in ages from seventeen to sixty-one—were uniformed from a precolor world in black dress slacks, white button-down shirts, ruler-skinny black ties. The Players tuned their strings—the drummer tightened the top screw of his cymbal—and destroyed any momentum, however small, generated by the introduction. Two minutes later, Lisa's white knuckles clutched the microphone, and her lips brushed the metal mesh ball. She drizzled, "Hi there."

The wiseasses snickered in the corner. The manager whisper-shouted from offstage, "Louder, dear, *louder.*"

"I'm, um, Lisa Zielinski, and these are the Stone Lake Players." ("Finally," the manager groaned.) "This is my uncle Stan." The fiddler lifted his bow. "And his friend Burt." The guitarist nodded. "And our neighbor Mr. Klu— I mean Charlie." The accordionist flexed the instrument resting on his medicine-ball gut. "His son Neal." The bassist smiled. "And my brother Kevin." The drummer ratted and tatted and ratted again. "Um, I hope you, I hope you . . ." She had skipped something, something that she had been told not to skip, oh, shoot. "Oh yeah, and I want, I mean *we* want—sorry—to thank Mama's"—Uncle Stan's hairbreadth nods led each syllable—"Ma-ma's State Fair Ale House for all-ow-ing us to play here. It's real-ly, um, nice. So, thank you."

Jesus friggin' Jesus, Barry thought. Where do they get these people? Well, Little Lisa Zielinski and Her Five Inbred Cousins couldn't be any worse than last night's five-thirty act, Rocking Ronnie Bamberger—in civilian life, a "tall" five-foot-five, glass-shiny bald real-estate agent. Every tune in his fifty-song repertoire had begun the same; Ronnie would push a button on a mail-order keyboard, which would trip a boom-boom-chick-chick mail-order beat; three seconds later, it would be joined by a preprogrammed bass line. Ronnie would step in front of the keyboard, adjust his headset microphone, and ask the crowd, "Are you ready to have some fun?" He would then swing a guitar clumsily from behind his back and render a pop standard Rocking-Ronnie style, that is, up-tempo and dreadful. How can he keep on doing that, Barry had wondered after the fifth same measure-by-measure lead-in. Yet some in the crowd, the fuzzy and the tottering, had swayed merrily to Ronnie's rockers. *This is the friggin' mainstream.* Barry heard a revelation coming down the track. *This garbage is so popular because people are desperate for good shit, the real shit, anything.* The revelation arrived toot-toot at the station. *The Hotels could—* Okay, we weren't like all that. But, but we *weren't* . . . and . . . we could like . . .

But before that revelation last night could harden into a resolution, Ed arrived at Mama's, as imprecisely arranged. Barry, a four-quarter competitor, had wanted to establish himself early, ignite a buzz, wait for the ladies. Ed's ideas differed slightly. "I'm leaving, jackass."

"What's your problem?"

"You." Ed's furies fell like a summer storm, unaware that it was ruining a nice afternoon.

"You're a psychotic."

"And you're a jackass."

"O-riginal."

"Shut up, will you. I'm going back to the motel."

"It's not even like six." Later, Barry did not approve of his sniveling tone.

"What's your point?"

"Don't you have like some organs to sell?"

"I'm done for today, jackass."

"Well, I'm not."

"Then get your own fucking ride back."

And Barry had to leave.

Little Lisa took a last breath for courage. Courage was the only attribute evident in the first number; it was a country song, Barry guessed, but who could tell? He could hardly hear her, and what he could hear sounded apprehensive and off-key. Afterward, Uncle Stan covered the microphone with his hand and whispered something pillowy to her. She blushed as thick and colored as the autumn leaves around Stone Lake, took another breath, glanced back at the band, and nodded.

And then it happened. Little Lisa and the Stone Lake Players melted American folk, German polkas, Irish jigs, Kentucky bluegrass, and Swedish waltzes into an overpowering alloy as old, as affirming as an A chord, as fresh as aurora. Uncle Stan wrote and arranged all the songs—he called them "traditional originals"—which were note-perfect played by the band, separate digits unimaginable apart, a dais for Little Lisa. When Lisa sang Stan's words—tablesawed, American words—of love or loss or redemption, her soprano gliding across ages and ranges, no one believed that she was not a woman. Yet when she sang those words in *that* voice, innocent and crystalline, everyone knew that she was still a girl. When the second song started, the bartenders froze and the chatter got shy. Before it ended, every eye had turned toward the stage. As the third song hit its stride, knees and toes bobbed and tapped, even knees and toes that were strangers to rhythm, born two beats out of step. During the fourth song, I-never-dance men grabbed I've-quit-asking women and started, Hail Mary, to congestedly dance. After the fifth song, the applause rumbled so loud—a single hosanna to the almighty for the Stone Lake Players—that the whole Fair must have stopped in time.

For as long as he could, Barry occupied his mind with the technical aspects of the performance—chord progressions, Lisa's phrasing—and he used as much jargon as he had bothered to learn or could still remember. They're not perfect, he concluded.

He was right: Burt on the guitar (he also played the tin whistle and the mandolin) sang backing vocals in a lampoony Southern accent as authentic as Mama's walls. For the benefit of the groupies in his imagination, drummer-brother Kevin hammed up his performance with arms a-waving, waving unnecessary. Little Lisa's voice was, okay, perfect—expressive, rangeful, mature—but it may have been too perfect, *another* soda-counter diva's on its passage through Svengalis one, two, and three.

"They're not perfect" didn't mean any of this, although Barry, who said it, wasn't sure what it meant. *They're, they're, they're . . .* He searched for the right word, a stickpin in a shag carpet. *They're, they're, they're . . .*

Old. Uncle Stan jellied jigs and waltzes into wigs and jaltzes, but they were infectious and flawless and *truthful* not because he jellied them but because the *them* was old. Stan connected memories— memories beyond him, memories of prairies and uncabined forests, sea journeys and old-country wails—like a child's locking blocks. The final constructions, the traditional originals, were his, but you could see the blocks' borders, hear history's ring; you could only look back. That's not like The Hotels, Barry pretended for a moment. Yet The Hotels, he knew, were old too— historians—an "interpretative alternative-tribute" band. And so was Rocking Ronnie. And so was the Crash and Bang Symphony.

Barry raised his head from his inward gaze. Kevin laid down the rhythm for the Stone Lake Players' encore, Uncle Stan's galloping, brain-burrowing "A Baby Too Few."

*Mother had a baby,*
*And Sister had a baby,*
*And Granny had a baby too.*

*We got to the table with ol' Aunt Mabel,*
*And now we got a baby too few.*

Jesus, Barry thought. He was in the record store; all the albums
ever produced taunted him from their cases; categories that he
had never heard of told him to give up.

*All'd been joking.*
*All'd been laughing,*
*All'd been singing along.*
*We got to the table with ol' Aunt Mabel,*
*And found one baby was gone.*

*A baby too few . . .*

It was last night's fantasy: The Hotels were reuniting. Now: what
was I even thinking?

*We looked in the cabinets,*
*We looked in the chimney,*
*We looked in the pots and pans.*
*For before the table with ol' Aunt Mabel,*
*The baby slipped out o'ur hands.*

They're better than me, an uncomfortable idea. *She's* better than
me, even more so. But, but, but . . .

*We went to the henhouse,*
*We went to the barnyard,*
*We went to the stables too.*
*"Don't blame us," cried all the critters,*
*The baby was lost by you.*

*A baby too few . . .*

Great was the before. Plain was the after. America, the story of the after becoming the before. America, the story of it not.

*We asked the reverend,*
*We asked the pastor,*
*Whether our God could.*
*But all them preachers said, "I'm sorry."*
*The baby was gone for good.*

And that was the way it was.

*Dreaming of summers,*
*Dreaming of rainbows,*
*Dreaming of skies clear blue.*
*All those dreams are now forgotten,*
*'Cause we got (we got a baby too)*
*We got (we got a baby too)*
*We got. A baby. Too few.*

The half acre under the blue tented tarp shook like a convoy-covered highway. The table bolts moaned, begging for relief. The manager hopped onstage and thanked Lisa (applause, hoots, hollers) and the Stone Lake Players (more applause, more hoots, more hollers) three times. After their fourth song, the manager had kicked himself for scheduling the band in the Rocking Ronnie Loser Slot. Well, he would have to rearrange the schedule for the rest of the Fair. Thank God it was only Tuesday.

Barry watched the stomping throngs. His fist hugged the plastic cup. *What am I doing here?* The last two years—his entire life, really—were made up of fumbled steps, partial decisions, uneventful events, good-time Charlie going with the flow. Now Little Lisa had knocked on the door and asked him in her perfect-pitch, perfect-range, perfect-friggin' voice to explain, if he had the time, the whole crazy universe. How can that dumb little girl and those whitebread hicks— How, Barry wondered, could he have agreed with Ed? And Cheryl Pfeffer? And immature? Barry hugged the cup tighter, love-crushing its sides. The cup discovered that love sometimes hurts.

The voice called out Barry's name.

# [ 7 ]

Ed had walked out of the South Exhibition Hall not visibly angry. Maybe, he had spent all his bullets of rage on tiny things, trivial things, and his machine gun was now empty; maybe he was in shock and would soon move on to other reactive phases: denial or blame, bed-wetting, God-disclaiming. Maybe—this is what Ed himself suspected—he would move on to a drunk with Barry and the girls at Mama's. Or maybe he would search for Barry all night, get blind drunk alone, and end it right there with the thrust of an All-in-One Knife—good night, sweet salesman— through his pathetic heart.

Ed was busted, but it could have been worse. He could finish the State Fair; he had already paid Otto Felder for ten days. However, to continue through Labor Day, as the original "first phase" had been conceived, would require real money, cash money from someone. Barring a visit from a fairy grandmother, someone would have to be his parents. The bigger problem, of course, was the debt, a debt that would still harass him after he received his you're-kidding-me commissions from Brackett. Sure, he owed thousands, not millions, and would pay it off eventually at eighteen annual percent, but he would have to find a job, something regular and punch-clock, something decidedly not on the road to greatness. Ed didn't want to think about those kinds of jobs; he didn't want to think—*Should I move?*—about his apartment; he didn't want to think—*Should I pay him?*— about Barry's salary; he didn't want to think about any of it for the same reason, perhaps, that he didn't appear upset. He was busted. And Orditz was dead. And one at a time wasn't working.

He passed through the Fair's byways, a ghost late for a haunting, and reached Mama's entrance, a yard-wide slit in a four-foot fence. The bouncer, his rear oozing lavalike over the sides of a bar stool, stretched his arm across the opening—Ed and the others would have to wait until the commotion settled down inside. Ed lifted himself on his toes. The drunks and the crazies, the sober and sane were chirping excitably; everyone was standing, except for one boy-man in long sleeves and pants, a free electron. "Barry," Ed shouted. Barry didn't hear. Ed cupped his hands and shouted again.

Leila hadn't dared—*What would he think?*—to look back at Professor Nancy as she left the Legionnaires' stand. She would just go to this stupid bar, she thought, and wait for five minutes. He would leave by then, for sure. Then she would walk to her car and drive home, climb in her bed and stay there all night; or she would call Yankel from the Fair—*I could*—and tell him in many-many words where he could shove or stick the second shift. Then she could stay in her bed all year, all life, and no pigs, no professors would ever bother her again. Others, in Leila's shoes, would have already crossed an invisible line that day, a line when one more thing horrible or strange could not possibly disturb them, when they wanted the day to continue because their curiosity about the *next* thing horrible or strange had overcome their fear of it. Yet Barry's face, an impression pinned beneath Leila's temples, had become a landscape's entre-cumulus sky— background, yes, but mood-determinant. And to Leila, Chubby and that face and Professor Nancy had whispered, licked, called, and recalled so quickly that she had seized the line and tied it around her waist. Don't ask me to decide, she cried, if I should let it go, hold it tighter, or double-dutch through its unseeable threads. Don't ask me to decide if I should relish the absurdity; don't ask me to decide. I have to go home.

When Leila reached Mama's, the bouncer stretched his arm across the opening; she and the others would have to wait until the commotion settled down inside. Next to her, a déjà-vuish-looking man shouted, "Perry." His dress shirt was untucked, and his tie was scissored, all wrong, the broad part behind his back, the narrow part in front. When his rising hands cupped around his mouth, he exposed two sweat oceans. Although Leila couldn't smell him specifically, she took two steps back.

Finally and unexpectedly, *bare* and *ree* had crawled through Mama's density.

Barry glanced over his back at the source. *Great. This friggin' crap again.* Struck now by deliberate deafness, he rejoined his beer, but a glimpsed image, one shutter's snap, turned him toward the entrance again. *Jesus Christ:* she was moving.

Jolting off the seat, Barry caught his leg between table and bench. As he unscrewed it, his cup fell to his belt, tipped, and spilled onto his thigh. *Like I friggin' need this now?* Barry didn't have time to answer the question. His left hand nudged elbows, knocked shoulders, pushed oxen; his right wrist tried to clean his pants. His strokes were hard and rough, too hard to go unnoticed, too rough to do any good. Ten seconds later, Barry reached the opening. He slid under the bouncer's arm and stood between the whale and his brother and The Girl.

Ed had watched Barry parting the crowd. "What the *fuck* are you doing?" he asked. All the outsiders, including Leila, heard the comment. Only Leila gasped.

"Once in your life." Barry, teeth sharpened, scowled. "Shut your friggin' mouth." He looked at Leila. She watched his wrist still attempting to complete its drying mission with a certain carnal gusto. She took two more steps back. Not again, the thought pierced as his body lunged as his hand grabbed Leila's arm between shoulder and elbow. "Please, don't leave."

"What the fuck are you *doing?*" Ed repeated with more justification.

The bouncer, who didn't like to get off his stool, got off his stool. "Yeah," he growled, "I'd like to know that too, buddy. What *are* you *doing?*"

"Please, I need to talk to you." Barry spoke to Leila alone. She, Ed, the bouncer, the others—a choir before the bellowing finale—dropped open their mouths in unison. That need, the way he said *need,* carried, it seemed, all creation's fate.

Leila closed her eyes and saw her yellow room. *I have to go home. I have to go home. I'm going home.* Then she said, "Fine."


It was six o'clock and, ninety miles to the north, Leila's Aunt Mary said something too. Every day, when her parlor clock cuckooed at that time, she repeated a little nonsense that she had heard once in a picture show, "Six o'clock and the babes are asleep." She addressed no one, of course, because no one was there, but it *was* six o'clock, and the babes were asleep. If that night they were dreaming baby dreams in baby tongues about Leila and Barry and Ed, the babes, optimists all, would have wished for profundity and resolution. Each, three, finding salvation in each.

In a few more hours, Mary would turn off the lamp on her nightstand—nine o'clock and the old lady's asleep—and wait, like she did every night, for her father's lullaby. "You can wish for this or that," he used to sing, "but the thin will be thin and the fat will be fat."

PART THREE

Barry acknowledged his luck: none of the hawk-eyed Mama's patrons had descended on his table. He sat on the side farthest from the stage, Leila across from him, Ed next to her, two feet away. Barry smoothed his pants, picked at the beer-on-cotton burrs; Leila traced figure eights on the table; Ed wheeled his head (to and then fro) and oriented himself to the half acre under the blue tented tarp. Each concentrated, scribe on scroll, on pants or table or tent, and Barry acknowledged his luck again: what were the chances that this girl and Ed, if you think about it, at the same time? Oh sure, he thought as he continued to pick-pick away at his pants, he probably shouldn't have grabbed her so hard—grabbed her at all—but there would be plenty of time to straighten that out; she was different.

Ed was confused: Barry had said he didn't know that girl. So what, he thought, was the last scene about? And the earlier scene? He didn't have time for this, and he waited, patience consuming, for Barry to dismiss the girl so that they, Barry and Ed, could talk about the obviously urgent matter that had brought him here. He waited, and he waited another half minute and finally, tired of the pulsing awkwardness for which he shared no responsibility, told Barry, "I got something to say to you."

"Whoa, dude," Barry said; he knew that he should have spoken first. "Um, excuse, me," his voice, rounded and experimental, petitioned Leila. Her finger hesitated, and she looked up. "I needed to talk to you"—he paused again—"because, um, you know, back there at the exhibition hall, the *South* Exhibition Hall, I think you like got something wrong." She said nothing, and Barry, distantly, appreciated her strategy; the silent treatment was determined, effective, shrewd. "Um, I didn't mean that you were wrong, you know. I just meant that like, if you think about it, there was a little misunderstanding."

She needed, *needed* to leave, needed to be anywhere but at this table with this guy (and that guy) and his hands and his explanations and his misunderstandings. She had forgiven Barry, she admitted, forgiven him for the lips and the tongue and the wink. She *had* forgiven him. But when he had grabbed her—her arm could still feel his fingerprint impressions, white and shrill— she had cursed her imagination, loud and final, bitterly and privately; she had cursed her never-learn brain for ever considering forgiving this guy. How could she have ever thought that this asshole was some gallant Roger who had just made a mistake? Why couldn't she have just kept her imagination empty? *It* had gotten her here. *It* pretended that this Roger was anything but what he was, a pig. As she continued to trace eights on the table, her deeper-grooved fingernails resisted in pain.

She looked at him with an immovable glare of a millennial boulder and said, "Don't worry about it." Barry slumped in his seat and conceded everything. No one spoke for another twenty seconds.

It festered, the injustice of the idea to Ed that someone else's concerns could be more important than his. He couldn't bear the goings-on between Barry and this lump of a person—an old girl-friend, probably—much longer. "I *said* I have something to tell you, something important."

"What then?" Barry snapped.

Ed had not planned this far. His eyes darted to Leila and back. "Um, it's kind of—you know." He didn't want to detail his financial problems in front of the s-t-r-a-n-g-e-r.

Barry didn't have time for his brother's games. "If it's so friggin' important, just say it."

"Don't tell me what to do."

"Then don't be like, 'I have to tell you something,' and then be like, 'I don't want to tell you.'"

"I'll *be like* whatever I want, jackass."

In the tabletop's gorge, the absence between slat and slat, Leila dug her nails, and she fixed her hopes on disappearing. How easy it should be: to float, to become a twisting, dancing gas. She didn't want to be here, the laws of the universe must understand. He was a jerk, a bully. They were both such bullies. *Never.*

"Do me a favor, Ed. Once in your life act like a normal human being."

"I'll do you a favor. I'll go back to the motel without you."

Leila placed two imaginary hands over her ears to protect them from the cross fire.

"Jesus friggin' Christ, dude, you're a freak."

"*Fuck* off."

"We're not sitting in some box." Barry glanced across the table. "*She's* sitting right here."

Last night, another person had explained that Leila was not deaf; now, she was not invisible. Ed and Barry and Chubby and Skinny could have all been the same character actors in the same matinee nightmare for Leila's wish or ability to separate them through the twilight. She needed to leave these people. She *wanted* to leave them, she rubbed her biceps, assuring.

"I can see who's sitting here," Ed declared. "I'm not a jackass dropout like you." The fire spat from the brothers' mouths was not yet hot enough to draw attention from Mama's other children.

"What's that like supposed to mean?"

"Are you too much of a moron to figure it out?"

"Why are you like such a bitter loser?"

"Excuse me," Leila said too softly.

"I got one reason. My brother's a moron."

"Here's another for you. You're a weirdo."

"Excuse me." Again, neither Barry nor Ed heard.

"How about this? How about *I* leave *your* lazy ass here?"

"Okay with me, loser."

"*Excuse me.*"

Barry and Ed's eyes locked on each other's first, a reaction as old as brotherhood: mutual malevolence turned to joint preservation at the smelled tip of trouble. The trouble was warranted, they knew; they had been acting dreadfully. It was Barry's duty to speak. "I'm sorry. Really, very. It's been like, uh, a long day, if you think about it."

"Don't worry about it," Leila mumbled again. Despite the instructions and the indifference behind them, Barry worried. "I have to go," Leila resurrected the reigning lie, "I, um, I have to meet some people."

Barry sat on his left fist, the grabbing fist, for he would not, could not . . . "You got to do what you got to do, right?" he said. He attempted to laugh—it ended up as an *eh-eh-eh* of a newborn's whimper—to prove that everything was like cool.

It was time for Leila to say something politely fallacious, insincere, or both—"I'll see you around" or "Have a good night then"—unhinge her legs, and walk out of Mama's forever. But she didn't. A feeling, a thought, an idea (possibly) arrested her; she had forgotten something, a contraction of her heart insisted, forgotten to turn off the stove, forgotten to take her keys, forgotten to say her prayers before bed.

Barry's jammed knuckles prickled with egalitarian numbness, finger indistinguishable from finger. He readjusted his fist under his bottom but didn't lift it. "Before you go," he asked Leila, appealed to her fated appearance; his larynx was strained by the futility. "Can I ask you one question?" She was different from the rest of them, from Ed, from his father. She was the same as he was. She was, she was.

Leila didn't say yes, and she didn't say no.

"Um, what's your name?"

She couldn't answer him, she knew; to do so would moor her to that table. On a day like this—she, tied to the line—he would undoubtedly proceed to ask her all sorts of awful, surgical, Rusty questions. And he was the same guy, the pig, who had licked those lips eighty minutes ago, the same bully who had manhandled her five minutes before, the same con artist who wanted to be best friends now, chuckling about some misunderstanding. No, she couldn't answer him. But she couldn't think of a painless way—*I'm sorry, I was never given a name*—to excuse herself from the question. So she dropped the anchor. "It's Leila."

Barry released his fist from under his body. "Oh, really. That's like a very cool name." Leila didn't say thank you, and she didn't say screw you. She tucked her amber hair behind her ear. "And, uh, my name's Barry." The other presence at the table fidgeted. "And that's my brother Ed." Leila's shoulders ticked, not offering Barry the definitive riposte of inaction or the candid ambiguity of a shrug.

The three returned, silent. Silence teaches different lessons to different people; it teaches poets about eternity, lovers about bliss, sinners about guilt. It taught Ed Steinke that everyone around him, then, was bored and would appreciate him talking, preferably about a subject uniquely interesting to him.

"Excuse me, Leila." Ed broke the table's lull; despite having heard her name a minute ago, he pronounced it *Lay*-la, not *Lie*-la. "I just have to tell my brother, um, something, and then it's all you, okay?" Ed's delivery was hardly polite, but it was urgently not violently disagreeable, a cold, not a cancer. When he had left the South Exhibition Hall—damnit, he would later recall, with his suit coat and briefcase there for the taking—he had abandoned twenty-four years of precedent and walked, ran almost, to Barry. But when he charged into the bathroom about to bladder-burst from a thousand gallons of water and a million gallons of booze, all the stalls were occupied, and the ancient attendant in the cuffworn tuxedo begged, Your pardon, sir, but you will have to wait. Ed swallowed. "Barry, we have a problem."

*We* have a problem, Barry felt the scream collecting in the butt of his brain. *We have a problem?* I have a problem—a brother from Mars who's got his head like so far up his ass that he forgot where he put it. Barry maintained his composure, but he wasn't going to volunteer sympathy. "Ed, I'm sure Leila"—he pronounced her name correctly—"doesn't want to like listen to your problem*s*." Cheers for Barry: Leila didn't want to listen to Brother Ed's problems, Brother Barry's opinion of how cool her name was, or Professor Nancy's pointless reminiscences of three-page stories.

"Well, fuck her and fuck you."

Barry slow-slapped his palm against his forehead. Leila resumed tracing figure eights. Barry, eventually, brought his hand down from his face. "Come on, Ed, please."

"Don't 'Come on, Ed' me. *I* came all the way over here to tell you something, and I get treated like a jackass because you got some gir—"

Barry's teeth became fangs, his nostrils flared, his face less human than lupine. "*Tell* me already."

"I really," Leila said loudly enough for the brothers to hear, "have to go."

"Please, don't go just yet." This was Barry.

"I'm sorry, but . . ."

"Please, just please."

"But this isn't—" Leila could feel in her muscles *Barry's* muscles tensing, corresponding to her under his shirt's long sleeves. She hadn't feared the licker of lips or the grabber of arms, but she began to consider the abstract idea that maybe fear wasn't an inappropriate sentiment.

"I know we're being rude here," Barry began. Slowly over the past several minutes, Barry had realized that his initial diagnosis of Leila's character—effective, determined, shrewd—was incorrect; her temperament was written on her frame: fragile-thin. He knew that he had to bring the discussion down, or everything, everything, everything would crumble, but he needed so little: only one kind glance, only one smile, only one neutral how-do-you-do from Leila that proved no coal-black, no hate was in her heart. "But it's been"—*What had it been again?*—"a rough day. I promise you my brother will behave himself."

"Fuck off."

"See." Barry laughed, capitulating. "That's how he says he agrees."

"Fuck off."

"That's how he says he agrees very much." Leila didn't join Barry's laughter but did note, detached, that he was sort of funny. The chatter of the rest of Mama's amplified, it seemed, as a hush fell on their table again. After ten seconds, Barry surrendered in full: "*Jesus,* go already." The tone, Barry worried, had been too rude.

"Well, I'm—we're—I'm busted."

"What does that mean?"

"Busted, you know."

"That doesn't like help."

"Just try to concentrate here, idiot." Ed pinched his fingers around an invisible tick at the center, at the perfect explanation, of being busted. He held it, eye-high, between him and Barry, and his focus switched from the tick to his brother. "We, I, I'm busted. We, I, whatever, having nothing to show for this summer except debts, and I don't mean a couple hundred bucks." With the word—the money—the dam was broached. "I mean *thousands*. We're not going to be able to go through Labor Day without some cash from somewhere, and even then there's like no way to, you know, to make a profit. Profit, hell. We'll be lucky to have anything left." When Ed had dashed from the South Exhibition Hall, when his stonewalled kidneys had felt moments from rupture, when he had removed his towel-covered waist and bared his financial failure dingle-dangle to a stranger, he had assumed implicitly that this would be cathartic. Ed had previously shown no faith in catharsis; he believed in the opposite cure for fear and doubt, the cure of the Cowboy, the Marine, the Farmer Who Awakens Before Dawn. You solved your problems by burying them deep in your belly and suffocating them with four feet of work and pride. But this hadn't been an average day for Ed. Orditz haunted with, "Does it matter?" The ledger teased, "You're busted." Vernon scoffed, "I guess I just ain't so smart."

He should have gone with his original instincts: he felt double shame then, double embarrassment. To reclaim some ego, he attached a postscript, sensitive and reflective, to his admission. "Does that make you happy, jackass?"

Barry knew that they hadn't sold many organs, but he didn't think they needed to. Ed had it all figured out: the zero case, the low case, upper case, downer case. Barry cringed at his recalled comments—his *loser*s, his *moron*s, his *disaster*s—which had been harmless until, lo and behold, they were true. He could only say, dry-throated, "Wow."

Like a sciencelab mouse in a sciencelab maze, Leila had followed the conversation for her polite, easy exit. She needed only one moment, one break in the action for her escape, but as she waited, something unfortunate happened: she listened. Three weeks ago, a bourbon-jacked man, one fall from the street, had come into the station. Five steps inside, he had railed a stream of anatomical insults at a lady friend, accusing her of numerous betrayals. The woman, who was so unattractive that the word *un*attractive felt generous (it was still related to attractive), had apparently cheated on the man, possibly right there in the parking lot, although Leila wasn't sure how that would have worked. Ed's rage, as she now compared the two, was different, a young man's rage, sober, lidded. She couldn't tell which was scarier, and she couldn't tell if Ed's behavior was typical—he was obviously having a particularly bad day—but his anger seemed so natural, his obscenities so regular that she felt a speck of sympathy for anyone who was obliged to accompany him as a matter of regular business, enough sympathy to force herself to remind herself that he, Barry, had grabbed her, had touched that tongue to those lips. She had, had, *had* forgiven him. But, maybe, you could explain that— *What's wrong with you?*

Barry was obliged to say something besides "Wow" and borrowed a line from Leila. "Don't worry about it." His brother glared at the advice, cheap and impossible. "Seriously, like don't worry about it," Barry continued. "If you think about it, it's just money. You have a lot or you have a little. At the end of the day, like who cares?"

"I don't think you *heard* me. I'm busted, the business is busted. It's not about money."

He had heard him. "Calm down."

"Don't tell me what—"

"Just listen. I'm not Mr. Businessman, okay, but I know things. It *is* about the friggin' money. You know, you're just like upset. But you have to think, you know, 'big picture.' There are things— I don't know—like *happiness* and stuff that are way more important than money." Ed grunted; he could not even begin to find the end-string of his balled, spinning disgust. Leila's sympathy for Barry, despite her brain's stuck-record disapproval, grew a centimeter taller. Whether or not he was making sense, he was trying, nobly trying, to steady a rickety man. Leila understood more than anyone else at the table, more than anyone else who had ever lived perhaps, how difficult it was to communicate using tools as inadequate as words. If Barry had been aware of Leila's thoughts, however, he would have taken exception to her condescendingly favorable, such-a-grand-effort-who-cares-about-the-results report card. He thought that he was familiar with a few truths about life, truths about priorities and virtue, fulfillment, success and failure. Now he was sharing them with his poor, night-lost brother. "You know, Ed, all this stuff you read, if you think about it, it's kind of whacked. Like this Orditz—"

"Orditz is dead."

"Huh?"

"Never mind."

"Anyway, it makes you think like this whole 'suit and salesman' stuff"—Barry moved his head in a small circle, apparently in relation to "suit and salesman"—"is what's important. But if you think about it, you don't need it. You don't need any of it. Like you"—Barry slowed down—"can create your own world out of different like thoughts and values."

"Are you ever going to stop talking, idiot?"

Barry paid no heed. "Dude, I'm talking about life here. This is like important. It's like so easy to just find another way, you know outside of it all—outside of all this. You can't judge yourself by like how much you make, or you'll never be happy. Take it from me." Ed coughed a one-note scoff. "All these guys at the Fair, they're just like trying to justify their worth with 'sales,' but they should do what makes them happy—if it's like selling junk, that's fine, but it doesn't have to be if they don't like want it to be. Whatever, though." He glanced at Leila. *You understand all this.* "They don't need to do what everyone says they should—they can do other things. That's the key, you know. Just don't"—Barry slowed down again and repeated the introductory phrase—"just don't let *their* rules define *you.*"

Leila strayed from the speech and found, like others before her, that when you dissected Barry's looks, you killed the good with the first incision. That nose, well, it was too big, and his shaggy crown—*Doesn't he own a comb?*—appeared to contain an awful lot of debris, and his blanched, whiskerless cheeks, when examined independent of his face, were sort of girly.

Barry took a hardy breath and was ready to fire another volley when Ed interrupted him with a pertinent question: "Well, what have you ever done?"

"What does that have to do with anything?" Barry was offended: this conversation was about the philosophized, not the philosopher.

"Who cares? *I* want to know. What have you ever done?"

Barry looked over Leila's shoulder at the stagehand bulldozing cords and cymbals and unplugged amplifiers into the corner. Ed and Leila also looked briefly and circled around again. Meanwhile, Barry had devised a plan to avoid answering the question: "What were we talking about?"

"Don't be a jackass."

"Well," Barry unfolded a second plan, "I think it's a stupid question, if you think about it."

"Oh, *really?*" Ed had been lectured long enough to fill a tanker of self-righteousness. "You can't sit there and say all sorts of things about how I'm wasting my life."

"I never said that."

"You did, okay. You did. So you can't sit there and say all sorts of bullshit, and when I ask you what you've ever done, say, 'It's a stupid question.' *That's* bullshit."

"You want me to answer your question?"

"We're waiting." Although Leila hadn't given Ed permission to answer for her, the hip-joined sentiment was accurate.

Barry gulped. "You know what I was doing . . ."

Ed cackled, base and sharp, victory-victory-victory. "You have got to be fucking kidding me. I mean, really, you are not, *not* going to say that. You were in a high-school band with a bunch of lazy jackasses. You guys didn't do anything."

"You're wrong."

"If I am, how come when everyone told you that you were too bad to play, you gave up?"

"You don't like know anything about it."

Ed chuckled, a deliberate sp-sputter. "I know more than you think I do. And I know that if you were really, you know, a 'musician'"—he signed his proof's final conclusion with a felt-tip flourish—"you wouldn't have given up just because people said they didn't like *one* demo tape."

"Oh yeah? Oh yeah, well—oh *yeah?*" Barry had watched the magician's trick from a balcony row only to find out that the magician had sawed him in half. His mother must have told his father, who must have told Ed. "Oh yeah?" he repeated once more; bearings, bearings, where are my bearings? "You're a loser, Ed."

"Is that right?"

"That's right."

"Says who?"

"Me."

"And who the fuck are you?"

"Jesus, dude, do you always like have to swear about everything?" If Barry had answered Ed differently—"not a loser like you," for example—the staccato duet might have continued indefinitely. If Barry had implied some violence—"someone who can like kick your ass"—a good fistfight might have ensued. (This would have been unlikely; the Steinke brothers rarely scuffled. Even as a child, Ed had proclaimed it childish to wrestle with Barry. When Gene, who had spent a good part of his own childhood in an older brother's headlock, learned about Ed's position, he worried for once that Ed, not Barry, was the funny one.) Yet Barry had played the mature card with his accusation of excessive obscenity. If Ed's next words weren't clever or biting, he would lose.

"Don't change the subject, Barry, just be— Hey, why don't you ask *her*?" The spectators applauded. The commentator raved. A master stroke. Truly inspired.

Through "that's right" and "says who," Leila's seams had tensed again, her back had straightened again, her eyes had stared again at her hands (again); she had blamed those hands, pleaded with those hands: push, push up, push me up, push my whole body up. *They don't even think I'm here anymore.*

"Why don't you ask her?" echoed, her voice, his voice, mingling, repeating.

Please, please, please just continue yelling at each other, Leila thought. Don't ask me. . . . She revived a favored tactic. She camouflaged herself in her surroundings, sat on her pack; a monkey she became, hearing no evil.

Ed rolled on. "Are you *deaf*? Why don't you ask your friend here?"

"Ask her what, you loser?" Barry shuddered before the oncoming disaster; Leila was different, like more artistic like him, she wouldn't be able to stand up to Ed's bullying; she needed someone to protect her. He clenched his teeth and ordered Ed, "Stop it, dude."

Leila thought that she had escaped; they still hadn't addressed her, only referred to her. She would gladly suffer the slurs of stupidity and invisibility and deafness—*Did he say deaf?*—if it relieved her from answering Ed's question. She wasn't even sure what the question was.

Ed, fed up with Barry's delays—"I'll do it myself"—turned to Leila. "Um, excuse me." She didn't look up. "I said, excuse me." She looked up, innocently. "Jesus," muttered Ed, who had transferred, from Barry, two dimes of contempt to Leila, Barry's road-bump of a girlfriend or plaything or *some*thing. He couldn't understand how this girl could just sit there, staring at her hands like some mute, cowering, broom-beaten kitten. He corrected himself; she *had* spoken; she had told them that she wanted to leave. So why didn't she? He placed his request to Leila, gingerly he thought: "Yeah um, I'm sorry to bother you, but my brother and I need you to settle, uh, a little dispute for us, okay?"

Leila didn't reply, and her face, her posture, rigid and brittle, didn't reply either, but Ed wasn't going to let Leila stand in the way of Leila answering his question.

"Anyway, we, um, want to know if you think it's a better . . . No, let me see, is it better to use your life to try to build a successful career in sal— business or to brag that you're a failed musician?"

"Come on, Ed. If you're like going to humiliate us, humiliate us fairly."

"I'm very, very, *very* sorry. Let's see. Is it better to use your life trying to build a successful career in business, for example"—his elocution was marvelously smug—"or, um, let me think how to say this 'fairly,' pursue an 'artistic' career even if it isn't successful? Is that okay with you, Barry?" Although Barry couldn't let Ed know it, he thought that Ed had framed the question, fingered punctuation aside, remarkably well.

Leila stalled. "Yes?"

"Yes what?" Ed asked.

She stalled again. "That's your question?" Ed didn't dignify that with a response. "Well, I don't know." Barry and Ed leaned forward, the natural reaction, and waited for Leila's opinion. Obviously, she didn't know. No one knew. Nevertheless, she would share her views on the subject, no matter how humble, bracketed, or qualified. Seven seconds later, the brothers leaned back, recognizing that nothing else was coming.

"See, Ed, she doesn't know anything. So just drop it."

Leila may not have spoken before, but now she was speechless. *She doesn't know anything?* The sympathetic boy that she had quit disliking minutes before sank into the body around those lips, the grabber, the insulter. He was unforgivable. She had to leave that place now or she was going to—the timer of her heart boomed loudly—explode. I don't know what you're trying to do, she thought, cementing her resolve, but I know that you're the same as everyone and that I don't have to answer your asshole, bully questions, asshole.

"She *knows*," Ed discussed Leila's same topic aloud. "But she doesn't want to offend you." He smiled: that was a good one.

"What are you talking about?" yelled Barry. The people to their left, smirking superior and tipsy, glanced at their table.

I don't have to answer, Leila thought.

"I'm talking about the fact that you're a goddamn quitter," Ed said untruthfully.

"And like what are you then?"

I don't have to answer, she thought again, too late for the last question, too early for the next. She surrendered again to the same daydream: words, words said often enough, everything crumbles before them.

"I'm out there, doing it," Ed read from his manifesto, "trying to do something with my life."

"Yeah, trying to make your dirty money so you'll like be The Big Man."

"Maybe, I should follow your lead and become a flunky pot-smoking warehouse jackass and spend my whole life thinking about nothing but doing girls."

"At least they'll talk to me, fat boy."

I don't have to answer.

"Who cares? 'Cause you're still a loser."

"*I'm* a loser? You're the one who's busted, *businessman.* You're the one who like talks the big game about Orditz"—"Orditz is dead" flashed, unexplained, through Barry's mind—"and some stupid friggin' article in, what's-it-called, *American Salesman.* And look at you. You're like a fat, sweaty, disgusting loser who's got nothing to show for like any of it."

"You know what, I'll get another opportunity, make *myself* one, and I'll make it soon enough. You can trust me on that, jack-ass. But you, you're going to just end up some poor, pathetic, poor"—Ed searched for a gem, something nastily alliterative, but came up short—"pathetic loser with a run-down shack and four kids and brag how 'cool' you once were. You're a *nobody.*"

"Better than being bitter and"—go for the sex, go for the sex—"whacking off."

I don't have to answer. I don't have to answer. Leila's chant imagined its own form; she could feel her table-glued palms gain-ing strength, gaining courage, rising like the snake slithering below the charmer's pipe.

"I'm bitter"—Ed would not answer the other accusation—"because look at these girls here." He threw his arm outward, showy and oversized. Pick any of them, the throw said, any of these women, short-shorted, eyes lined in blue. "But not you, Don Juan." Cain twisted the knife just to hear Abel scream. "You have your *girlfriend* here. Isn't that right, Leila?"

Barry bowed before a genius of evil. "Jesus, you're incredible."

"I'm not the one you want to be complimenting, Barr-*y*. Isn't that right, *Lay*-la?"

She tied her eyes by fiber and chain to the table. I don't have to answer.

"Hello?" Ed bobbed his head up, down, left, right, to check if Leila was conscious. Barry, immobilized, could not prevent the disaster.

"Hello?" Nothing.

"Hello?" Nothing.

"Hello?" And Ed poked her arm, a forefinger knock-knock on a miniature door. Most people would have found the poke— not a particularly hard or hurtful poke—merely inappropriate. To Leila, whose eyes were fixed on the table's wood, burgundy and weather-worn, the poke came like a train on a daisy. She recoiled; off the bench her body jumped and landed a half foot away. Her heart skipped three beats, gone forever, and rushed two hundred alternates in the minute that followed. Ed's poke was Barry's lips and Barry's hands and Professor Nancy's *hands* and Rusty's sex; it was Chubby's conceit and her grandfather's indifference. "What!" she cried.

"Isn't that right, Leila?"

"I don't have to answer. I don't want to be here anymore. I just want to leave."

"Who's fucking stopping you?" Ed demanded, yelled, challenged. People on both sides of them gawked. "*I* don't see anyone stopping you."

"Please, Ed." Barry's voice climbed volume, climbed pitch.

"What?" Ed shouted. "If she wants to leave, then she should *leave*."

Barry's eyes met Leila's. His were the same brown eyes that, ninety-five minutes before, had noticed a girl blushing, hair-stowing behind her ear. Hers were the same gray eyes that, ninety-five minutes before, had returned the flirtatious glances. Yet those eyes, all four eyes, no longer dreamed of flowers and soft dinner lights; now they only begged for release. One pair begged to be delivered through a vapor of prayers to a bedroom that was hers, hers and still. The other begged for a moment of free joy that made everything else wait in turn. A third pair of eyes at the table, another pair of brown eyes, which ninety-five minutes before had looked only to fill an emptiness of sales, pretended to need nothing. The mouth under Leila's eyes did not open.

Hopeless, the mouth under Barry's eyes pleaded, independently, one last time, "If you have one beer with me—with us, I mean—I swear to God, that I will not like ask you to stay any longer after that. One beer, you know. Like five minutes tops. . . . It's just that, that I've had a—we've had a—a bad day, and I don't want you leaving thinking that I'm like some sort of monster. Okay?" Ed didn't know what Barry was doing, Leila didn't know what Barry was doing, and Barry didn't know what Barry was doing. But the offer—a window slams, a fly slips below—came as Ed's shouts still ricocheted in Leila's skull. Had the devil's offer come later—not much later, a minute maybe—Leila might have reacted in an unprecedented manner. She might have stood up and socked Ed with the frenzy of the wronged and the strength of the repressed. But Barry's offer didn't come a minute later; it came when Leila's wires were crossed, her brain disconnected, her will vulnerable and, lucky for Barry, compliant. The deal, Leila thought if thought played a role, presented the least resistant solution: in five minutes, the brothers would let her go, and then it would all be over, *then* she could go home, and then she could— *What?*

She shrugged.

Initially, Barry didn't recognize the shrug's intent. After Ed's display, Barry wanted to left-hook for Leila, dissolve into the

ether for (or with) Leila. When she didn't leave but, in fact,
cocked her head so-so and raised her eyebrows the same, her
meaning became evident. "Great." Barry's face brightened. "I
mean, thanks. That's like, wow, great." But there was a proce-
dural problem. Someone had stolen his pitcher, and his cup had
gone to the sticky graveyard on Mama's floor. Well, Ed would
have to buy the new pitcher; Barry obviously couldn't leave her
alone with him. "Ed, can I ask a favor?"

No response.

"Could you get us a pitcher?"

Clear response: "No."

"Thanks a lot." Any other time, Barry would have balanced
more venom with less sarcasm, but now he needed restraint; the
cracks in the ice were growing louder; the water-blanket was
creeping drop by gallon by drop. But restraint didn't solve his
problem. "Um, Leila, I'm going to just like go to buy a pitcher.
Please don't—" He stopped; it was too late for that.

The cattle were tail-swinging in their sheds; the vendors of the
South Exhibition Hall were counting the day's take; the push at
the dairymen's had narrowed to a tinkle; the fairgoers' youngest
had cried waah-waah long ago. Their parents were now carrying
them among knives and syrup and potato-run clocks to cars and
cribs and homes. It was nighttime at the Fair, and all the roads
ended at Mama's or The Grill Haus, Captain Kruger's or Happy
John's. Mama's half acre was noticeably more populous, more dis-
sonant than an hour before; the bartenders now were gears in a
great beer-pulling machine, one hand a pitcher, the other a tap.
Barry, who had pushed himself within one peopled row of the bar,
would have to wait eight minutes before the pert blond on the
other side noticed him. *Like what the hell am I doing?* He was
puzzled. He was Barry Steinke; he was cool; he was hardly desperate for sex. Anyway, capricious fate had showed its other, sallow
face and had already eliminated the possibility of love or lust or

light petting with Leila. She like detested him or feared him, both if she was smart. But she was diff— Get over it already, he scolded himself. There was nothing going on here. Nothing was like going to happen. He decided, waiting, that now he only wanted for the evening to end as the afternoon had begun: Ed, recently changed into pure hate, reverting to his average angry self; Leila, recently changed into an enemy, becoming, abracadabra, a stranger again. And as long as he was going to get everything he wanted, he wanted The Hotels, Cheryl Pfeffer, Gina-Tina, Little Lisa, Rocking Ronnie, revelations, resolutions to climb back into their caves and hibernate for his life's long winter. Really, though, the *only* thing that Barry wanted right now was beer. The bartender flew past him once more. Two sets of boxcar shoulders, watermelon heads, and spaces-between-where-necks-used-to-be stood between him and the bar. He waved his hand above his head, only to magnify his impotence. He tried to check the table to see if Ed had strangled Leila or she, within her rights, had gotten to him first, but two more refrigerators blocked that view too. Barry waited for mercy from God or bartender, whichever came first.

"How are we all doing *tonight?*" The manager's voice scratched from the speakers. Looking back, the manager knew, was less glum than looking forward. "How 'bout them Stone Lake Players, huh?" The wiseasses in the corner, now the presiding officers of the Little Lisa Fan Club, whistled and hurrahed. "I think this next person will, ah, keep the *party going on!*" The manager's conscience, however enfeebled, made him stop there. "So here she is, Colleen *Zim!*" Colleen, wearing sandals and a flowered shapeless sundress perfectly shaped for her freckled shapeless frame, stepped onstage, an acoustic guitar in tow. Only six hands, two of them her brother's, clapped. Colleen considered herself at the forefront—or tail end, depending on the season—of one of the periodic revivals of Women's Folk. As

she had retired her unique voice two years ago, it was not clear
what made her folk particularly womanish other than the
assorted organs beneath her dress. Her songs were pleasant
though with enough minor chords to make them vaguely intellectual, sort of blue, and remarkably ill-equipped to bring Mama's
its third-*l* loud.

As Colleen came to the bridge of her second song, which
sounded exactly like the chorus, which sounded exactly like the
verse, which didn't sound that different from the first song, one
of the giants tapped Barry on the shoulder and nodded at the
waiting bartender. "Finally," Barry exclaimed to no one in particular and ordered two pitchers, not an unusual ratio for Mama's—
the giants were on pace to drink two each—but future-necessary
for Barry after Leila left. The giant handed him the pitchers.
Barry passed the bartender the money through the same conduit.
"Hey, dude," he shouted over Mama's clamor, "could you get me
three cups." The incredulity on the giant's mashed-potato face—
he was either incapable of understanding English or stupefied
that Barry would mistake him for a barmaid—whittled a foot off
Barry's height.

He started the long walk back. He could already picture the
gory details that awaited him: blood on the wood, bodies on the
ground, relatives blubbering, detectives probing. "Can you identify your brother, Mr. Steinke?" the coroner would ask as he
uncovered the two body sheets. Barry, pointing: "He's the one
who's not the woman." Barry slalomed through the crowd, a
pitcher in each hand, beer unspilled, three cups snapped in his
bite. He almost lost the cups twice trying to inspire some of the
more sponged obstacles to move. ("Excuse me," he said. "Eh
who he," it came out.) He almost lost them again when he arrived
at the table. The colors and muscles and vessels of Ed's face,
lately crimson and strained and a pinprick away from a pop,
appeared—*What the?*—normal. Ed and Leila were talking.

When Barry left the table, he left Leila and Ed in familiar mental moods. Leila parked her mind at "one beer." *One beer.* She
didn't think, supposedly, about flying-fleeing, reappearing in her
yellow room. One beer. She didn't think, purportedly, about the
day, the lips, the grab, Ed beside her, Professor Nancy. One beer
was the easy solution: five minutes tops—he *prom*ised—and then
she could leave. Yes, leave, Ed agreed extrasensorially. He hated
her there, frozen next to him, hated her as the guilty man hates
the judge, not because the judge holds his fate but because the
judge is fair. He also hated the Brackett Corporation and hated
Vernon Warbler and hated Otto Felder and hated *talking about
it.* He should have drowned all his busteds in the South
Exhibition Hall. Yet he had raved like an idiot, sworn like a madman, yelled like a jackass, and now this *Lay*-la or *Lie*-la or *Lee*-la
thought he was all those things, and she was right. Ed and Leila
sat motionless together, head-down twins. *Does it matter?* Ed's
thought lighted on another madman. Does it fucking matter? I'm
screaming this, I'm screaming that, Orditz is dead, and all I can
do is go off like some . . . I'm through. Yeah, it matters. The court
asked the witness if that was his official answer. *It matters because
that happens.* The magistrates scratched each other's heads. *If
someone tries something in this world, these people, these bastards
judge him for being a-a-a nut.* Twenty-four years in the northland,
twenty-four years as the namesake of Grandpa Kroeger, deco-
rated veteran and confirmed man of sacrifice, ordered Ed to stop
whining. He stared through the table's slats and sampled ways to
clear his mind, but the table's hush and Leila's presence, her mute
judging presence, still burned. He needed to say something—
small talk, big talk, chitchat on this-that—for he couldn't breathe
the sulfuric silence for another second. "Yeah, pardon me." Leila
held her breath. "Um, I was, um." Barry had already asked her
name so what could he. . . . "What do you do?"

Leila didn't know what to make of the question, a cabbage that fell from the sky. This is not part of the deal, she complained silently but forcefully to the authorities. One beer—that's all, don't you understand? I don't have to answer. I have to leave. After five seconds of adhering to these principles, Leila muttered something faint, if only to signal the question's impropriety.

"I didn't hear you."

Leila hurry-drove the answer through her throat again. "I work at a gas station. In the store."

"Oh yeah?" Ed thought about that and said, "Retail, that's a good business." And they both began to laugh. They didn't giggle or sniggle or titter or snitter or flitter away to any thesaural stand-in. They laughed true laughs, true laughs of a child in a sea of clowns. Their first laughs came together, and because they came together, they were good, released it all, the chants and the judgments, the embarrassments and the slights. "Retail, that's a good business" was patented in have-I-gotta-deal-for-you car lots by toupeed men with checkered sport coats and checkered morality, white and cucumber-green. It was believed by immigrant romantics, families who traded in four generations of savings for a Stop & Shop, families whose American dream was a six-hundred-foot square of cigarettes, snack cakes, and milk. Retail, that's a good business. What a stupid thing to say.

Shampoo companies (and breath-mint manufacturers) would have had Ed and Leila believe that one never has a second chance to make a first impression. If this propaganda was true, and one could *never* recover from bad breath or dandruff flakes, then the peak blocking the reversal of Ed's first impression on Leila was unscalable. Fortunately, this fact on first impressions was bunk. Barry made a good first impression on Leila and reversed it with his tongue; Skinny made a good first impression on Leila and reversed it with his friend; Rusty made a good first impression on

Leila and reversed it with himself. And Ed made a bad first impression on Leila, as bad as possible without revealing his privates or admitting a certain aw-shucks fondness for murder or blood, and reversed it, at least muddled it, with inanity.

Leila and Ed's laughter lasted forever, so it seemed; after the initial uncontrollable propulsion, it spilled on, perhaps too intently, for ten seconds more. Neither wanted it to end because the pause, the precarious pause, came next. The pause would give Ed—*or* Leila, but it would have more likely been Ed—the opportunity to catch everything foul laugh-released and drink the bitter mix again. Ed picked at a notch in the picnic table and said softly, "You know, uh, all that stuff back there, I'm kind of, you know, um—"

"Don't worry about it." Leila knew what "um" meant.

"'Cause, you know, it's been kind of a—"

"That's obvious." They both laughed again, an ordinary laugh.

Something to say next, something appropriate and consistent, hovered beyond Ed's fingertips. Sixteen months ago, tired of panning for love dust, Christy Kanko—Barry used to call her Skanko, inevitable because of her name and only half-contradicted by her appearance—had broken it off with Ed for the third and final time. The desert had stretched from that day until this one. Of course, Ed talked to women every day: the young married mothers who formed most of his potential customer base, the young married mothers who wore the comfort of marriage and exhaustion of motherhood on their abstinent sweatshirts and sensible shoes. But they didn't count. And sure, Ed had talked to those bitchy girls conjured by Barry when the brothers had gone out together earlier that summer. Yet he had had no desire to really converse with those girls; they could see him only for what he was, not for what he would ultimately be. But this girl, her laugh, seemed different. He should probably just explain, you know, what's going on. . . . And so the film began without previews, without warnings, without the totems of the producers' propriety. "This guy Orditz died." Ed wasn't loony enough to bring up the busting again, and he figured that this was the next most relevant topic. "And I've kind of been thinking about stuff because of that." Scientists, behold: Leila's eyes did not glaze over in apathy when Ed uttered the great man's name; they squinted in confusion. Ed, it was clear, spoke not in paragraphs but in disjointed sentences, thoughts separated by years and moods and miles. "Oh yeah, sorry." Ed stopped picking at the notch. He looked up, not at her, awkwardly next to him, but not away from her either. "He was this famous author—really famous author—who wrote this seminal book, very seminal book about sales theory—*and* technique—called *Classic Sales*. It set the stage for a lot of other things."

Leila couldn't believe that this guy was really famous. She, for one, had never heard of him. She also couldn't conceive of what kind of other things he set the stage for: computers, democracy, television? Yet it wasn't important, was it? She preferred this to the shouting and, for that matter, the thinking. "That sounds, um, like interesting."

No one had ever said it sounded interesting. "Yeah, really it is. There are a lot of books about sales, you know."

"Really?" There was no reason that there couldn't be.

"But most of them," Ed continued, "are just how-to books. Not that Orditz doesn't, or didn't, contain practical advice." For all Leila knew or cared, it could contain all sorts of practical advice. "But its *really* important part is—was, I don't know—in the second part, 'Part Two,' which put sales and salesmanship in a larger, philosophical framework."

"Hmm," Leila said. *Just think*. Salesmanship in a philosophical framework. Fascinating.

"But anyway, he died, and I just found out."

"I'm, uh, sorry to hear that." Then it was like a death, thought Leila. Those are rough.

"Oh no, it's not a big deal. I guess," Ed said as *does it matter* bawled from the crib. He plugged it, hastily, with a pacifier. "You know, his best work was already behind him."

"Hmm." Just think. Already behind him.

This conversation on the late Alfred Orditz provided Ed and Leila with the easy solution. It wasn't the easy solution of Leila's acceptance of Barry's beer; that was the choice among a set of options that provided the least amount of pain. Leila and Ed encountered their easy solution by embodying an old secret: life is easiest in the shallow and the present. It may, in fact, be its natural state; oceans all flow to the shoreline; puddles all descend with the dawn. When, with the laugh that dislodged the bone in the throat of the day, Leila and Ed stumbled into the shallow and the present, they realized that it was comfortable, proud, artless like all natural states are. Orditz and *does it matter* needn't be deep. "Who's fucking stopping you?" was a lifetime past.

Their words skipped from nothing to Orditz to nothing again. "Anyway," Ed went on, "like I said, *Classic Sales* was an important book, um, very seminal, but he died kind of under 'odd' circumstances."

"Hmm." Just think. Odd circumstances. Remarkable. The moral of Ed's story wasn't totally obvious, but Leila, nonetheless, nodded thoughtfully.

"But you don't really want to hear about this."

"Hmm." Just think. I don't really . . . "No, that's all right."

Ed was wading in new waters; his unanticipated success in airing thirteen sentences about Orditz (or fragments thereof) beat the previous record, Christy Kanko excluded, by thirteen sentences. Leila's civility did not, however, delude Ed about Leila's level of interest. So be it. The shallow and the present whispered a hint. Ed asked, "Have you been at the Fair all day?"

"Since four."

"Hmm," Ed said. Just think. Since four. Unbelievable.

Leila wanted to avoid another all-thumbs interlude and struggled to force the words through her mouth's rusted crust, but five
thousand hours reciting the chopped, straight language of the
American service sector—yes, no, come again, thank you, one
dollar, two dollars, three fifty-five—had coated her mouth, her
tongue, with tarnish and dust. Reactive comments like the ones
with Yankel and Professor Nancy were not too hard, but she
creaked and clicked before exposition. "I usually go on
Tuesdays."

"Hmm." Just think. On Tuesdays. I would have never
guessed. *Where's Barry?*

"I went to the exhibition hall. That's where, um, I went before
the livestock buildings. Cows . . ."

"Hmm." Just think. Cows. Moooooo. Where the hell's Barry
with those beers?

"And then I got some corn . . ."

"Hmm." Just think. Corn. *If he doesn't—*

"What's goin' on?" Barry interlaced his mumbled announcement with a stuttery, whimpery laugh. Ed and Leila looked up,
together and relieved. In a single motion, Barry had set the pitchers
down and somersault-spat the cups before anyone noticed where
they had been. Barry couldn't begin to imagine an appropriate
reaction; he had left a hurricane and returned to an idyll,
returned maybe to an eye.

"Oh, we're just talking about the Fair," Ed answered, his
manner casual, confiding, warped. Ed and Leila had apparently
become an old married couple just jawin' about the high price of
socks.

"Really?" Barry asked.

"Yeah. Leila usually goes on Tuesdays." At that, Ed and Leila
both smiled a confederate's smile. Barry poured three beers and
handed one to Leila. Her nod thanked him, and she took a few
sips. It was an appropriate beer, light, domestic; its slogan, like its

flavor, was the shallow and the present. Following her lead, Ed and Barry also drank. After a long minute in which they rotated glancing at Colleen Zim, Barry eye-measured Leila's cup uneasily; she had already finished a third of it.

"Um, Leila, Ed said you like go to the Fair on Tuesdays. Usually." It was the nearest thing Barry had to a thought.

"Uh-huh."

"Yeah, that's cool. We used to like come ourselves every year too."

"Uh-huh."

"I really liked it." Barry had still not adjusted to the new order at that picnic table. It was what he had wanted, everyone to revert to his average self, but those kinds of wants don't normally come true. "Yeah, our dad," Barry started a story, insecure of its direction or details, "used to like only give us ten dollars a year for the, um, midway, but our mom would always bring extra money and like slip it to us when he wasn't looking."

"Uh-huh."

The opening had not gone horribly, so Barry continued. "One year, Ed like cheated me out of most of the money that my mom gave me. Remember that?"

At Leila, Ed smiled with more leaking arrogance than was good for his or his brother's reputation. "Not really."

"Anyway, I was like really mad. Remember?"

"It's your story."

"*Anyway,* I told our mom that Ed stole it from me, but Ed was like, 'He's lying,' and like, 'I haven't taken anything,' but she couldn't do anything about it because my dad was only ten feet away. Remember what happened next, Ed?"

"No."

"Okay, you do. But whatever. Our dad's like, 'What's the matter?' Our mom's like, 'Nothing,' because she didn't want to explain about giving us extra money. Not that it was a big deal or anything. So anyway, Ed knew he had won—he was only about, I don't know, twelve and then I must have been then like, I guess, eight— and to be really mean, he pinched me right here." Barry petted the triceps on his left arm. "I started to cry. My dad's like, 'What's the problem?' I didn't say anything because, um, I felt like everyone was against me. So I ran away right down, you know, the center-space-thing between all the games."

"Uh-huh."

"And it took like an hour for them to find me. Wasn't it about that?"

"Something like that."

Barry had tried for the whole pointless story, a story he didn't want to tell as much as they didn't want to listen, to elicit some response; he had tried to let Ed or Leila's admission, explanation, retraction hatch on its own terms. He had failed. "Excuse me." His eyebrows sank to convey the situation's severity, his attention-must-be-paid complaint. "I left to get some beer, and you're like yelling," he nudged his head in Ed's direction, "every word in the book. And I had to beg you," he nudged it in Leila's, "to stay here because"—*careful, dude, careful*—"you had some friends to meet, and then I come back, and everything's like okay. So can someone tell me what's going on?" Both Ed and Leila raised their shoulders: your guess is as good as ours. Barry, tension's tendons pulling his neck's wrapper taut, ordered himself to keep it under. He demanded firmly but under, "I want to *know* what happened."

Ed felt sorry for his brother, so emotional, so unstable, so close to the cliff's edge. "Calm down. Nothing 'happened.' We just had a little laugh over something." Ed was being deliciously cryptic. "It was no big deal, I swear."

"Is that true?" Barry asked Leila. Ed's explanation may have been delicious in the baking, but it was rotten in the eating.

"Uh-huh," Leila agreed without devoting too many thoughts to any of the questions involved.

"It's been a long day for me too," Barry pardoned himself.

"No problem," Ed, generous and merciful, accepted Barry's almost-apology. "Have another beer."

It was the end of the summer, and the mild strolled through the blue tented tarp, under the watts and glow of dusk and man. It was the end of the summer, and night was falling and fall was nearing and the three at the table all thought, *Okay, okay. Okay but what?* they all worried and wondered. No, this is okay, they packed the wonder and worries beneath their feet. They were locked here, locked in the shallow, locked in the present, and wished for nothing but order and peace, acceptance and ease. And they had found it, they had snatched it, they had smothered it, afraid of the autumnal breeze, the hour before, the worries below. It was the end of the summer, and the setting sun shone the shallow, and it was the end of the summer, and the rising moon brought the present, and it was the end of the summer and all three wished, all three wished to pocket the time.

Barry filled Leila's cup—she didn't protest—and then his own. For a while, they had been lost in the end of the summer, lips closed. A previous discussion of the Mama's empire—all, of course, had been to a Mama's before, Barry a half dozen times—had expired two minutes ago. Barry risked another noise. "Leila, are you from here?" She said yes and asked the same question. "No, we're from up north." He named the city; Leila asked which part. "We're from the, uh, west side," Barry, not yet restored, answered in rough clips. "It's not like, um, there's that many sides." The others shed not a tear for the miscarried joke, and Barry rushed, "We live in Kopekne Green."

"That's kind of a funny name," Leila noted halfheartedly.

Barry agreed full-heartedly, maybe even double-heartedly. "Yeah, there's like this whole thing with this guy Bob Kopekne." Despite having heard the tale of Kopekne Green at least a dozen times, Barry had never troubled himself to learn it. He admitted, "Like I don't really know it that well. Ed does, I'm sure." Ed did and told Leila about the D day resolution, Norman towns, the government veto.

I wasn't in Italy on vacation, Peter Luden had sometimes grouched. He had left it, always, at that. She didn't think that he had been on June's Joe-blooded sands, but she wasn't sure. With little forethought and unexpected aplomb, she declared, "Yeah, all those guys do is like talk about World War Two."

The brothers shook their heads in agreement. "Seriously," Barry warmed, "if you think about it, if they hadn't gone to war, they would have like *nothing* to talk about."

Leila this time nodded in agreement. "It's weird, living totally in the past."

Her nods encouraged Barry. "It wasn't even like great, if you think about it. They killed like a lot of people—Japanese people and Chinese people and stuff. Like really racist, you know. Most of it was just for . . . For *whatever*. It wasn't cool, if you think about it."

Ordinarily, Ed would have corrected Barry fact by mangled fact, but that night he wasn't going to poison the pond of the shallow and the present with anything as trivial as the truth. "There's this guy who owns this restaurant-supply outfit I used to do sales at," Ed introduced a main character. "He was always talking about 'in the service' this and 'in the service' that, you know. So I always figured that he was some bomber pilot or something. But one day he's arguing with his wife, right there in the showroom, and claims how he got treated with more respect, you know, 'in the service.' And she screamed, get this, 'The only service you were in was in Delaware.' I guess he had a desk job there." Leila and Barry liked that story; it seemed to prove the point.

A time-out was called; the coaches weighed offense, defense against the ticking game clock. Barry finally called a play: "You know, our grandpa was in the navy in the Pacific." Barry thought Leila might need more information. "Um, in World War Two." Leila and Ed didn't like that story; it came from nowhere; it had no plot; it didn't prove the established point and may have, in fact, showed sympathy for contrary views. Barry recognized the first and last objections and jumbled the issue further. "And he's always like telling us—our dad does it too—that we don't know what it's like to sacrifice because we never had to fight for our country. Once, he was even like, 'You should join the army.' Can you believe that?" Barry looked at Leila to see if she could believe that. She looked at Ed.

Ed summed up the collected analysis: "Yeah, there are a lot of people with strange fucking ideas." Realizing a short breath later his renewed unsanitary choice of words, Ed waited for a rebuke. It didn't come. Ed wheeled around, torso up, to watch Colleen's anachronistic, pantomime strumming; during the same fifteen gangly seconds, Leila looked at her finger, which seemed ready to revive its once-flourishing career tracing the figure eight. Beaming, Barry raised his cup. "I propose a toast."

Ed smiled quizzically and Leila smiled bashfully and Ed thought, "What's he up to?" and Leila secured her hair behind her ear.

"Here's to no more wars."

"To no more wars," Leila and Ed repeated, tipped their cups, and drank.

"You want to know who else pisses me off?" Ed, swallowing, extended the offer. Barry knew a lot of other elses pissed Ed off:

men, women, the young, the old, friends, relatives, neighbors, strangers. "I mean in the same way." Barry puffed, impatient. "All these people, these former 'hippies'"—*hippies* was physically quoted—"who are always going on about how great a time the sixties were."

"Is that right?" Barry asked.

"Of course it's right."

"Why's that?"

"For the same reason. They're always so-so-so *critical* of everything."

"Sure, dude," Barry allowed.

"There's *no* question it is, Barry." Ed didn't actually know any former hippies. The earlier "they" had faces and names—Ed Kroeger, Peter Luden, Bob Kopekne. This "they" were only shadows and specters. But there were other voices, media voices, woven-in-the-fabric-of-youth-culture voices—Ed had just heard Colleen voices—which served as targets, as surrogates for Ed's ire. Those voices echoed still, judged still, and Ed felt their sting. Only a half hour before, his own brother had delivered a rambling monologue of cheap, tub-distilled protest songs. *Don't let their rules define you, dude, man.* During Ed's unabridged sermon that began then—it was encompassing, integral, an exaggeration— Leila and Barry did not participate actively enough to indict themselves before a boom-baby tribunal. They did, however, sprinkle enough ayes to satisfy Ed that his sentiments were, more or less, acceptable. Barry, truth be told, had nothing against Ed's marks. (He had always thought that any generation that had left sexual liberation and overdrive guitars to the next couldn't be that bad.) Yet a so-critical they—yes, *that* generation—had pestered him his whole life; his parents, his teachers, friggin' Tim Knudsen, the V-neck-sweatered managers at Lincoln Paper. Leila too scrambled Ed's they and her they—those pitying mothers who spoke too loud and too slow, those mothers and Professor Nancy.

"Abso*lute*ly," Ed agreed eagerly with a truism that Leila had eventually (and sluggishly) added near the end of his monologue. "They're still rah-rah about some stupid fucking revolution"—it was improbable that Ed knew anyone rah-rah about any kind of revolution—"but look at them. They're just a bunch of sellouts. And they lecture us about no values, no direction, no responsibility." Ed's eyes caught Barry's and proclaimed, Inclusion, brother, we're in this together, but Barry's eyes, his swallow, resisted. "And that's just bullshit. Because we work. We try to make something. Just look at—" New-and-improved Ed decided to save his supporting points, most of which were examples from his career in sales, for another occasion. Deliberating what to do next, abutting a panic, maybe jealous, he was struck by an idea. He filled the three cups— in the middle of Leila's cup, he switched to the second pitcher— and lifted his own. "Here's to um." Ed had not plotted the next part, which turned out to be the hard one. "Here's to, um, no . . ." His first thoughts seemed less graceful than Barry's toast of unity and good cheer. "Here's to . . . here's to no more revolutions."

"To no more revolutions," Leila repeated mildly and indrawn, thinking that it was her fault. "To no more revolutions," Barry repeated one beat later through a queasy part-smile, thinking that it was his fault. Ed, watching the others, thought it was his fault too: with every nip at the bodiless whipped cream, the three revealed more of the pie below. The pie wasn't inedible, but it was the afternoon, hard and dirty, with a mud-custard and a pebble-crust. With every gluttonous nip, with every unmindful word about the world outside Mama's tent, the moment approached when only the pie remained. Ed, his own toast could not mask, was busted; Barry, who lived his life in the whipped cream, needed to remind himself that these were the free-joy minutes that made everything else wait in turn; Leila wanted to go home, she intermittently, privately insisted and maybe even believed. *These guys are the same as before.* This change of mood, silent but copied three times, could perhaps be attributed to the presence of a certain rascal, son of barley, skin of hops, body of water, brain of yeast, but neither Leila nor Barry nor Ed was willing to admit it yet; they all came from German stock, which had long ago sown, strand by strand, an estimable tolerance for dunkels and bocks into its genetic code.

Leila worried first and spoke first. "So what are you guys, um, doing here?"

Barry answered, "We're like salesmen for this organ company."

Leila realized she knew that. "Duh, that was a stupid question."

"No, no," Barry shined his armor, "it's not. Like because sometimes guys are independent salesmen, and sometimes they're like commission salesmen, and sometimes they're regional salesmen. It's actually pretty complicated stuff." Ed inspected Barry's dome. Where in it precisely was he manufacturing this garbage? "Um, right, Ed?"

"I wouldn't want to argue with you."

Leila prayed that her next question would be less embarrassing. "Have you been doing it for a while?"

"Not really." Barry answered this one too. "Just since the middle of May." Hearts reposed, passengers watched the cloudscape roll again, the captain announced the turbulence was through. Barry seized control of the table with a pair of anecdotes, one about a Mrs. Wajciechowski, "Krakow-birth'd-and-born," who had tried to haggle Ed down to "no penny more den four hund'ed dollar," and a badly told one in which Barry accidentally kicked out the Brackett's power cord, whereupon two customers accused the brothers, in story if not in fact, of being "like crooks." Barry provided the bulk of the narration; he swelled with the mission-accomplishing depiction of the true-life adventures of traveling-organ salesmen in Region Nine. Ed mutteringly confirmed two or three details, but at the beginning of a third anecdote, his brother's increasingly lavish festoons reminded Ed, as his stomach rocked back unwelcome to debts and commissions and scarlet sums, that he would rather not discuss the lives—adventurous, true, or not—of traveling salesmen in Region Nine. Barry was embroidering a gory, third-hand tale about a knife salesman who had cut off the fingers of one heckler when Ed interrupted him. "But we're not really doing that anymore."

"What's that?" Leila knew that they were really doing that two hours ago.

Ed rewrote his last lie with another one, three-quarters the size. "I mean, we're almost done with it, and then we're—well, at least, *I* am—going to do some other things. Some other things I have been looking into, for a while here."

Barry cringed; the rekindled wrath of Edward Steinke was about to punish him for the sin of insensitivity. But, Barry absolved himself, I'm in a groove again. Why's Ed ruining it again? She's beginning to like me—again? She is different from you, Ed, Barry longed to explain to his brother in private conference. She's like me. I understand her. And she doesn't have to take your crap. Barry prepared to charge the ridge of Ed's interruption, but somewhere between brain and mouth, planned and delivered, most of his nastiness withered. "Like what?"

"Huh?"

"Like what? What kind of other things?"

After three seconds when the scales could have tipped either way—textbook drama—Ed smiled. "Hell if I know." He laughed, and they followed.

Leila's cheeks felt the frost first, which may explain why she asked the next question, one forward *and* theoretical. Either of those types would have been shocking enough, but the combination was dangerously close to being neither shallow nor present.

Between two halves of a postlaughter grin, she asked whomever cared to answer, "Then if you had a choice of any kind of job in the world, what would it be?"

Barry had been glancing intermittently at Colleen. He now stared purposefully. Oh, Granny, what occupied eyes you have. Better not to answer you, my dear.

"What?" Ed didn't understand the question. This drew the required restatement. "Um, that's good. I mean, interesting. *Any* kind of job?"

Leila's mouth rose between giddy and self-satisfied. "Uh-huh."

"*I* would say . . ." Ed's italicized delivery of the vertical pronoun affected more certainty than he had. "Me, *personally?*" This wasn't the time to ponder whether five years of Orditz, five years of fortitude had been long enough. "I don't know. I think I would continue in sales."

"Oh." Leila's interest, may it rest in peace.

Aware that his answer would not compete for the most inspiring ever said by man—I would be a cosmonaut or the king of Peru, a lion tamer in my very own zoo—Ed hoped that Leila, if nothing else, could appreciate its rationality. "Because, you know, there are no other jobs out there."

"Uh-huh . . ." She glanced at Barry, side-eyes, whose performance continued. Nothing, he was sorry, could draw his attention away from the impossibly engaging Colleen Zim.

"There are no good jobs out there for people like us, you know, with all the big companies laying off, excuse me, *downsizing*"—Ed's wide-mouthed sarcasm paled next to his father's sneering pronunciation of the word—"and all the really good business ideas used up."

"But you have a good job, right?" The ingenue batted her eyelashes.

No, Ed thought, but her question posed other problems besides the answer. "I didn't mean there are no more good jobs. I just meant that there are no more jobs, you know, that have some, uh, meaning." Ed winced at the last word's prissy lace.

"Like teaching?"

"I guess, like teaching," Ed conceded, "but *I* meant like other kinds of jobs, jobs that aren't just there for the check so you can buy some stupid house." Ed held himself at the stupid house. "Not that that's wrong or anything. I just don't see anything for *me* other than sales, which, I don't know, leads someplace except to my parents'—you know, their kind of life." Barry made a noise, part sigh, part honk, all loud, all deliberate. On strike, he would not go back to work until this conversation ended. *Jesus Christ. Why's Ed always talking about stupid friggin' sales?*

Leila understood Barry's stance, if not its depths, and tried to steer the conversation toward a conclusion. "I know what you're saying," she turned the wheel slowly, "'cause like I'm thinking about leaving my job too." That very afternoon, she had told Yankel, in her mind at least, to go choke on the second shift. "But I dunno, maybe you're right. Maybe there are no more jobs that, you know, are something." Full stop. "Maybe."

Beaten by apathy, Ed raised his cup to sympathize with its last droplets. As the cup neared his chin, he tilted it toward Leila and mumbled, "Yeah, whatever. To no more jobs, right?" Leila was skeptical about whether the toastmasters would approve such a cheer-puncturing cheer, but she didn't want to offend Ed. "To, um, no more jobs," she repeated and drank. She looked at Barry, who, open-mouthed, expressionless, a fortress, was still impersonating someone who had not listened to the previous discussion. You won, her look argued. Management has ceded all your demands.

Barry mumbled, "To no more jobs," with the same leaden lips as his brother's.

The three exhaled, smiled, waited, glimpsed. Colleen finished her masterpiece, "indigo, indigo," her six-handed fan club applauded, drunken shouts dotted Mama's nearly seven o'clock rattle, and with a masterful application of the law of heat, Barry took control of the conversation again. "It was like pretty hot today, huh?" At the year-end ball of the shallow and the present, the weather always reigns as the queen of the dance, and Barry, Ed, and Leila read their lines on cue. First came the temperature, then the humidity; someone mentioned the sun, the breeze, the night, the forecast, the will-feel-nice cool. All the platitudes must have aggravated Ed's sensitive bladder. He excused himself.

Barry's eyes followed Ed; Leila's eyes followed Barry's. When Ed melted into the crowd, Barry's eyes returned, and Leila's, which had lingered too long, were caught waiting. Neither spoke. Then they both spoke at the same time. Unraveling their words, Leila insisted that Barry go first.

"No, you." It went on like this for a while. "It wasn't a big deal," Barry chuckled. "I was just going to say that I'm like sorry for my brother." He needed to be more specific, he thought; there were pallets of reasons to be sorry for his brother. "For like that stuff about sales and jobs."

"I didn't mind," Leila confided. Colleen's fans applauded at the end—or the end—of her performance. Before she dismounted her stool, the stagehand was already arranging the microphones for the next act.

"It's been such a crazy day," Barry tried to explain. He and Leila reciprocated *yeah*s and *uh-huh*s, smiles and tucks and scratches, reprised the riff of crazy day. They lobbed inattentively back and forth, and then Barry stopped—a disordered thought had become, was becoming, lucid. Leila had drank—*What was it?*—three, four cups of beer. The original one, okay, was the bargain's part, but the others were on her own. *She wants to be here.* The idea mushroomed into a nuclear sky, under which nothing else could live. "You know, Leila. I'm like glad you stayed."

Boom, the lightning-struck tree crashed. *One beer.* That's all you were supposed to do. These are the same guys with their lips and *fuck*s and. . . . She stared at the table, and her thoughts reversed: don't be stupid. He's just being nice, you liked him before, you had forgiven him (once). You always panic, you always run, and that's why you're always—she knew what was coming and dreaded its entrance—alone. Don't act drunk, the original speaker returned to the podium. You know who these guys are. They're problems. You heard him, didn't you? He's just looking for some gir—, *some girlfriend.* That word was even more horrible than *alone*: girlfriend, noun, someone to pounce and lick; girlfriend, noun, someone to ignore while you root for third-down conversions. *You don't need any part of this.* Time's up. Next speaker. *Why can't you just lighten up?* You like him. You know you do. He's forgiven, was forgiven. Beer, remarkable beer, continued to insert thoughts into Leila's brain and remind her that it had inserted those thoughts; it then inserted opposite thoughts and informed her, sadistically, that it did that too. When she was finally susceptible to all sorts of evildoings, the beer, in a classic technique of self-propagation, promised to end the confusion if she had another beer. So Leila drank a quarter cup.

To the outside world and the inside Barry, her silence was a downcast canvas, vexing and blank. Barry figured that he had kicked his foot into his mouth again.

Leila's disputants agreed on one point: she had to say something. It had been a half minute. "Yeah, um," she began, following their precise instructions. "Do you, um . . . " The beer must have hijacked her tongue. "Do you, um . . ." That would be the only explanation for not finishing the question with "know the date today" or "prefer cakes or pies" or "have ten fingers and toes." That would be the only explanation for, "Do you, um, have a girlfriend?"

Barry smiled. Her comment was a non sequitur, of course, but the kind of non sequitur that advanced a conversation by hours, the kind that cried, Enough with the salad, let's get to the meat. He had a rule when it came to that question: regardless of the truth, he replied, "Well, sort of."

Leila didn't see Barry's smile. I didn't say that. I didn't say that. She caught her breath for more. I didn't say that. I didn't say that. She stocked the bomb shelter with canned peaches and beans, ready for a lifetime of repetition.

"It's like kind of complicated," he went on.

At some point, Leila came to be aware that Barry was actually answering her question. Whatever gave him the idea to do that? "Huh?" she stammered.

"Oh, I said, it's like kind of complicated."

"Huh?" Her mind wobbled across the half acre.

"You know, your thing, it's like kind of 'tricky.'"

"I don't know."

Barry didn't think that that had made much sense, but he reserved judgment for later. "There's like, um, one girl. Maybe."

Leila's brain tripped. "Um, where do you work?"

It was Barry's turn for "Huh?" He was seconds away from reciting a well-practiced speech on relationships, girlfriends, boyfriends, and their associated complications in the modern world. The speech usually made him seem elusive and/or available, sensitive and/or strong, but as he was priming his voice box, she asked him—that? "You know, like selling organs." The two calm points of fact were coated lightly in peeve.

"Oh yeah."

The well-practiced speech was to be heard after all. "So like I was—"

"I meant before."

"What?"

"You said that you've like only been doing this since May."

"What?"

"What did you do before?"

Full disclosure, Barry decided, would most effectively dispense with this cramp. "I like worked in a warehouse for a paper-goods company."

"Uh-huh."

"So anyway, like I was saying—"

"I work at a gas station, uh, in the store."

The from-nowhere suddenness, the finding-your-own-name-in-the-newspaper surprise made Barry misplace, for a moment, the well-practiced speech. "Really?"

"Uh-huh," she corroborated her previous statement.

"What do you do there?" The work of the pallet crew on the rare moons when it was work was dull, but it must have been better than working at a gas station.

"I'm like a clerk." She wasn't even like a clerk, she was a clerk, but she didn't want to split hairs.

"Do you like it?"

Leila grinned as her tippy-toes touched the ground; even the beer didn't quarrel. "Are you kidding? It *sucks.*" They both smiled, knowing and itchy and mirrored.

Attributing unrequited mystery to Leila's occupation, Barry probed in predictable directions. "Are you like going to school or something?"

"Uh, no." She looked over Barry's shoulder, into the boxed emptiness of mid-distance, but then she focused again, almost on Barry's eyes; Leila had recently discovered the art of changing subjects. "Do you like your job, your *old* job?" she asked him about one, both.

Regarding the old job, "Do you like it?" was not something that the dudes of the pallet crew lolled around asking one another. The job was a job. Now, regarding the Ed job, well that was irrelevant. Summer break was over—it wasn't a thought but a reaction, not conclusive but lodged—and after Labor Day, he would register for another semester at Lincoln Paper or a place just like it and stay there for who knows how long for God knows what reason. Or maybe he wouldn't. But all this was immaterial; Barry answered as he was bound to: "It sucks." Laughs, laughs. He abbreviated a censored history of the pallet crew. She told him that the second shift was a solo shift, and she, that canvas, filled for Barry with details and shades, with a girl in polyester uniforms and grease-stained collars, a girl whom you asked to fill 'er up. Barry, to beer-aided Leila, was no longer just the eternal organist, a bolted-down fixture of the South Exhibition Hall; he was a midget in a warehouse, a hairy bead in a vault stacked to the ceiling with logs and barn rolls of paper. Neither was sure if this made the other more or less.

"Uh, like what do you do all night then?" Barry asked.

She lowered her voice. "Almost nothing. *Really.* I don't know sometimes how I stop from going crazy."

"Yeah." Barry nodded. "It's tough." Leila saw his eyes brim with compassion—brown, illimitable, boyish eyes that knew from whence they spoke.

"Of course, *you* understand," she said, and when she said the word, it was true. He understood, understood, understood, understood. He understood about second-shift loneliness, understood about flip-flipping through magazines in the night's high dead hours, understood about staring at yourself time-lapsed in a black-and-white monitor, understood about a stillness, a quiet so deep that handsome thank-yous were remembered for months and Chubby's whispers were never forgotten. And he understood about a girlhood room in a long-dead house. He understood, it was tough.

"Totally, it's tough," Barry reinforced his point, and they laughed again, not at some slapstick bonk-giggle exchange but at themselves, secretly, symmetrical. Barry was like so wrong, he now knew, for worrying about friggin' Ed. He had been right all the time: she was like him. Leila also chided her own stupidity: she was right to begin with, right to have forgiven him, right to laugh now, right to understand that the lips and the grabs were nothing, were more than nothing, were normal. He topped off the cups, and she rested her chin on her palm, her elbow on the table, and sighed. He looked behind her at the stagehand plugging and pushing enough cords and speakers, it seemed, for a fifty-piece band.

"Barry . . ." It was the first time that she had used his name. She had said it, objectively speaking, sisterly, familiar.

He bent forward. "Yes?"

"How do *you* do it?"

He bent back. "Do what?"

"Get through the days?" The inside-her speakers cleared their throats, rolled up their sleeves, prepared for another beery debate. But before opening arguments could begin, Leila remembered: he understood.

Barry lied, "I don't know."

"You *don't?*"

"Well, you know, I like think about other things."

"What kind of other things?"

There was an obvious response, obviously delivered: I think about three other things—getting laid, getting laid, and getting laid. Barry amused himself with this, momentarily, and then responded plainly. "You know, personal things." In Leila's chest, the debating speakers tuned their rhetoric, did deep knee bends for pirouettes. *Why can't you just shut up?* What can't you just get up . . . ? Why can't you just— "Because," Barry continued, "like you got to think about something, right?"

Barry understood, Leila remembered, understood about Rusty and her grandfather, jungle dreams and a nonorphan's fate.

He was right too, again; you did have to think about *some*thing. "Do you think about it all the time?" Leila asked.

Barry, baffled, emitted, "Huh?"

"The personal things?"

Barry looked in his cup for explanations afloat in the foam. Leila could be acting coy, he supposed, and could be making a pass at him. She *could* be like doing any number of suggestive things.

Leila—or the beer—confessed, "I've stopped thinking about it."

"Huh?" She must be completely drunk, Barry thought. How else could—? She was still the same person who fled, traced eights, said nothing.

"About it," Leila said, hushed. Barry showed no sign of recognition, and Leila wondered, Was that how it would happen today? Was this what I've never done before? Was that why I am what I am? She folded over, her voice two feet from Barry's ear, and whispered, loud, through a windy breath, "Love."

His mouth curling like a cat on a sofa, Barry removed the well-practiced speech. "Oh *yeah.* You see, you—"

"Are you the ones who ordered the brewskis?" Barry and Leila looked up. Ed was carrying two full pitchers in his hands and a grin, collegial and ignorant, on his face. Barry knocked twice on the table and flashed a tight smile at Leila; she tucked her hair behind her ear and flashed one in return. Self-satisfied, Ed had completed his tasks, bathroom and beer, with no interruptions from *does it matter* or the busted ledger's sneers. He sat down. "What were we talking about?"

"Nothing," Barry shut the door. The wiseasses in the corner began to electrify, louder and colliding. "I mean like, yeah, we just finished. There's not much, I like mean *no more* to be said on, whatever."

Barry, Leila could tell, also knew that they had been close, so close to something, so close to knowing what that something was. But with Ed here, it was better, Leila and Barry both thought, to wait and to blabber about the weather here-and-there or the weather at the Fair or the air or their hair or the best-cream-puff-I-swear.

Ed went ahead and said what was on his mind: "I was doing some math." While waiting for the pitchers, he had drooled at the sight of the bartenders' bountiful green harvest. He then happened upon the notion that joints like Mama's made lots of money. He wanted to bounce some preliminary—*very* preliminary—ideas off Leila and Barry. "With certain locations in particular, I figure—"

She faked a cough. Of course, she knew that it was better to talk about certain locations in particular or certain months of the year or certain moons of Jupiter or certain provinces of China, but she wanted her and Barry to talk about certain shallow-and-presents, not Ed. She looked at the pitchers, then at Ed, then at Barry. "Oh, I got it." She grabbed the three cups—she pinched Ed's in the middle of a drink—and set them in a row. Trying to hoist the pitcher over the cups, she knocked two of them down. She set them aright, filled them—she overfilled Ed's, but the table absorbed the excess—and handed them back one by one to their owners. Although she had not chosen the ending, she nodded to the tented roof anyway and indicated that she, Leila Genet, had a toast this time.

She didn't have to say it. Yes, Barry and Ed had toasted to other things equally odd, but she didn't have to say it. Yes, it was only a silly, Silly, but she didn't have to say it. Yes, everything was the same—the truth was the same—whether she said it or not, but she didn't have to say it. It may not have been her fault. It's hard to believe that four words—four tipsy, playroom, joking words—could have done all that. So maybe it was the manager.

"How's everyone doing tonight?" he had just asked. Maybe it was the band. Maybe it was the cup. But she didn't have to say it.

She lifted her cup. She said it.

"To no more love."

Someone had spiked the manager's personality, normally enthusiasm and ham on the rocks, with sincerity. "How's everyone doing tonight?" he asked. "You're *going* to be doing great because Mama's has a special treat for *you*." He winked to offstage right. "Those of you who were here two hours ago heard something *real* special. But hold on, hold on. First things first"—counterfeit concern—"Glass Factoire will not be appearing tonight." Alas, there had been no spiking; God was shining on the manager that night. John Glass, the saxophony front man of the scheduled act, masters of pretentious, poorly played jazz, had fallen ill, according to the band's marble-mouthed guitarist, from either "tobacco pasta" or "the bad kielbasa." The manager continued, rolling on the balls of his feet, "If you were here, if you weren't here, who cares? You're here *right now*! Ladies and gentlemen, let's give it up *one more time* for Little Lisa Zielinski and the *Stone Lake Players!*"

A mustard-gas thrill, transparent and visible, passed over some, passed into others. The corner wiseasses erupted as the band mounted the stage. Veterans explained to rookies, strangers promised strangers: the Stone Lake Players were no ordinary folks. Veterans at least tried to explain to rookies; individual voices had been demoted to freckles on the collective, expanding din. From then on, one could barely hear one's own words, and the band had not yet begun to play.

When Leila gave her toast, Ed repeated "To no more love," and half his cup chuted gaily down his gullet. Leila drank a smaller amount. Barry drank not at all. To no more love, he bristled. What kind of a friggin' toast is that? When Leila gave her toast, the manager had almost finished the introduction. As Ed and Leila drank, the manager presented the Stone Lake Players. *Great. These people again.* Barry yelled to Leila, "What did you mean by that?"

"Huh?"

"Like what did you mean by that?"

"By *what*?" Leila yelled back.

Barry pointed to his rounded mouth. "The toast."

"You're like going to have to talk louder. I can't *hear* you."

Barry did not talk louder. "Just drop it."

The mustard-gas victims at the back of the bar compressed forward, and Leila lifted her knees off the table bench and spun toward the stage. This is fun, she confided to the ether; the disputants were banished; alone was disarmed; it was clear now: there was going to be no more second-guessing that day. It would not happen tomorrow. Leila was still proud of the toast, *her* toast. She assumed that Barry had thought it was pretty cute. And Ed too. Why not? Ed too. Leila could see only the performers' disembodied heads, and she stood up to see their presumed embodied areas. The Stone Lake Players, never great at capturing the moment, were still sound-checking their instruments. Leila sat down again, facing the stage.

Barry had saluted Leila's turn with a "Fuck you, then." *To no more love.* She had been so cheery when she had said it, but what was she cheering? If she had meant no more sex—that was what *he* had been talking about before Ed arrived—that was one thing. But Barry didn't think that she had been talking about sex. He thought that she had been like talking about that other kind of love. "Why do men chase women?" Cheryl had once asked him. "Because it's filling," he had answered. Yet he knew that there was more, then, now, always, a constant. It—Barry was thinking about both kinds of love, not always distinctly—wasn't just filling, it was *the* filling. It was the filling that made life not hollow. It was *the* filling that meant that it was unimportant if he stacked pallets and she pumped gas, the filling that could fill the days of organ sales and no more jobs. *To no more love.* If that was true, Barry guessed, then that's it. To no more love. Why did she have to say it then? To no more love. What kind of toast is that?

The Players opened with the second song of their last set. *You ain't no puppy/And I ain't no kitten/Don't pre-tend you're too young to be smitten/Yahoo (yahoo), I do (I do), yahoo (yahoo yahoo).* Knees and toes and hands, bounces and taps and claps swirled in confectioner's red and white. Ed had also screwed his body around to face Little Lisa; three minutes later, he reversed along the same line. "Hey," he shouted for Barry's attention. "Hey." Something had been eating at him. "Hey." He set down his beer and waved his arms in a crossing pattern. "Hell-*low*." Moving his cup out of the way lest he tip it over, he bent across the table like a worn swimmer climbing out of a pool. "Why didn't you drink back there?" Ed had noticed; Leila, apparently, had not. Barry, who had leaned ten degrees forward in brotherly compromise, swayed past the perpendicular by twenty. Christ, he thought as he shook his head, he's asking me *that*? Ed's elbows waddled closer. "Hey, why didn't you *drink* back there?"

Barry swung closer to his brother. Nose a forearm from nose, he screamed, "'Cause you're a loser." *You ain't too big/And I ain't too little/We're gonna meet right here in the middle/Yahoo (yahoo), I do (I do), yahoo (yahoo, yahoo).* Barry had become accustomed to Ed's outbursts, more from the well-documented effects of desensitization than from any faith in Christian tolerance. With the roles switched, Ed proved still sensitized. "I'm a loser? *You're* a fucking loser."

Barry lifted himself from his seat. Nose now a long hand from nose, he rebutted, "Oh yeah, what's all this"—mockery mixed with scream—"'to no more jobs' shit? Can't you ever in your entire friggin' life like stop talking about sales? Like don't you understand? It doesn't matter."

Ed riffled through a next possible line as a pain pierced his bent bloated stomach. That pain joined his kidney pain, the punishment of the back of the work of the life, and the pains merged, then alternated and whimpered. Ed leaned upright, just in time to read ". . . so you can bite me" on Barry's billboard lips. Ed didn't try to shout over the noise. He flipped Barry the most expressive finger, attacked a mouthful of beer, refilled his cup, and noticed the table quivering as Leila, like a cooperatively sedated dance partner, moved to the Stone Lake Players. This is so good, she was gushing over the band, perhaps, or the half acre under the blue tented tarp. Her bobbed and beered frame begged for oxygen. In a daring, ribald move, she glanced behind her—not long enough to see Barry's lemon-sour face—and thought, This is good too. You'll hold me up/And you I will carry/Today's the day that we're getting married/Yahoo (yahoo), I do (I do), I do I do I do. Ed, rather than look at his brother for another blink, twisted his body—knees under chin, over knee, under knee—to a view of the stage. In midmove, the pain winced. His thoughts competed for his own attention against Mama's applauding rumble, a union of cries and rapture, crashing through his ears. Where does that jackass get off telling me, me, anything? I'm carrying him, supporting him out of my own money, and he says shit like that. As the Stone Lake Players ignited their next song, Leila sprang up for a better look at Uncle Stan's fiddling fingers tap-dancing along the board, his bow surfing the bridge. Her spring knocked Ed's shoulder, and Ed directed his inner snarls to the right. This one is exactly the same. I see it in their little goo-goo eyes, talking about me. But I'm going someplace and these losers aren't. At their gas stations. Ed wrung "gas stations" with such revulsion that it would have shamed an earthlover sworn to the overthrow of the car. At their *goddamn paper crews.* They, they, they think that the whole world's going to kiss their ass. Well, *wrong.* (Barry, rapid-fire, drank a cup and a half of beer. Leila clapped to a rhythm of her own.) *Jackass, jackass, jackass*—Ed could no longer control the tornado inside—*doesn't know what he's talking about with his "It doesn't matter."* Barry had said that, hadn't he? *What the hell does*—Ed chased a pronoun: he, I, we, they—*what the hell does he know about anything?*

*Fuck them all,* the unscheduled intermission ended and began.

Because it does matter, because I'm not like him, Ed entered the second act. I'm not about to wind up like him and—he snatched a glimpse of Leila—*them.* Two losers living in some house with fifty kids and dirty dishes and dirty clothes and dirty everything on nothing but—he knotted the word with gas-station disgust—*love.* Ed felt obliged to share his clairvoyance, and he pretzeled around to face Barry again. "Hey. . . . *Hey.*" Some people, it was clear, never learn. "Hey." He waved his arms, the crossing pattern now a flailing pattern, if there was any pattern at all. "Hey, motherfu—"

Barry ordered Ed to stop with his most expressive finger, and so the matador fluttered his cape.

Blasting from his seat, Ed lurched forward, but he wasn't as careful as the last time, and as he was about to explain to his dear brother where he could put his expressive finger, he upset Barry's cup. The cup was only a third full, but the final drops of the spill's delta landed on Barry; specifically they landed on his upper thigh, which had recently and finally dried out. Barry looked at his thigh, looked at the cup, looked at Ed, (glanced at Leila), looked at his thigh, looked at the cup, looked at Ed, picked up the cup, and threw it sideways and upways and downways in his brother's direction. Given the poor aerodynamics of an empty plastic cup and the nature of the throw, skeletal, chicken-elbowed, ungainly, it was unremarkable that the cup traveled a foot to the right of and three feet above its intended target. Barry, seeing this, joined his traitorous hands to the sides of his head, hoping this would alter the cup's course.

Leila had again intook the night's mood and mild and swayed with the crowd to Little Lisa's waltzing third song. This is good, she reprised. This is good, a new chant prepared to end the day. Then the cup hit her on the back of the head. She looked first at Ed, snickering, and aimed by his hitchhiking thumb, she turned around. *I don't care.* Sitting now, she tried to tell Barry with her eyes and silent brow, That didn't hurt, it was a cup, funny, funny. But Barry, whose own cheeks started to feel the freeze, couldn't make out funny-funny. He could only see a face, blank.

Barry, however, understood the message of Ed's cackling teeth, jaundiced by the halogen moons. Leila couldn't hear what Barry then said or what Ed then said, but she could see, anyone could see, their hate-narrowed faces, their flickering, furious mouths, their clenched ugly paws. Barry's fist ground into the tabletop; grain-flecks of stain chipped onto his skin. She thought, How come they don't know that this is good? Why can't . . .

But the music of the Stone Lake Players encased the world in curtains and blare. And Barry's fist ground still, and the table chipped still, and Leila could not bear it anymore. She watched her hand, then, cover his. Then—What would she do? What could she do?—she unclenched it, finger by finger by finger, and rubbed his middle knuckle with her thumb. Just listen, she begged silently. Just listen.

Barry tried to translate the tongue of her thumb and her face. *The noise.* He shut his eyes. *All the noise, I can't*— He opened his eyes, but they did not return to Leila. They stared down a black-walled tunnel at Ed, still shouting.

It doesn't matter, Ed cried his eureka. Don't you see? It doesn't matter. He did it and— Ed noticed Barry's hand, now open and limp, in Leila's hold. He burped, and the recall and the foul of the too-fast beer and the too-long day swam to his nostrils. His face collapsed, lips on eyebrows, ear on ear, and he said, accidentally it seemed, "I want to go home." His head slumped. "Let's go home."

It came back, let's go home, no more love. Leila didn't have to say it then, and *Ed,* Barry thought, had said it now, but whether through eye or mind or sodden imagination, it came back, let's go home, no more love. Leila's pleading continued to orbit Barry's knuckle. Let's go home, no more love. He tugged his arm away, tentatively, and she clutched tighter. To no more love. His second tug was stronger and— He hid his hand, freed, on his knee. To no more love. For a few beats, Leila missed what had happened. Everything was so fast, so blurred, so loud, so confused. Then she beheld Barry's forearm, a rainbow past the horizon, leading to an invisible end. She tucked her hair behind her ear, but this time only for a moment, only to think. She placed her palms against the table, she looked at Barry, and she pushed up.

It was only after Leila had stood up and walked away that Barry stopped gazing through the table at his hidden hand, at his knee. When he finally collected himself, resurrected himself, Leila had disappeared—she was at the point of disappearance— into the oblivious, shameless, slavish, bouncing, enraptured sea under Mama's tented tarp. Barry jumped up and shouted, "Wait."

She floated to the bathroom through the canned-fish crowd. The previous occupant stepped from the one-stall closet, and Leila, unaware of the four women waiting, glided pace-unbroken inside. She latched the door, listened not to the affronted knocks, and looked in the mirror.

The width through which it came, at first, was a papercut. The brine trickled because of Barry, *for* Barry—probably—and for the

intangibles, for Ed, for the ill-remembered. It was for not happening today, for not happening today. For never going to happen.
Then it was a gash.

When she was finished, the faucet turned off and her face
water-wiped, she looked again in the mirror. "Oh, Leila," she
slurred, "you can't stay here all night."

She got in her car—in her drunk, it wasn't safe—and drove
onto the interstate. Soon the road would enter the suburban
prairies, the planted rows of cream-sided ranches and matching
colonials, punctuated by flat farms and rust-rusting factories,
gleaming office parks and replicate malls. But there would be no
mountains or oceans; there would be no bomb blasts or demon-
strations. All the wars had been fought, and all the revolutions
had turned. Yet no one—not Leila, not Barry, not Ed—had bothered to celebrate.

The once-twilight sky like the summerend day was black and
blue, but Leila didn't turn on her headlights: she thought she
could see fine. At her exit, only one stop from the Fair, a green
sign's reflecting arrow directed her more up than right. She let
the exit pass, sort of smiling.

# ABOUT THE AUTHOR

GARY SERNOVITZ was born in Milwaukee, Wisconsin. He now lives in New York. *Great American Plain* is his first novel.

SERNOVITZ
2001
(New Sticker)

1655330